DARK EUPHORIA

What Reviewers Say About Ronica Black's Work

"Ronica Black's debut novel *In Too Deep* has everything from nonstop action and intriguing well developed characters to steamy erotic love scenes. From the opening scenes where Black plunges the reader headfirst into the story to the explosive unexpected ending, *In Too Deep* has what it takes to rise to the top. Black has a winner with *In Too Deep*, one that will keep the reader turning the pages until the very last one."—*Independent Gay Writer*

"…an exciting, page turning read, full of mystery, sex, and suspense." —*MegaScene*

"…a challenging murder mystery—sections of this mixed-genre novel are hot, hot, hot. Black juggles the assorted elements of her first book with assured pacing and estimable panache."—*Q Syndicate*

"Black's characterization is skillful, and the sexual chemistry surrounding the three major characters is palpable and definitely hot-hot-hot…if you're looking for a solid read with ample amounts of eroticism and a red herring or two you're sure to find *In Too Deep* a satisfying read."—*L Word Literature*

"Black is a master at teasing the reader with her use of domination and desire. Black's first novel, *In Too Deep*, was a finalist for a 2005 Lammy. …With *Wild Abandon*, the author continues her winning ways, writing like a seasoned pro. This is one romance I will not soon forget."—*Just About Write*

"The sophomore novel [*Wild Abandon*] by Ronica Black is hot, hot, hot."—*Books to Watch Out For*

"Sleek storytelling and terrific characters are the backbone of Ronica Black's third and best novel, *Hearts Aflame*. Prepare to hop on for an emotional ride with this thrilling story of love in the outback. …Wonderful storytelling and rich characterization make this a high recommendation."—*Lambda Book Report*

"This sequel to Ronica Black's debut novel, *In Too Deep*, is an electrifying thriller. The author's development as a fine storyteller shines with this tightly written story. …[The mystery] keeps the story charged—never unraveling or leading us to a predictable conclusion. More than once I gasped in surprise at the dark and twisted paths this book took."—*Curve Magazine*

In *Flesh and Bone*…"Ronica Black handles a traditional range of lesbian fantasies with gusto and sincerity. The reader wants to know these women as well as they come to know each other. When Black's characters ignore their realistic fears to follow their passion, this reader admires their chutzpah and cheers them on. …These stories make good bedtime reading, and could lead to sweet dreams. Read them and see."—*Erotica Revealed*

"Ronica Black's books just keep getting stronger and stronger. …This is such a tightly written plot-driven novel that readers will find themselves glued to the pages and ignoring phone calls. *The Seeker* is a great read, with an exciting plot, great characters, and great sex."—*Just About Write*

"Ronica Black's writing is fluid, and lots of dialogue makes this a fast read. If you like steamy erotica with intense sexual situations, you'll like *Chasing Love*."—*Queer Magazine Online*

Visit us at www.boldstrokesbooks.com

By the Author

In Too Deep

Wild Abandon

Deeper

Hearts Aflame

The Seeker

Flesh and Bone

Chasing Love

Conquest

Wholehearted

The Midnight Room

Snow Angel

The Practitioner

Freedom to Love

Under Her Wing

Private Passion

Dark Euphoria

DARK EUPHORIA

by

Ronica Black

2018

DARK EUPHORIA
© 2018 By Ronica Black. All Rights Reserved.

ISBN 13: 978-1-63555-141-9

This Trade Paperback Original Is Published By
Bold Strokes Books, Inc.
P.O. Box 249
Valley Falls, NY 12185

First Edition: May 2018

CREDITS
Editor: Cindy Cresap
Production Design: Susan Ramundo
Cover Design By Tammy Seidick

Acknowledgments

My publisher, Bold Strokes Books, took me under their wing all those years ago and held my hand, teaching me so much. I'm eternally grateful all these years later as I continue to learn. Thank you to everyone at BSB.

Cait, who has been there through it all and still sticks around plying me with love, humor, and grace. You are my Rockstar.

My editor extraordinaire, Cindy Cresap. We've come a long way, woman. I love your notes, your suggestions, and your humor. Keep it all coming!

My readers, what can I say? You all continue to encourage me to write and I'm forever grateful for your support, your kind emails and your gifts. (Especially when they contain chocolate!) You lovely people keep me chasing the dream! Please, don't ever hesitate to email me at ronicablack@gmail.com I'm patiently waiting for someone to send me wine…is that possible? Legal? Here's to dreaming!

Dedication

To my best friend and love, who has believed in me
from that very first short story.
I love you.

PROLOGUE

Thunder cracked, and the crowd of well-to-do guests pointed in awe at the growing storm as they exited the Valle Sol Country Club for the evening. The guests from out of town panicked and ran hunched over like dusty wet humps scattering into the flashing darkness. Gowns and tuxedos were ruined, but nobody wanted to stay to wait out the storm. He understood their urgency though his own feelings of urgency had nothing to do with the storm. His was all about his companion and the need to get her home before he either passed out or she wised up and took off. Passing out seemed more likely with the way he was feeling.

He pressed a trembling hand into the small of his companion's back and tried to ignore the tingling in his arms and the wave of dizziness that washed over him. His knees weakened, but he blinked and regained focus and a little strength. They neared the bottom of the front entrance stairs, and blowing dirt assaulted his skin and eyes. His companion laughed and twirled as if the storm were feeding her senses.

Despite the blowing dust, he could still see enough of her to know how lucky he was. Most women needed a little encouragement, like a small hint of his great wealth, a tiny promise of a yacht getaway, or the opportunity to ride in his Aston Martin. Sure, they played coy at first, but they almost always came along. This one, however, was suddenly ready and willing, with little to no braggery or promises he never intended to keep. Maybe it was because she was high-class pedigree just like he was. Or maybe it was because she already knew him. Regardless, the word jackpot came to mind, and he laughed like he was drunk. He brought his hand to his mouth and belched and tried to recall all he'd had to drink. His stomach hurt and his body warmed from toe to forehead. Maybe he was coming down with something.

He pushed the thought away and focused on the woman's high, tight ass as he ushered her into the waiting limousine. The sequins on her beige skin-like dress sparkled and teased as she moved. He swayed slightly on his feet but caught himself and slid in next to her. The door closed behind him, and he inched closer, unable to shake his painful grin. It was so strong it felt like it was cracking his cheeks, yet he couldn't relax his face. A small part of him knew he should be alarmed at his loss of physical control, but his libido killed it in an instant.

"My God, you are gorgeous," he said with difficulty, draping his heavy-feeling arm around her shoulders. Wind shook the car, and fat drops of rain splattered against it. The dizzying scent of her perfume mingled with the smell of wet earth, and he wanted more, needed more.

He kissed her graceful neck and fell against her, which only caused her to laugh.

"Mm, you do like to move fast don't you?" Her eyes flashed against thick lashes, and he felt a twitch in his hardening cock. Something was still working fine. Thank God.

"I do. I thought you were game too?" He ran his hand up the bare silken flesh of her leg. He knew who she was, her reputation. She was definitely game. She shuddered and he licked his lips.

"Oh, I am," she said. She lowered the driver divider and gave the man instructions on where to go. He didn't bother to pay attention. He only knew they weren't going to his place. The car started.

"Where…" he touched her lips, "are you taking me?"

She crawled onto his lap. "Does it matter where we go?" She teased him with light kisses, and he felt his body go completely limp. It felt magnificent. He laughed at the tickle of her kisses but then went breathless as she plunged her tongue in his mouth with dominance. He groaned and tried to pull her closer. When they parted, her lips glistened with dark red and he tasted blood. He struggled to finger his sore lip. She'd bitten him and he hadn't felt it.

"Too rough?" she asked.

He shook his head though his heart pounded. "No way."

She raised a hand and ran a sharp finger down his forehead. Something warm dripped into his vision. He fingered it, saw the dark red once again.

She laughed and held up her hand. The glint of sharp metal on the tip of her finger caught his eye. She'd cut him and now she was licking the piercing end of the metal with her snakelike tongue.

"You still up for this?" she asked as the car sped up. She loosened his bow tie, leaned in, and licked his neck. "Or do you want to get out?"

He swallowed the rising lump in his throat and her knee pushed into his groin. He tried to home in on her face, but the edges were beginning to blur. For a second he panicked, but then she morphed back into reality and he felt the hard grin again. Nothing was going to ruin this. He'd waited too long for this one.

"Hell no," he heard himself say. "I'm going where you're going."

The car accelerated again as she laughed and tugged on his shirt.

"That's what I wanted to hear."

Chapter One

Thunder boomed overhead, and Homicide Detective Maria Diaz jerked even with a woman pressed tightly against her.

"Sorry." Maria laughed a little, embarrassed. But the woman, whose name was Tina or Trina, didn't seem to notice.

"God, I want you." She licked delicately around Maria's ear. "You taste so good. Like candy."

"Really?" Maria closed her eyes and tried her best to relax and react to the sensual moment. But the flashes of lightning promised more thunder, and the woman's groans promised more of the dull make out session. Maria winced as the woman laughed into her neck. She thought about pushing her away, but instead she balled her fists and willed herself to feel…anything. What was wrong with her?

"Oh, yeah." Tina pressed her denim clad thigh between Maria's legs and cupped her breast. "And you've made me wait so long, I've been doing nothing but thinking about it." She thumbed her nipple through her shirt, and Maria's breath hitched, as she hoped for more pressure.

"Someone else is excited too," she said. Before Maria could stop her, Tina knelt and lightly kissed her nipple through the fabric. Frustrated at the lack of progress, Maria grabbed her head to pull her away, but Tina took it as a sign of passion. She smiled and Maria knew the dimples had crumbled dozens of hearts. Just not hers.

The woman searched her eyes for reciprocal hunger, and then her face fell. The dimpled smile was gone, and once again Maria felt like shit.

"Listen, Tina…"

But Tina shook her head in obvious anger. "Not again. Do you realize how long we've been doing this?"

"I'm—"

"And my name is *Trina*. With an r." She pushed away and ran her hands through her hair. "You're kidding me, right?"

Maria had been putting on the brakes, date after date. But her job as a homicide detective with the Las Brisas County Sheriff's Office took up much of her time, and she was often exhausted after work. And truth be told, she rarely dated and knew she was terrible at it. But her partner, Silas Finley, had set this one up, insisting she relax and have a little fun, as well as an orgasm or two. But she just hadn't been able to feel much of anything for Trina. For her or the countless others people had set her up with. All she wanted was her bed and a good night's sleep. She'd pay for it at this point.

She eyed her watch and lowered her arm quickly. The face of the watch was blurry and she couldn't tell the time. "It's late." She didn't know what else to say. And why was her vision acting up again?

"Don't you mean early? It's nearly four."

Trina had taken her to a late-night dinner and a club. They'd danced and Maria had pretended to enjoy it. She knew she was supposed to like it, so, why didn't she?

"I have a long day. And—"

Trina backed away. She held up a hand. "Let me guess? You're exhausted. You can't do this now. Maybe another time?"

Maria touched her own lip and sighed. She still felt the moisture from the kiss, but that was all. Nothing earth-shattering or heart skipping. That was what she was supposed to feel, right?

"Don't bother even voicing it." Trina turned and headed for the door. She reached for her jacket and then fumbled impatiently with the locks. It was still storming badly outside, and Maria knew she should ask her to stay out of sheer politeness, or to at least wait out the monsoon. But when she opened her mouth, nothing came and she closed her eyes in defeat.

"Oh, don't worry. I'll be fine in the storm," Trina said with a bite to her voice, as if she'd read her thoughts. She yanked open the door. "Please don't call me again. And tell Silas, tell him he's a shitty friend to suggest such a shitty date." She slammed the door, and Maria jerked at the impact. She heard Trina crank her truck and peel out of the driveway. Strong wind shook the windows and lightning flashed, showing an empty space behind Maria's two vehicles.

She sighed with relief. She didn't know what her problem was with dating, but she was too damn tired to try to figure it out now. She crossed to the kitchen and retrieved the Patron from the freezer. She made herself a double on ice with lemon and lime and downed it. Her cat, Horace, jumped onto the counter and stared at her with his large yellow eyes. She stroked his long curly mustache and scratched his gray head. If cats could talk he'd do so with a thick British accent and he'd tell her like it was while soothing her with the promise of tea and biscuits. But instead, he just flicked his tail and purred.

"I just didn't feel anything," she said. "I mean, it's better than leading her on, right?"

He meowed and she nodded. "Right, I did let it go on too long. But still, I was trying. I mean I was really hoping to feel something."

She thought about a refill but decided she was well worn enough to sleep peacefully. She deposited her glass in the sink and bypassed her living room with an unfinished puzzle on the coffee table, along with various crossword books with worn corners. Empty water bottles were lit by low lamplight, illuminated brightly every second or so with lightning. Lately, when she couldn't sleep, she'd get up and work her puzzles. She considered it her only addiction. She just had to work them until they were finished; otherwise it left a gnawing in the pit of her stomach.

She stripped when she hit the hallway and allowed her clothes to fall freely behind her, leaving a trail of melancholy and fatigue. They joined a small pile of weary and another pile of insomnia. She'd pick them up eventually, but for now, they were markers of

CHAPTER TWO

Jesus Christ, what a mess," Maria said as she maneuvered through the hot, muddy desert in her old faded red Jeep Wrangler. The canvas top had been eaten by sun rot years ago, so they were having to drive with the constant tickle of drizzling rain. She'd hoped it would help cool the heat of the early morning, but it just seemed to encase it, making the heavy air thicker. It felt almost ominous, as if promising a truly gruesome scene ahead. Like they were trapped in a macabre snow globe of sorts, trapped inside a piece of the disturbed Las Brisas desert with little air to breathe and no way to escape. She wiped the damp from her face and shook the thought away. But inside, her stomach clenched with anticipation. Just what lay ahead, she did not know. She just knew it was bad. Very bad. And the victim was wealthy.

She adjusted her mirror as the Jeep lurched forward in the unforgiving terrain.

"Thank God you still got this thing," Silas Finley said as he gripped the upper bar of the Jeep. He'd rolled up the sleeves of his dress shirt and his tie was askew. Sweat had weighed down the front of his hair, and he smashed it away from his forehead. The rain dotted his angular face and he adjusted his sunglasses, which he wore rain or shine, with his free hand. "Are we going to arrive in one piece?"

The Jeep shimmied and she gunned the engine and drove out of a menacing ditch. She could see the mud fly up behind them in the rearview mirror.

"At this point, I don't know." The monsoons had hit them hard the past week, and Las Brisas was covered in strewn palm limbs, broken roof tiles, uprooted signs, and downed power lines. She clenched her jaw and drove on, squeezing the wheel. Monsoons, she was used to, but having to drive off-road in the early morning dawn was new to her. And the way it was going so far, she realized she didn't enjoy it at all, even if she did love her Jeep. And as they bounced along, she realized she was glad she'd kept the Jeep, even if it was for nostalgia.

After Finley had called and ruined her hopes of sleep, she'd hobbled from bed and stumbled into pressed khakis and a short-sleeved blouse. She'd laced her hiking boots, snapped on her phone and gun, and pulled her hair back into a quick ponytail. She'd had to dig through the junk drawer in the kitchen to find the keys to the Wrangler. So when she'd arrived at Finley's, he'd looked impatient with a limp, wet newspaper held over his head and a covered cup of coffee in his hand. He'd looked like a drowned rat, tired but intense. A look, according to him, they'd both perfected lately. He was more concerned over her look than she was his. According to Finley, she was too young to be so fatigued. He, at least, had the excuse of late forties and a house with a baby. While she had nothing and no one to wear her down.

But thankfully, he hadn't sparred with her that morning. They'd ridden in virtual silence, both of them mulling over what lay ahead in the desert. Neither one of them were morning people so she'd been grateful for the silence.

"The aviation unit is bringing in the sarge by chopper," Finley finally said, sipping his coffee carefully as they crawled over more rough terrain.

"Must be nice," she said as she changed gears. Sergeant James O'Connell was all about appearances and perfection. He was often on their asses for being late, underdressed, or not solving cases quickly enough. She glanced down at the spots of mud peppering her shirt and forearms. She didn't mind getting dirty; her job often required it. She just hated the looks her sarge gave her when she was less than presentable.

Loud thumping came from overhead, and she looked up to see the police chopper landing not far ahead. Finley shook his head and she scoffed. As usual, the sarge would show up looking pristine as always. How did he do it?

She downshifted as they neared a huddle of police vehicles with what appeared to be an old barn behind them. Uniforms wove in and out and one uni was winding the yellow crime scene tape around the area, using nearby bushes and trees for support. Crime scene technicians hurried like ants in their white head-to-toe protective garb. And a handful of plainclothes gave their attention to the helicopter as it landed.

Maria killed the engine to her Jeep, and they crab walked to the small crowd out of habit, expecting biting wind and dust from the chopper blades. But today there was no loose dirt to blow into their faces. Today it was just hot, humid wind and the piercing feel of drizzling rain. The coroner, Dr. Judy Haddock, welcomed her with a smile and a quick brush of loose strands from her blond bun. She was damp and glistening and somehow beautiful despite it all. Maria's heart lifted and she found herself returning the smile. Haddock was like a mentor to her, and she was a hell of a lot more attractive than her sarge or Finley. At one time, Maria had had a fierce crush.

"I've already done my initial and my walk through," Haddock said. "So go ahead when you're ready." She drew closer and Maria's heart rate nearly tripled as she leaned in and retrieved Maria's small container of VapoRub from her back pocket. She held it in front of her.

"You'll need this, trust me. Even if your old man wants you to tough it out for the crowd."

Maria nodded, speechless. She could smell her light perfume, weighed down and stimulated by the rain. If they'd been different people with different jobs, she'd drop everything to ask her out. But, as it was, she didn't have crushes and she didn't date colleagues. She didn't have the time or the emotional availability of mixing business with pleasure. And the fiasco with Trina reminded her of that. Even if she hadn't been a colleague.

Haddock gave her a wink and left her to stare into the rain. The cool drops fell lazily onto her face, and she wished she could close her eyes and relax into their dance. But instead, she looked alert and straightened as her sarge emerged from the chopper like a huge clown from a tiny clown car. Standing about six foot five with a hefty frame that once held firm muscle, he walked away from the chopper like he was the most important man on earth. His confidence was obvious and alluring, and every other person there was watching him in quiet amazement. He demanded respect in a quiet way, simply by how he held himself. She respected that about him, and even though he was often a pain in her ass, she was in awe of him.

"Here comes the Hulk," someone whispered, but the laughs were short and stifled. The Hulk was the name the rookies called him, and rarely did she hear it from anyone else. They just knew better. And she wouldn't be caught dead referring to him as such. She'd seen his temper on more than one occasion. One time too many, in fact.

As if he could read her mind, the sarge caught sight of her and Finley at once, just as he smacked a crime scene technician on the back, encouraging him to hustle back inside the barn.

"Diaz, Finley." He pointed to the ground, and Maria often felt like a dog being called to its owner. They stood in front of him and attempted to straighten their appearance. By the look on his face, they failed, and Maria heated at being less than perfect.

"You'll need to clean up before the press arrives." He looked around with narrow eyes, studying the empty land beyond them. "Scratch that. We'll keep them from landing. If they come, it will be by vehicle. Hopefully, you two can be done before then."

The sarge was the one to always handle the press. He had the ability to calm, soothe, and charm the most dangerous of snakes. But he wanted his team looking sharp at all times. He continued looking around as he ran his thick thumbs up and down the length of his suspenders. His navy dress slacks and matching blazer were spotless, and he'd even taken the time to already cover his wing tip shoes in clear plastic. She looked to Finley who merely shrugged in defeat. What could they do? He always one-upped them.

She fought back a smile and was just enjoying the scent of his trademark Realm cologne when they moved closer to the barn and all three of them grimaced as the slap of decaying flesh hit them.

Maria turned and spread some VapoRub beneath her nose and then tossed the small container to Finley who did the same. They did their best to hide it from the sarge who preferred to "man it out." For Maria, it was bad enough the smell would linger and attach to her hair and clothes; she didn't need it invading her brain as well as she tried to work.

"So, this one's a whale, huh?" Finley said as they entered the dark and damp. The sarge spit and wiped his mouth. The scent was overpowering, sneaking in on the tails of the VapoRub. It was even getting to the sarge. Flies swarmed where she couldn't yet see. One landed on her and she swatted it away. The air was heavy, moist, menacing. She thought about a mask, but her claustrophobia wouldn't allow it. She needed to breathe, free and clear. But it was difficult.

They moved farther in and she noted the bare wood-planked walls. The barn didn't appear to have been used in years. It was a wonder it was still standing with the wooden beams so old and weak. How had it withstood the monsoon winds? The sarge led them around some tire mark evidence and stopped. He looked at them with serious brown eyes.

"I'm going to be frank with you two." Someone was playing with the portable standing lights, turning them off and on again. It caused Maria to flinch and refocus. She reached for Finley's arm to stabilize herself as their sarge continued. "This will probably be the case of your careers." The lights came on and stayed on, and Maria blinked again to focus on the form spotlighted in the center. "Diaz, Finley, meet Mr. Hale Medley. Heir to the Medley Hotel chain."

Maria's first instinct was to take a step back. Finley caught her, and she quickly regained her resolve. But the figure remained, imprinting into her brain. It was a scene she knew she'd never be able to erase or forget.

The deceased male was nude and sitting in a worn, flannel patterned cushioned chair. His arms were bound behind him and his feet were tied together. A rope wrapped his chest and chin, holding him in an upright position. His eyes were half open and a red ball gag was in his mouth with his swollen tongue protruding around it. His belly was bloated and discolored and looked as though it could burst at any moment. Those were the little things she forced herself to take in. The large things, the real eye catchers, were the wide gaping cut to half his neck and the thick carving in his forehead.

She stared while her mind computed. Despite the cut to his neck, there was no blood. Despite the cuts to his forehead, there was no blood. Flies swarmed, and she could see where what did drain from his body had seeped into the chair and onto the dirt below. It was as if he was melting into the chair. She fought turning her head. She'd seen worse in the way of decay, but never had it been such a presentation. This was for them. A sick play of sorts, with the body center stage.

Finley coughed and the sarge cleared his throat. She wasn't the only one affected.

"What's...what's on his forehead?" Maria asked as the crime scene technician hovered around the body taking photos.

"Jackson!" The sarge snapped. "The forehead."

Another technician rose from next to the body and pushed the man's head back with two careful gloved fingers.

Maria gasped.

The word HORNY had been carved into his forehead.

"Yes, my little warriors," the sarge said. "This will be the case of your careers."

Maria closed her eyes and fought dizziness. The lack of sleep was getting to her, but she couldn't let on. Instead she steeled herself and opened her eyes. Hale Medley stared back at her with a clouded, cold stare. And she admitted what she always hated to admit.

The sarge was right.

Chapter Three

W ho found the body?" Maria asked, forcing herself into "the zone" as she called it when she narrowed in on her crime scene. She moved closer after she covered her feet in blue booties and snapped on a pair of gloves. Behind her, she heard the other plainclothes enter, their banter echoing in the small enclosure. Her sarge shook hands while her hands shook as she tried to write in her small notebook. She lowered them and glanced around to make sure no one saw. But Finley's blue eyes were bright and staring right at her. He approached slowly and leaned in.

"You all right?"

"Mm, fine." She cleared her throat.

"Did you go for that checkup?"

She sighed. "No."

He nodded in frustration. "Okay, we'll talk later. In the meantime, I'll take notes and you can get them off me later." He opened his notebook, made a few notes, and then clicked on his handheld recorder. He rounded the body and began to speak while she drew ever closer, wanting a better look at the forehead.

"Diaz?" the sarge called, interrupting her inspection. He placed a hand on a young man's shoulder. "This is Everest Miller. His grandfather owns the ranch nearby. He'll tell you what you need to know." Maria stepped away from the body and faced Everest, who looked like he was green around the gills.

"Do you want to step outside?"

He shook his head. "No, ma'am, I been around dead things before. I'm all right." He tugged on the brim of his white straw cowboy hat. He appeared to be in his early twenties with a boyish face and a sad attempt at a five o'clock shadow.

"Even so, seeing someone, a murder victim, it can be overwhelming."

He refused to look anywhere near the body. He kicked at the ground. "Yeah, I—I was real shocked at first. Thought it was a dummy at first even."

"So you were the first to find him?"

"Yes, ma'am. I come up here to check my rabbit traps and to check on the fence after last night's storm. My dog run in here and my horse stopped out front and refused to go any closer. I climbed off and whistled for Remington, but he didn't come back out. So I came closer and that's when I smelled it. I thought maybe it was an animal, like maybe a coyote come in here to die or something. But the smell was too strong and I knew when I walked in here I'd find trouble."

His voice shook and he turned to spit. For a second, she didn't think he'd be able to continue. But then he regained control of himself and he tugged on his worn hat again, as if the snugger it fit on his head, the stronger he'd be.

"Like I said, when I first saw—it, I thought it was a doll. It was so pale and shiny like in the early morning light. And then I drew closer and shined my light on it, I nearly fell over backward. I scrambled to back out and I kept calling Remi, but he was—he was—you know—messing with—gnawing at—"

She stopped him with a gentle hand to his upper arm.

"Who identified him, Everest?"

He blinked as if he'd totally lost focus. "Uh, that'd be the deputy who first arrived. He found the wallet nearby and opened it with his pen."

"Did you know the victim?"

"No, ma'am. Never seen him before."

"Have you seen anyone or anything unusual around the past few days?"

He shook his head. "No, I didn't see anything, but a couple of nights ago, I heard—" his voice caved. "I heard, well, I thought it was coyotes. It was—like loud—screams." He lowered his head, and his shoulders shook as he cried. Maria squeezed his arm. "I didn't know, you know? You hear wild animals out here and when coyotes kill they yip and yowl and make all kinds of noise."

"It's okay, Everest."

"I mean, what if it was him?" He looked at her with pain filled eyes.

She led him out of the barn and back into the rain. He kept his head low while she stared up at the sky and into the falling rain. She hoped, for the briefest of moments, that it would wash everything clean and gone and that Everest hadn't seen what he'd seen or heard what he'd heard. She wished she could go home and strip and slip into a bath and fall deeply asleep in her cool bed. Oh, how she wished.

"I'll never be able to sleep again if it was him."

She turned him so he'd look at her. "Everest, from what I could see...he wasn't killed here. There isn't enough blood from the wound in his neck."

Everest nodded slowly. "You think?"

"I'm pretty sure. But regardless, it's not something for you to think about. You're an innocent bystander. And you did the right thing by calling this in quickly." She pulled out her cell phone and had him enter his name and address into her contacts. His hands trembled, and when he finished he looked embarrassed. "You did good, Everest. Real good. Now go see if someone will get you some coffee and a place to sit."

She watched him walk away and then reentered the barn. She approached the body and knelt next to Finley. "No body hair," she said, studying the shaved legs, arms, chest, and scrotum. Even his head was completely bald.

"Nope."

"Was he this well-groomed or is this ritualistic?"

"I'm guessing this was our killer's doing. Guy's clean as a whistle. Forensics said they've found next to nothing. He appears to have been thoroughly washed, maybe even bleached. And check this out." Finley held up the dead man's fingers behind the chair. "They even pulled out his nails."

"Jesus."

"That was done post mortem," a voice said next to them. Maria looked up and smiled at Dr. Haddock once again.

"I thought I heard the voice of God," Finley said, giving her a wink.

Haddock pulled on some gloves and knelt with them. Her thick blond hair was still wound into a bun, and she had on her typical dress slacks, rubber boots, and tailored blouse. Her glasses rested on the tip of her nose, and Maria always had the urge to gently push them back for her.

"See the lack of bruising and trauma to the nail bed?" she asked as she encouraged them to look at the fingers which had turned a dark crimson from settling blood. "The nails were pulled well after death." She stood. "So were the toenails. There's no healing." She lifted the dead man's chin more and made a ticking noise with her tongue as she studied the forehead. "These marks, however, were not. They were cut into him while he was alive and some time before death. See the scabbing and the attempt at healing?"

Maria grimaced. They were very deep cuts. It had to have been extremely painful.

"But the perp went to a great deal of trouble to groom and clean the body afterward. This was done somewhere very private, where they had a lot of time. I'm thinking we won't find much of anything on him."

"Time of death, Doc?" Maria asked.

Haddock took a step back and removed her gloves. "I'd say forty-eight hours. And he's been here exposed to the heat and damp for a day, possibly a little more." She paused and scanned the body again as if it were softly speaking to her. "He also has some liver mortis along his back and shoulders, suggesting he was lying flat for a time after death. Probably while he was being cleaned."

"What about cause of death?" Maria asked. "Was his throat slit while alive?"

"Could've been. There's a great deal of trauma and more than a few attempts. We'll have to clean him up a bit to get a better look."

Maria noted the leaking nose, mouth, and gaping wound. He was decomposing quickly from the inside out.

"He was bled out and then bathed," Finley said.

"To hide evidence," Maria said. "They may have been amateurs in killing, but they were good at getting rid of forensic evidence."

"I'll oversee the medical examiner who does the autopsy. I want the best of the best on this," Haddock said. "I've never seen anything quite like this. Certainly not in Las Brisas."

"There may be more," Maria said as she studied the body. Someone was trying to make a statement. And they were deadly serious in the way they chose to make it. She had a feeling they weren't done talking.

"This could possibly be a female perp," Finley said, standing next to Haddock.

"I'd say more than one," Haddock said.

Maria backed away and stood next to them. She wasn't sure on more than one. A single pissed off female could've pulled this off with careful planning. But why? Abuse? Violence? Revenge? And why all the trouble? It was unusual for women to kill hands on. So why didn't she poison him or shoot him?

Finley answered, as if he'd heard her.

"The killer wanted to make him suffer. And they wanted to shock whoever found him."

"Yes," Haddock said. "And shock us, she did."

"If this is a woman, she is one twisted bitch," he said.

"Twisted, yes. But intelligent, more so. She's one smart, smart woman," Maria said. She knew the time it took, the planning, the blood draining, the cleaning, the moving of the body. If the killer were a woman, she'd be hell to stop if she chose to continue.

"She is clever," Haddock said. "During my walk through I found small tire marks. Indicative of a dolly or a hand truck. He wasn't drug in, he was wheeled in and then placed in the chair."

"Which is in the center of the barn, ready to shock whoever entered," Maria said.

"Precisely."

"And the killer wanted us to know right away who he was by leaving the wallet next to the chair."

"Yes, where the hell did that come from when they left literally nothing else on the body?" Finley asked.

Maria reached for her phone and took photos. Finley did the same, only he made his way backward from the body, photographing the crime scene techs as they took casts of the tire marks.

When they finished, they gathered next to the Jeep under the gray sky. Maria wiped the VapoRub from her nose and tossed the hand towel to Finley who did the same. She always carried a kit with her to every scene. Water, VapoRub, towels, gloves, dry T-shirts, socks, and rubber boots like Haddock wore. She didn't use them much in Las Brisas, but she was always glad to have them when she did. She tossed Finley a water and a fresh wet towel. He wiped his face and neck and cleaned his shades before slipping them on. She wiped herself down with her own towel, trying to rid her skin of the mud flecks.

"This is a goddamned nightmare of a case," Finley said, kicking his boots against her tires.

"You said it."

"Horny? Can you imagine the field day the press will have with this one?"

"So, we don't tell them."

"Yeah, like that won't leak."

"Let's hope it doesn't. It's critical to the case."

He brushed off the legs to his pants and climbed in. He gripped the roll bar, ready to go. Maria asked the question that had been on her mind since she'd seen the word horny. "If the killer wanted to make him suffer, and he/she is attacking his libido, why were the genitals left alone?"

Finley sighed. "I was wondering the same."

"That tells me this killer has self-control and deliberation. And that…is very, very scary." It meant the killer would be more than careful and more difficult for them to catch. Intelligent, yes. Oh, yes, the killer was intelligent.

"Now we've got to go find this psycho who thinks he's a little too horny," Finley said with a scowl. "From what I know about him, that won't be so easy."

"He a dog?"

"A big one."

"Great."

She packed up her kit and placed it in the back. She took several swigs of warm water and caught sight of another plainclothes running toward them. It was Martin Biggs, another detective in their unit. She wasn't surprised to see him. No doubt the sarge would pull out all the stops on this case.

"Diaz," he said, catching his breath as he stopped at the Jeep. He bent with his hands on his knees. "Glad I caught you."

"What's up?" Finley asked.

"I've got a big lead for you."

"Oh?" Maria perked up and Finley removed his shades.

"This Medley guy," he breathed. "Big damn deal. Very, very wealthy. Big time playboy. Liked his women a lot. High class, high pedigree, prostitutes, it didn't matter as long as they were hot and willing."

"Sounds like we'll be busy," Maria said.

But he held up a hand. "There's one you should know about. One he tried to get for years, but she always turned him down. I guess it caused a feud between them, and at one point she even threatened to kill him."

He straightened as he caught his breath. "Her name is Ashland. Avery Ashland."

"Holy shit," Finley said. "*The* Avery Ashland? Of Ashland Resorts?"

"That's the one."

Finley slid on his shades and looked to Maria.

"Get in the Jeep, Diaz. This case just went from shit show to shit fest."

She climbed in and started the engine. "What's going on? Who is Avery Ashland?"

He laughed. "Very soon, you'll wish you never, ever wanted to know."

Chapter Four

Avery Ashland. Maria thumbed through the information on her phone. Owner of Ashland Resorts Incorporated. Had inherited the popular resort chain from her late father, Paul Ashland, and remained mostly a silent partner in the business with the exception of Euphoria, which had been her own brain child, which she owned and ran freely on the outskirts of Las Brisas. Euphoria was well known to be an elaborate, expensive, private resort where Avery Ashland threw lavish parties and hosted numerous private get-togethers. Maria had heard of Euphoria and of the swanky rumors, but she'd never ventured out to take a look. It was way out of her price range so she'd never given it a second thought. Now, she couldn't be more curious, and Finley hadn't done a very good job of explaining anything to her.

"So it's big?" she asked, glancing over at him as he drove.

He nodded and took a long draw off the straw of his gas station soda. "Enormous. The resort itself is large, yes, but she owns acres and acres of land around it."

"Wow."

"I'm telling you, you've never seen anything like it."

"And people actually travel here to stay?"

"Uh-huh. It's private and exclusive. Meant for the richest of rich and for those with a certain taste for…eroticism."

She laughed at how ridiculous he sounded.

"I'm serious."

"As in sex?" She looked out the window, suddenly understanding just what Finley had meant when he'd said the case had turned into a shit fest. Sex was already a huge variable in their murder, they didn't need more to add fuel to the raging fire the press would no doubt build if they caught wind.

"Yep. Private sex parties. At least so I've heard."

"So you've heard. Like when? While shooting the shit with the guys?" She rolled her eyes and tried to play it like she found the whole thing ludicrous. She'd only heard of such things in movies and television shows. She'd never had to investigate a sex party or deal with one in real life. So who's to say he was right?

She looked down at her hands. With all the debauchery she'd seen in her days on the force—prostitution, drugs, trafficking, and numerous other things she'd rather forget about, she found herself surprised at how little she knew about legal private sex parties and swingers' clubs. It made her feel more than a little prudish.

"We turn up here." Finley pointed to a large gleaming sign set in stone on the side of the road. It read Euphoria. It shimmered in the sun and she swallowed at the expense and high quality of the sign alone.

He turned and drove down a long winding paved road. Soon the desert turned to gravel, deep purple in color which matched the surrounding mountains. Narrow paved trails led through the gravel, and as he drove, they led back to lush fields of grass and trees.

"It's like an oasis."

She stared at the cool looking green grass and all the shade the trees provided. A quick glance at the thermostat awed her even more. It was a hundred and eleven degrees outside, yet by the look of this tropical paradise, it seemed as though they were on the shore of some beautiful island. She pointed as they came upon a group of swimming pools off to the left, sparkling blue with waterfalls and wide white sun beds under wooden cabanas. Oh, how she wanted to dive right in and swim and relax in the cold water.

"There's the resort," Finley said as he pointed.

He stopped her Jeep Cherokee and they both stared. The main resort tower was massive and at least two dozen stories high. It stood stark white with red Spanish tiled roofing and highlights around the windows. Lush looking vines climbed the stuccoed walls while heavy looking palms, elaborate statues, and crystal blue fountains brought the whole package together, leaving Maria excited and completely overwhelmed.

"Damn, this is definitely not Kansas anymore, Toto," she said to Finley.

"Gee, hon, we should've brought the Bentley," he said as they pulled up at the entrance on a cobblestone path. He grinned and climbed out as a man in a white uniform held the door for him.

"Good, afternoon, sir. Can I get your bags?"

Maria climbed out her side and inhaled the fresh, clean smelling air. Misters lined the awning, cooling the entrance. Another gentleman nodded politely to her, wanting to park her vehicle. "Be careful with her," Maria said. "She's priceless."

"Yes, ma'am."

Maria grinned at Finley. "What the hell have we gotten ourselves into?"

"I told you," he whispered, tucking her arm under his. "See why I insisted we shower and change?"

"Mm-hm." They walked into the large entrance through tall, heavy looking wooden doors and into the considerably cooler resort. Maria stopped and blinked and everything came at her in warm colors. From the burnt red of the Spanish tile flooring, to the wooden ceiling with truss beams, to the rich hues of the accent furniture to the red patterned rugs. All of it contrasted with cool, smooth white walls and a huge stone fireplace surrounded by deep brown leather couches.

"Close your mouth, you'll attract flies," Finley whispered with a nudge.

"I can't help it. This is so beautiful. Look at the colors on the artwork. And look at those indoor trees. Man, I wish I lived here."

In the far corner, an antique grandfather clock chimed the quarter hour.

Finley tugged on her.

"Now be confident," he said. "And remember, smile."

She tore her eyes away from the décor. "What do you care?"

"Trust me on this."

They crossed to a shiny tiled counter.

"Hi." He smiled unabashedly at the young female resort worker. "We're here to see Ms. Ashland."

The woman laughed as if they were joking and then stopped. "You're serious?"

"I'm afraid so."

"Do you have an appointment?"

"No."

"Then what makes you think you can see her?"

"We're old friends." He leaned causally on the counter. "Did I forget to mention that?"

The woman stared at him for a long, hard moment.

"Names?"

"Oh, we want to surprise her."

She rolled her eyes. "Sir, Ms. Ashland doesn't see random visitors. You have to make an appointment."

"And I do that where? With you?"

"No. And if you really knew her, you'd know that."

"I see." He slipped his hand in his jacket pocket and pulled out his badge. He set it on the counter. "How 'bout now? Can I make that appointment? How about for, say, right now?"

She slid the badge toward her and picked it up. "Just one moment." She turned with the badge and crossed to a telephone on a beautiful antique wood desk, lit by a green bank lamp. She spoke for several minutes and seemed to be flustered. When she hung up she didn't bother to force a smile.

Instead she returned the badge and dug behind the counter for a key on a gold palm tree keychain. She slid it to Maria.

"Take the elevator to the top floor. You'll have to use the key to gain access to the penthouse."

"Thank you," Maria said.

"Just you," she said. "Your husband can wait here."

Finley read her name tag. "Look, Kelly, I'm not her husband. I'm her partner."

"Whatever you want to call it, you can wait here. She'll only see the woman."

Finley turned and elbowed her. She caught sight of several cameras.

"We're homicide detectives and I'm going with her," Finley said.

Kelly rolled her eyes and held up her hands toward the camera. The phone rang from the desk behind her. She answered but did not speak. She hung up and returned.

"Fine, go ahead. But I'll need to see your badge first, ma'am."

Maria dug in the pocket of her short dress jacket and handed it over. This time the woman wrote down the information before returning it. "You can go ahead," she said.

Finley held out his elbow. "Shall we, dear?"

She took his arm and they crossed the long walkway to the elevator where they nodded at the man who opened it for them. They stepped inside without him and Finley inserted the key and turned it, allowing the penthouse button to be pressed.

"Why does she only want to see me?"

"Just play along," he said. "Remember, be confident and smile."

They continued in silence and she glanced down at her pencil skirt and dark hose. Her blouse was lavender and her short jacket matched her skirt. Finley had insisted she wear her hair down so it rested in waves along her shoulders. Now she was beginning to wonder why.

The door opened and they stepped into a hallway, this time covered in ivory tile. Finley led the way, whistling at the expensive art on the walls. They stopped before a set of large dark double doors. A security pad of some sort flanked the doors. Maria's heart began to beat fast like it did when she first shot her gun in the field. Adrenaline surged through her, but she had no idea why.

The doors opened and an older woman in pressed pants and a casual blouse showed them inside. She had a gentle smile and her salt-and-pepper hair was worn in a long braid. Maria returned the smile and thanked her as she led them to another large room with high ceilings. And though the room was somewhat dim, Maria made out the lush rugs, colorful art, hand sculpted statues, and expensive yet more modern furniture. A vase of fresh flowers sat atop a shiny grand piano.

"Ms. Ashton will see you in here." The woman opened another set of double doors and Maria squinted at the bright light coming from floor-to-ceiling windows. A dark figure stood before them in a pair of pin-striped pants, sharp looking heels, and a sleeveless blouse. Her silhouette looked like it had just stepped off a painting. Her form long and sleek and elegant.

The woman didn't speak at first, just held her cigarette near her face, and for a second Maria wondered if they had the right woman. The tall blonde appeared to be lost in thought, as if they weren't even there. Surely someone who knew the police wanted to speak to her would be more keen to their presence.

"I suppose you came to talk about Hale?" she said before inhaling her cigarette and blowing it out toward the window. She brushed back her hair and finally turned. She walked with confident long strides, and Maria felt herself heat as she took in the angles of her face. She forced herself to look away as the woman offered them a seat and then sat on the white sofa across from them. She crossed her legs and stubbed out her cigarette in a crystal ashtray.

"Yes, we came to discuss Hale," Finley said. He reached for his small notebook and began to write.

"I'm not interested in what you have to say," the woman said, halting him.

"You." She threw her voice toward Maria. "Who are you?"

Maria met her eyes and she felt them penetrate. They were light brown in color, almost gold, alive and seeking. Maria felt exposed, as if the woman could see right into her soul. She blinked, hoping to break the focus, but the woman didn't flinch. Maria glanced away and forced herself to speak with the confidence that was slowly being pulled away.

"I'm Detective Diaz," she said.

A quick glance back to the woman showed Maria that her stare hadn't changed. She was looking at her as if she were devouring everything about her.

"I'm Avery Ashland. Pleasure to make your acquaintance."

Maria nodded, not quite trusting her voice.

"Diaz," Avery said with a low, throaty rasp. "Hispanic?"

"Yes." Suspects rarely asked personal questions. They usually only wanted, needed, to know about the case at hand. Where they stood. How much trouble they were in. And could they maneuver out of it. This, this was new.

"Of course. The dark hair, olive skin, I knew right away." Avery paused, fumbled with a case on the coffee table, and plucked a long, slim cigarette from a blue and white package that read Vogue. She lit the cigarette, inhaled, and said while exhaling, "They're French. Would you like one?" She spoke directly to Maria. She didn't give Finley a second glance.

"No, thank you."

"You don't smoke."

"No, I don't."

"Of course not." She looked her up and down. "You have to stay in tip-top shape. Be ready for anything." She grinned. "That means no on anything unhealthy. And by the looks of your body, I'd say you stick to that quite well."

Maria fought a blush. She looked at Finley who cleared his throat and tried again to enter the conversation.

"Ms. Ashland, we'd like to ask some questions about Hale Medley."

Avery stood, rounded the coffee table, and extended her slim hand to Maria.

"Come, Detective Diaz." She smiled.

Maria took her hand and stood along with her, not liking the way she stood over her. It was a power thing.

"Promise me you'll call me Avery. Ms. Ashland sounds so ancient." She slipped her hand into Maria's elbow and began to lead them away. "I understand you wish to talk about Hale?"

Maria shot a glance back to Finley who shrugged. He stood, waved her on, and began snooping on his own.

Avery led them toward a back room in the open, airy penthouse. More double doors led to a vast master bedroom. Maria halted at the door.

Avery only laughed. "Relax, Detective. I don't bite."

Maria watched as she entered the room, crossed to a deep closet, entered, and emerged completely nude, tossing a sun dress onto the bed. "I simply wanted to change into something more comfortable as we talked." She eyed her with a crooked grin. "Surely you can understand that?"

Maria burned and struggled for breath. She'd seen plenty of nude women in the locker room and on film. And of course, she'd had a handful of lovers. But seeing Avery's long, lean body glowing in the afternoon sunlight sent lightning bolts straight to her center, into her gut and all throughout her skin. She was burning alive in her stupid kitten heels.

Avery slid the dress on over her head and straightened in the mirror. She turned her head.

"Would you mind zipping me up?"

Maria had to find the nerve to speak. "I think you should ask someone else to do that."

"Who? That Neanderthal partner of yours? No, thanks."

"What about your housekeeper?"

"Nadine?" She laughed. "Good heavens, no. Where's the fun in that?"

"I didn't realize this was about fun."

"Oh, it's always about fun." She walked toward Maria with graceful strides like a runway model. She stopped inches from her, smiled softly, and turned, exposing her bare back.

Maria inhaled deeply as she felt the electricity between them. She could reach out and run her fingertips along her spine, tease her ripple of muscles as they moved, kiss her freckle near the bottom. She shivered with a desire so strong she almost lost her balance.

"Please?" Avery asked with a whisper. "Just a delicate little zip."

"I can't," Maria said, unable to hide the quiver to her voice.

"Why not?"

"I—"

"Here, give me your hand." She reached back and found Maria's hand. "Let me help you." She placed it at the bottom near the zipper. "There."

Maria pressed her lips together and clenched the zipper. She tugged upward and covered her back. She dropped her hand slowly, as if she'd just completely splayed open her insides and Avery had seen them all, even picked through them to find the parts she wanted to see most.

Avery turned and floored her again with her eyes. "Thank you." The corner of her mouth lifted in amusement. She took Maria's hand and led them through the bedroom and out onto the terrace. The rain had stopped, but the sun was winking through the clouds as if it couldn't decide what to do. Avery offered her a seat and then eased onto a reclined lounge. She crossed her ankles and slid on a pair of expensive looking shades.

"Would you like a drink?" Avery lifted a receiver and spoke French into the phone. She hung up and sighed. "I hate the rain. It brings such trouble. Wouldn't you agree?"

Maria leaned back and tried to relax and get her bearings, but she couldn't. She was stiff as a board but as wet as the ocean. Avery had gotten the one-up on her, and she didn't know how to recover. So she did what she'd learned to do as a child. She acted tough.

"Are you referring to Hale?"

Avery stared off into the sky. "I suppose I could be." She sounded unshaken, calm.

"If you don't mind my asking, how did you know we were here to talk about Hale?"

Avery turned toward her. "Because he's dead, isn't he?"

A chill went up Maria's spine. "How do you know?"

Avery chuckled. "Come on, Detective, don't play coy. I might like it."

Maria fought against the inner turmoil of fear and desire. It was swirling and gaining strength and bringing her down fast. She imagined drowning right there in a chair on a terrace of a penthouse. Drowning without anyone to know, anyone to help or even grieve.

Avery was studying her, and when Maria didn't speak, she did. "Hale has long been a nemesis of sorts. And I make it a point to know my enemies and know them well. If they succeed, I know. If they fail, I know. If they die—I know."

"How?"

"Friends."

"Friends?"

"Yes. Good friends. Friends who have access to information."

"As in police investigations?"

She laughed into the sky. "I know he's dead, Detective. Isn't that all that matters?"

"You don't seem too upset by it."

"Would you be if it were your enemy?"

"I don't have enemies."

"Oh, I don't believe that. I'm sure you've broken hearts all over Las Brisas. Question is, how did I not know about you?"

"Why would you?"

Avery looked at her and removed her shades to place the tip of the arm in her mouth. "Because you're stunning."

Maria looked away, but Avery continued. "And gay."

Maria whipped her head back and stared into her. "How—I—"

"You nearly came out of your skin when you first saw me. And then when I was nude and asked you to touch me—I thought you were going to fall over with pent-up desire."

Maria stood and hid her trembling hands behind her back. "I think we're done here."

"What about my dear friend Hale?"

"We'll be back," she said as she turned and walked through the bedroom and back through the penthouse to find Finley. She found him snooping through a tall bookcase.

"We're going." She didn't wait for him to catch up.

"Guess what I got?" he said. "A lifted print and a cigarette butt."

"Great, wonderful."

"Wait. What happened? What's going on?"

They reached the elevator and stepped inside. She squared off with him.

"She's gay."

He blinked as if shocked.

"And you used me to get to her."

"I—I'm—"

"How could you not tell me?"

He grabbed her shoulders. "Because she would've known. She would've sniffed us out. And she would've clammed up. We had to do it this way."

"We?"

He sighed.

"What the hell have you gotten me into, Finley?" She leaned against the elevator wall as dizziness came again. "What the hell have you gotten me into?"

Chapter Five

A very lifted the phone receiver and sipped from her glass of Chateau Margaux 2010. It was slightly chilled, just as she liked it, with hints of blueberry and black currant, just what she needed. She knew it would only take a glass or two to completely relax her, and she needed that after her enticing encounter with Detective Diaz. She swallowed another decadent sip before Bobby Luca, her private investigator, answered. Then she spoke softly and swiftly.

"Detective Diaz. Female. Las Brisas County Sherriff's Office. Find out all you can about her."

She replaced the receiver, stood, and stared down at the front of the resort. She saw a dark, older model Jeep Grand Cherokee speed away like it was running from hell itself.

"Oh, Detective Diaz. They sent you all fresh and squirming on your sweet little hook. They knew I'd bite, but how did you not know you were the reason?"

"Avery," Nadine said, carrying a plate of fresh fruit and cheese.

"Just set it down, please," she said. "Unfortunately, our guest is gone."

"I'm sorry to hear that."

"She'll be back."

"Shall I prepare a meal then? For this evening?"

"No, she won't have an appetite…for food. She'll be more interested in information."

"Would you like me to inform the staff?"

"No. I want everyone to behave as they always do. I want everything run as it always is."

Nadine seemed to hesitate. Avery noticed and grew frustrated.

"What is it? You've been with me since I was a child, yet you still hesitate to speak your truth. Spill it, woman."

Nadine cleared her throat. "Are you sure you want to go ahead with tomorrow night's festivities?"

Avery cocked her head. "Yes, why wouldn't I?"

"Because there might be police presence."

Avery sipped more of her wine. "Everything will continue as planned."

Nadine nodded.

"And, Nadine?"

"Yes?"

"I want to know the second Detective Diaz shows up."

"You're sure she will?"

Avery couldn't help but smile. "Oh, yes. She won't be able to help herself."

"Avery?" Nadine asked.

"Yes, Nadine?"

Nadine played with her hands. "She seems nice."

Avery met her gaze. "Yes, she does, doesn't she?"

Nadine excused herself and Avery deposited her wine glass on the table. She entered her bedroom, stripped once again, and ran a bath in her oversized Roman tub. She slid into the slick porcelain and bathed with her fragrant sliced soap and Prive shampoo and conditioner. When she finished, she climbed out and stepped into a satin robe to air dry. She was combing through her hair when a knock came from her bedroom door.

"In," she called and sprayed on her perfume. She'd made it herself on one of her many trips to Paris. She was in dire need of a new bottle.

"Mm, I can smell you already," Lana Gold said as she entered in a long white cotton dress and sandals. Her red hair was pulled up into a twisted bun and loose strands hung down to tease the moisture on her shoulders. "Won't you ever tell me what's in that perfume of yours?"

"No."

Lana came to stand behind her. She wrapped her arms around her and stared into the mirror with her. She kissed her neck and teased her ear. Avery closed her eyes at the sensation and then opened them with a ferocious desire. Toying with Diaz had turned her on, and she wanted and needed nothing more than to get off.

She shoved Lana back and tore off her robe. She threw it at her and walked to the bed where she lay down and called to her with a curled finger.

Lana tossed the robe aside and climbed onto the bed.

"I want your mouth on me," Avery said, opening her legs and stroking herself. "Now."

Lana lowered herself and began kissing and teasing the sensitive flesh of her inner thighs. But Avery couldn't take it. She grabbed her head and pulled her onto her aching cunt. She made a loud noise as Lana's mouth hit her, all hot and wet and heavy.

"That's it, fuck yeah." She bucked her hips and held fast to her. She clenched her eyes and thought of Diaz and her lusciously curvy body in the tight pencil skirt. She thought of her flashing dark eyes and stubborn set to her mouth. Thought of her trembling hands and trembling lip that she failed to hide. And mostly, she thought of the heat on her cheeks and upper chest as she burned with poorly harbored desire.

"Oh, God. Oh, fuck yes." She writhed into the pleasure and imagined Diaz between her legs. But when she opened her eyes, the delicate bubble of the fantasy was pierced and she sat up, pulling Lana away.

"What?" Lana touched her mouth and sat back.

"My vibrator. Where is it?' She had to come and she had to come now. She was nearly ready to burst.

"Why?"

"Just get it."

Lana leaned over and dug through the nightstand. She found the soft, pink, vibrating dildo, and Avery took it from her, switched it on, and held it to her flesh. Her head and neck arched as the pleasure returned, and she laughed into it, closing her eyes once again to think of Diaz. As the pleasure mounted, she pinched her own nipples and arced up into the phallus. When she felt Lana fasten to her breast, she didn't protest, but rather came up off the bed in orgasmic spasms.

She came and came and came again, calling out for the one she wanted, the one who currently eluded her.

"Who's Diaz?" Lana asked before she had completely come down from her climax.

Avery lay still with her heart pounding and her breath struggling to go in and out. She rolled out of bed and slipped back into her robe. She felt hot and tingly and alive. Her chest heaved in spent heaven. She felt wonderful.

She returned to the bathroom and finished getting ready. Bobby would arrive any minute with news on Diaz.

"Avery?"

Lana reentered the bathroom. "Another woman?"

Avery combed her hair and examined her dewy skin. "No. Not yet." She turned and planted a lingering kiss on Lana's lips. "I have an appointment. I need to get ready."

"Now?"

"Yes, now."

"But we had plans."

"Well, we'll have to reschedule."

"Avery, I came all this way."

Avery stared at her in the mirror. "Lana, you know how this goes, how this plays out. We aren't exclusive; we see who we want to see when we want to see them. And right now, I have an urgent appointment."

"With this Diaz?"

"No, you'll be glad to know it's not with her. It's with Bobby."

Lana's stern face softened. "Oh."

"Yes, so I'll call you later, okay?"

Lana nodded, studied her for a moment, and then turned to leave. She paused at the door.

"Are you seeing Bobby about Hale?"

Avery stopped styling her hair. "I'm sure the subject will come up."

Lana hesitated at the doorway and then left the bathroom and the bedroom. Avery heard the door close behind her. Lana was a little possessive, and though she'd told her time and again they weren't exclusive, that didn't keep Lana from hoping. Avery suspected it was because they'd known each other so long and had experienced so many sexual liaisons together, it seemed likely they'd end up together. But Lana couldn't hold her attention, and relationships of any sort she steered clear of. That is, except for her nieces. But that relationship was private and so very special. She shared it with no one other than Nadine. She thought of the beautiful detective and wondered if she'd consider a relationship with her. Her heart fluttered, and a warm feeling overcame her. Just as it had all those years ago with Bryce, her first female lover. It was a warm, tempting feeling, but it left her feeling vulnerable so she forced herself to laugh and straighten her posture.

She'd eat the detective alive. And then some.

The determined detective was so ripe and full of harbored desire she'd surely pop at the slightest touch.

The realization caused a grin, and she thought how very much she'd like to tease that pop out of her. Make her beg for it. Plead. Pant. Go fucking mad. She knew she could do it. It was her specialty and it was what drew married woman after married woman to her, night after night, on the arms of their wealthy husbands who were up for a little fun of their own. Of course, the fun ended up being all hers, but she couldn't let on just how much fun she was having in taking their wives to the very edge of desire.

She returned to her lounge chair on the now sunny patio and settled in, already a little turned on again. The breeze had kicked up, as had the smell of dirt and rain, promising another monsoon. Usually, she dreaded the monsoon season because it wreaked havoc on her evening events. But lately, she'd embraced the storms, even standing outdoors to smile up into the lightning as it lit up the sky. Her mood was new, but she knew exactly the cause. And it wasn't just the introduction to the beautiful detective. It was the death of Hale Medley.

She grinned as she rested her hands behind her head and crossed her ankles to stare into the sky.

He wouldn't be causing her any more trouble.

Ever again.

CHAPTER SIX

I feel like I'm trapped in a thick leather mosquito net," Maria said as she lost her balance stepping into the impossibly high heels.

"Well, you look hot and that's all that matters." Finley straightened his bow tie and grabbed her arm to steady her.

She looked at herself in the mirror and grimaced. She tugged at the thick black straps of her dress which were squeezing her and barely covering her most private of parts. "I hate it. I'm changing."

But Finley held firm. "Ah-ah-ah. No, you aren't."

"I look…I look…"

"Hot."

She scoffed. "This is not me, Fins. I feel like a mummy."

He leaned forward and examined his close shave. "Precisely. We don't want you anywhere in the picture tonight. Not the real you, that is."

"I'm not playing some little sex kitten. You can forget it."

He laughed. "Can't you at least try?"

She glared at him as he slicked back his hair.

"No."

"Just flirt a little."

"She won't buy it. She already saw the real me. And I wasn't happy."

He rested his hands on her shoulders. "Perfect." He turned and left her in the restroom.

"Wait, what?" She followed him, stumbling a little. "I'm so confused. Can't I just go in as myself?"

He sat on his bed and a baby toy squeaked. He pulled it from beneath his bottom and tossed it across the room. "No, we'll stick out like a sore thumb. We need to blend."

She rolled her eyes and Paige entered with a six-month-old Silas Junior on her hip. She whistled and Finley rose to kiss her.

"Don't you look dapper?" She smiled and the baby shoved a teething toy in his mouth. His eyes were bright like Finley's and his cheeks were red like a cherub. Maria's heart surged, and she promised herself again not to ever let anything happen to Finley.

"I feel like a freak," Maria said.

Paige laughed. "Hardly. You'll knock 'em dead, girl."

Still not even close to being comforted, Maria pawed at her hair which was up and teased. "What about my hair? My makeup?"

Paige touched her arm. "Maria, you look good. Really good. Honest."

Maria closed her eyes and breathed deeply. "Okay."

Finley clapped his hands. "Good. We'd better head out if we want to beat that storm." He again kissed Paige, this time on the cheek, and he did the same with baby Silas. He blew a kiss as they walked out the door and down the hallway to the garage.

"You're lucky, you know," Maria said.

"Yep." They entered the garage and climbed into the black Lincoln SUV Finley had rented for this evening's event. Maria inhaled the new car smell and fought running her hands over the leather seats. She had very little experience with luxuries, and it was difficult to hide her admiration. Growing up, they'd had one vehicle for a family of six. It was an old panel-sided station wagon and she'd hated it. Now, though, she wished her parents had kept it. It had brought them through many good times. And if she closed her eyes real tight and remembered, she could almost smell the cracking vinyl seats and worn carpet.

"I don't think I've ever had a new car," she said as Finley backed out of the driveway and drove into a wall of deep blue sky.

A vein of lightning shot through, letting them know they didn't have much time before blowing dust and rainfall.

"No?"

"No."

Finley tapped his thumb on the steering wheel. "Well, embrace it. We'll be pretending to live the high life while we investigate Ashland."

"I'm not okay with this approach."

"So you've said."

"And I resent being the one dangling in front of her."

Finley laughed. "We didn't do that. She made up her own mind the second she saw you."

"Which you knew would happen."

"Well, I confess, I had hoped. Makes this a whole lot easier."

"Maybe for you."

"You'll be fine. Just let her wine and dine you. Let her talk. See where it leads."

"I plan on asking her point-blank questions."

Finley sighed. "Diaz, come on. Play the game a little."

Maria stared into the storm. Wind battled the car, and the trees bent to face off with them as well. They were headed for one hell of a storm. And it had nothing to do with the impending monsoon.

Maria squinted through the rain- and dust-splattered windshield, trying to get a better view of Euphoria and the people arriving for the private party. But the wipers were only smearing things, and she sat back and groaned with impatience.

"Easy, there, partner. We'll get in soon enough." Finley adjusted the AC and sat back in his seat.

"I just want to see what kind of people are ahead of us."

"Rich people. Very rich people. And they've come to play."

Finley had done his best to bring her up to speed on Ashland's private parties, and what she'd heard had her nerves working overtime. She tried to wipe her moist palms on her leather skirt but to no avail.

"So this is going to be like a swingers' type thing?" She prayed she'd heard wrong. That Finley had been mistaken. While she'd learned Avery Ashland was into this sort of thing, she'd hoped that by some miracle she wouldn't have to confront it. If she did, she'd hoped she'd at least have more time to get a better handle on her suspect. But here she was, being thrown to the lions one day after meeting her and nearly coming in her pants over her.

She palmed her forehead, nerves firing off worse than they had with the worst of offenders.

"Something along those lines. No one inside the department really knows for sure. We've only heard the rumors."

"Great. We could be walking into an orgy."

"Only if we find the right room." He looked over at her and grinned.

She smacked his arm. They eased forward in line and were finally under the awning at the entrance. Valets hurried about in their white outfits, soaked through to the skin. Her door was opened quickly, and she startled.

"Madam?" A valet held out his hand for her.

She took a deep breath and climbed from the car with his assistance. He helped to balance her on her heels. She looked around quickly for Finley who sauntered up to her side.

"Relax."

"I'm trying."

"Try harder. You look fantastic, now act like you know it."

"I'm not used to looking fantastic."

"Ha ha. Nice try. You know you always do. Have some confidence for Christ's sake."

"Okay, fine." She straightened her back and held her head high.

"Good, now smile."

She forced a smile.

"Not like that. You look crazy."

She relaxed her face and Finley nodded and led her inside. They moved slowly behind others and were waved right through the entrance, which surprised them both. The lobby was lit with low golden light, and soft music played. Voices rose as someone behind them was denied entrance. Finley had to pull her onward as she tried to take in the commotion.

"I wonder who that was," she said.

"Probably some perv trying to get in to get his rocks off."

Maria saw a man in a suit and tie being led back out by two men in white. He was yelling, but she couldn't understand him and most of the other guests seemed to ignore him.

"Come on." Finley followed the crowd to the long counter of the front desk. Employees handed out envelopes to the guests, and she was surprised when one was handed to her.

"What is this?" She fumbled with it.

"Open it."

Finley was bouncing on his tiptoes, one of his more annoying nervous habits. Her hands trembled and she handed the envelope over to him. He slid his thumb into the corner and tore it open. It contained an elaborate invitation to the evening's ball and a room key was also provided.

"A little presumptuous, isn't she?" Maria asked. "She knows we aren't together."

"Maybe it's for you alone."

Maria took a deep breath, and they entered the elevator to go to the fifth floor. The other guests standing next to them looked similar in tuxes and designer dresses. They all offered soft smiles, and a few held hands. One couple kissed. They looked like any other people you would pass on the street. She'd never peg them to attend something like this. Whatever this was. Finley squeezed her hand in reassurance and she tried to relax. But when the doors opened, they faced off with more security. And this time they were stopped.

"Ms. Diaz." The man, who was large and muscled, gave her another envelope. He waved Finley through. She tried to follow, but the man stopped her and nodded at the envelope. She clawed it open and found the elevator key to the penthouse.

"Your presence is requested," he said with a bow.

She tried to call to Finley, but he had already disappeared into the darkened hallway. Blue lights accented forms and figures, but she couldn't make him out.

"Damn it." They'd been there five minutes and they were already separated. She slammed the envelope against her thigh and then turned back to the elevator. She texted Finley on the ride up.

I've been sent back to the penthouse. Help!

She rode in silence as guest after guest exited well before the penthouse. The doors opened as she tucked her phone into her clasp, and she took an awkward step out.

"Hello?"

The doors closed behind her. Her eyes adjusted, and she saw a single candle lit near the large double doors of the penthouse. She picked it up and walked inside as the doors clicked open. She came to another candle in front of the vast doorway to the living room. She walked inside and saw a tiny glow of orange coming from the sofa.

"You made it."

Maria sucked in a quick breath as she recognized Avery Ashton's voice.

"Please, sit."

Maria rounded the facing couch and sat, placing the candle amongst two others on the coffee table. Avery leaned forward and was lit up in all angles and shadows. The sight took Maria's breath away, and she had to battle to get it back. She might have gained control of her breathing but she couldn't control her staring. Avery was just too striking.

A coy smile came across Avery's face as she watched her in return. She seemed to be enjoying herself, and she sat back, crossed her legs, and sucked on her cigarette.

"You look exquisite," she finally said.

Maria looked down nervously and smoothed down her leather dress. She felt like she was going to pop out of it in several areas.

"Don't worry," Avery said. "I don't think you're in any danger of exposing yourself. It seems to be a...perfect fit." She grinned again, and Maria's heart pounded.

"You look nice as well," Maria said, trying to sound calm and polite. Avery glanced down at her white sleeveless body suit, cut deep at her cleavage. A gold chain hung there with a locket shimmering in the candlelight.

"Mm, a compliment. Thank you." She leaned forward and tapped the ash off her cigarette. "I thought for sure after our last visit, I wouldn't hear such kind words."

Maria fought squirming. "I can be nice."

"Can you?" She laughed. She again took another drag. "Why are you here, Detective? I mean, why tonight of all nights? Surely you didn't come to play. Or did you?"

Maria searched for an answer. The large room was quiet and dancing in candlelight. Beyond the open curtains, she could see Las Brisas lit up in all its glory. The diamond in the desert.

"You know why I'm here."

"To talk about Hale?"

"Yes."

"But you thought, what? You'd come dressed ready to swing just in case?"

"I simply wanted to fit in."

Avery belted out in deep laughter, and it stroked Maria's spine like the touch of a light feather. "My dear, try as you might, you will never be able to fit in."

"Why is that?"

"One, because you're gorgeous, and two, because you have absolutely no clue that you are."

This time Maria did squirm.

"I've embarrassed you."

"No, I'm fine."

"Would you like me to escort you to the party? After all, I'm sure you want to see what exactly goes on here don't you?"

"I'd rather talk about Hale."

"Hale attended the parties. Aren't you curious as to what he experienced?"

"My partner's downstairs. I'm sure he's taking enough notes for the both of us."

Avery stood as if dissatisfied with the answer. She held out her hand. "Please, allow me to show you around."

Maria hesitated but then stood alongside her. She kept her hand to herself. Avery chuckled at that, but then placed her hand at the small of her back to escort her back to the elevator. They rode in silence to the sixth floor, and Maria squeezed her clutch for dear life. She knew she was about to walk into a sex party, but she honestly had no idea what to expect.

"Please," Avery said, offering her to exit the elevator first. Maria did so and Avery was right back by her side, leading her past the obedient security guards to the blue lit hallway where every room door was open allowing noises of pleasure to escape.

"Don't you want to look inside?" Avery asked in a whisper.

Maria clenched her jaw and stood firm. "No, thanks."

But Avery gently cupped her elbow and turned her to look inside an open doorway. She stood a little behind her and spoke in her ear. "It's okay to be curious, Detective. After all, it's your job to be curious."

Maria shivered at the feel of her hot breath. She let out a small noise of helplessness that caused Avery to press into her.

"Tell me. What do you see?"

The room was lit in the back, near the patio door. She could see shadows of people on the bed. A woman whose perky breasts were in profile, writhed on the mattress while another figure was between her legs, on their knees, bobbing up and down, driving the woman crazy. Another woman was near her head, holding her arms back.

Maria swallowed the rising lump in her throat. She couldn't move, couldn't speak. The figure between the woman's legs stopped and stood. She was tall and built, and she climbed on the bed to straddle the prone woman's face. She laughed and began to gyrate against her mouth while she made out with the woman at the head of the bed. Maria wanted to turn away, the image too much. She leaned back into Avery and warmed at the firm feel of her body, of her breath. Maria hadn't had sex in a long, long time, and at that moment, the lack of human contact made itself known.

"It's something else, isn't it? Watching like that?"

Maria cleared her throat and turned. When she tried to walk, she stumbled in her heels. She cursed in pain as her ankle turned and Avery caught her.

"I've got you," she said. Maria straightened as her skin heated against the strength in Avery's arms. "Can you walk with me? Let's sit you down."

Maria tried to shove her away. "My leg's just numb is all. I must've pinched a nerve." But Avery held firm, and Maria reluctantly allowed Avery to help her back to the elevator and back into the penthouse. When they arrived, Maria looked longingly toward the couch but instead was brought into the master bedroom. The table lights automatically came on as Avery sat her carefully on the king-sized four-poster bed. Maria leaned back and felt the ultimate softness of the gray crushed velvet duvet. But she hissed in pain when Avery knelt at her feet and removed her shoe.

"I'm fine, really. I should go." The pain was scaring her a little, leaving her wounded with possible deadly prey at her feet.

Avery seemed to ignore her. "This looks bad." Her long, nimble fingers carefully moved around her painful ankle. Maria jerked a few times, and her skin broke out in gooseflesh. She cursed herself for reacting so easily but blamed it on not being touched with such delicateness in ages.

Avery looked up at her, seeming to sense her thoughts. Her eyes sparkled in the lamplight, and Maria saw something she'd never expected to see. Empathy.

She stood and picked up the bedside phone to speak. "Yes, can you bring us an ice pack, an Ace Bandage wrap, and some wine? Thank you, Nadine."

Maria tried to move, but the pain stopped her and she winced. She crawled fully onto the bed and tried to relax. Her ankle hurt, but the strange numbness to her leg bothered her more. And as she tried to maneuver again, a pinch in her upper back thigh made her cringe. A Charley horse. What was happening?

"Shh, stay still. You need to ice it and elevate it." Avery maneuvered a pillow beneath her foot and propped it up.

"I'm fine." Maria flexed her foot by pointing her toe and the Charley horse released, but she was nearly nauseous from the pain it had caused her ankle. Still, she put off complaining. She just needed to get out of there and get home.

"Stop it. You aren't fine and it's stupid to play tough. You'll only hurt yourself worse."

"But—"

"Your partner is being entertained. When he's through I will send for him. In the meantime, you need to sit back and relax. I thought those heels were ridiculously high for you."

Maria pushed out a breath. "They were."

"Then why wear them?"

Maria met her eyes but didn't answer. She couldn't.

"Ah, to get to me, was it?" She laughed and then her voice softened. "You look very sexy in that dress, Detective, but to be honest, I liked the kitten heels and the other outfit better."

Maria blinked with surprise at the sincerity.

"You do?"

Avery nodded. "Yes." She stood and slipped off her own designer heels. "Only someone like Hale would prefer an outrageous outfit like the one you're wearing. And Hale was a very, very bad man. Trust me, you don't want that kind of attention. Tell your sources to do their homework better."

Maria fought for words. Who exactly was this woman and how could they have been so wrong in their research? She thought back to what Finley had said about the department only knowing of the rumors, that no one really knew what to expect where Avery was concerned.

While a sense of warmth came over her in realizing that Avery may indeed be a good person, another more sinister feeling came as she realized she could be a murderer. The painful truth was they didn't know. And if they didn't even know what Avery was really attracted to, then they sure as hell didn't know whether or not she was capable of murder.

She cringed, but not from pain or discomfort. It was fear trying to force itself through. But she kept it at bay just as she'd trained herself to do. She kept it close to the surface though, to remind her to be on her toes.

Avery slid off her watch and rings and placed them on the night table. "Oh, come on, Detective, I know you've all looked into me. Into everything about me. But you still don't know me. No one does." The sparkle in her eyes was gone, replaced by a cold indifference. Maria knew she should leave. She was physically impaired and in the room alone with a possible killer. A cunning killer. But she remained, knowing it was probably her only chance to delve deeper into her psyche.

"I see."

"And…I must confess I've looked into you too, and we seem to be similar in that regard."

"You looked into me?" Maria swallowed the lump in her throat carefully.

"I haven't received the full report yet, but yes, I've read up on you a little. Did you think I wouldn't?" She unzipped the back of her body suit. "Fair is fair."

She turned and wordlessly asked Maria to unzip the rest by turning her back to her. Once again, Maria took in the tanned, toned back. She reached out, tempted to touch her, to graze her fingers over the etched muscles, but she stopped herself and just unzipped her. She looked away when Avery turned and stripped down to her panties. She walked into her closet and returned in a satin robe, rubbing lotion on her hands.

"What are you doing?" Maria asked. The scene was all too familiar. It was her own nightly bedtime routine.

"Getting comfortable." She sat and rubbed the lotion on her long, bare legs. Again, Maria had to look away. It was difficult enough to be in her room where all her lovely scents lingered and in her bed where she lay her beautiful body every night, but this, this was madness. An unwelcome desire was threatening to battle her reserve and carefully put away fear.

"Why?"

Avery stopped and stood. "Why not? You're injured and I'm done socializing for this evening."

"But you have a party going on."

"Oh, trust me, it will go on without me. And I've seen all I need to see for this evening." She winked at Maria. "I think you did as well."

"I saw enough."

"Enough to turn you on?"

Maria shot her a glance. "Somehow I think you knew women would be in that room."

Avery shrugged. "So what if I did? I do know what you like. That is one thing that wasn't that hard to find out." She grinned and sat at her feet again.

Nadine entered, saving Maria further embarrassment. She handed the things to Avery and then placed the wine glasses on the night table. She'd already popped the cork and she poured them both a glass. She handed one to Maria.

"Oh, I don't think I should."

"Drink it," Avery said. "It will help dull the pain."

Maria took the glass and sipped only a little. She nearly groaned at how good it was. "Thank you."

"My pleasure," Nadine said with a soft smile. "Anything else, Avery?"

Avery leaned in and kissed her on the cheek. "Not tonight, Nadine. Thank you."

Nadine exited, leaving them alone once again.

Maria wanted to soften at seeing the two interact. Clearly, Nadine meant something to Avery. They definitely needed to do better research into her. Tonight alone she'd been more than surprised by a few things.

Avery gently placed a thin towel over Maria's ankle and set the small bag of ice atop it. "How's that?"

"It hurts a little."

"Can you feel the cold?"

"Starting to."

"Good."

She began to gently rub her shin in a massaging motion. "No pantyhose with that leather dress."

Maria couldn't move her leg, and her heart raced. She prayed her skin wouldn't react to the touch, but it was too late. She was blushing and heating.

"Feel nice?" Avery traced her fingers up and down. "You have really nice legs. Just the right amount of muscle."

Maria jerked involuntarily, and she cried out in pain as the muscle in her upper thigh contracted. Avery stopped and crawled to sit next to her.

"Sorry, I couldn't help myself."

Maria clenched the soft duvet. "It's okay. It's going now."

"I can't help it, I want to touch you." She took her hand and kissed the back of it.

Maria fought for breath, but another rush of pain snapped her back to reality. She decided to be direct, to force the rising desire away, to see Avery for who she really was.

"Why is that? Is it because I'm unattainable? Because I'm a detective investigating you? A game of sorts?"

Avery blinked but still held onto her hand.

"Is that what you think?"

"You tell me. Is it true?"

"No…" She dropped her hand and looked away. "I genuinely like you."

"But you know you can't have me. You know I can't reciprocate. So why waste your time?"

She leaned forward and stared into her eyes. "I'm not known for taking no for an answer, Detective. And who says you can't reciprocate? Your boss? Fuck him. He doesn't own you or your feelings."

"He owns my paycheck."

Avery laughed.

"And I'm telling you no, Avery. From my lips to your ears. It's not going to happen."

Avery leaned in next to her ear. "See, I don't believe it's you telling me no. It's that Goody Two-shoes cop in you. It's your badge. Your colleagues. It's not you. I saw the real you downstairs. You want it just as much as I want to give it to you."

Maria shuddered and sucked in a quick breath. Despite trying to hide and fight the growing desire, it rushed back in and slapped her in the face. Avery felt it and angled her face so that her lips gently brushed Maria's. She moaned softly and kissed her again, this time firmer, more direct, and Maria dug her nails into the covers at the soft, hot feel of her. She wanted more than anything to answer the kiss with one of her own, but she knew she couldn't. She had to pull away, and when she did, Avery groaned.

"Don't go," she said, opening her eyes. "You feel too good."

Maria stared into her, searching for truth, for motive. She saw only want, need.

"Ahem," a voice came from the doorway.

Avery turned with anger on her face. Finley stood with a hand in his pocket. His concerned eyes bored into Maria.

"I didn't mean to interrupt."

"Like hell you didn't," Avery spat. "You can go. You aren't needed here."

He stepped inside, noted Maria's ankle, and came to her side. "I think maybe I am. And don't be mad at Nadine. I forced my way in with that pesky little badge of mine. What happened here?"

"Those damn heels. I twisted my ankle."

He lifted the ice and towel and examined her without touching. He whistled.

"You really should do better at protecting her," Avery said. "Making her wear a ridiculous outfit that only a man would fall for was asinine."

He reared back as if struck. "Hey, lady. Easy does it."

"It's not his fault," Maria said. "Not totally."

Finley glared at her. "You looked hot. How is that a bad thing?"

Avery scoffed. "Anyway, Detective, as you can see she's being cared for. So you aren't needed."

He forced a smile. "Actually, I am. I'm taking her home."

"I'll see to it that she gets home."

"Like hell."

"I really should go," Maria said. She lifted her foot, winced, and swung her legs over to hover over the floor. Finley came to her side and helped her stand. He wrapped her arm around his shoulder. "Where are your things?"

"My clutch is on the bed and my shoes…screw the shoes."

"They're Jimmy Choo. We're taking them. I got those for Paige for Christmas. Cost me a small fortune."

"Fine."

He balanced her and left to grab her things. Avery stood by watching with a disappointed look. She stared into Maria, silently pleading with her to stay.

"Thank you for your help," Maria said. "It really was very nice of you."

"I'm sorry I couldn't do more," Avery said. She followed them to the door. "I'm sure I will hear from you again, Detective Diaz?"

"You'll most likely hear from me," Finley said over his shoulder.

"Then don't bother. I won't speak to anyone but her about Hale."

Finley shook his head in obvious disbelief. "Whatever you say, lady. Whatever you say."

Chapter Seven

I don't care who you have to fuck or fuck over to get the information, just get it." Avery ended the call and threw her cell phone across the room to bounce on the couch. She rubbed her temple and sank into a goose down stuffed chair. Nadine graciously handed her a cup of hot coffee and some aspirin.

"You're going to get high blood pressure if you keep on," Nadine said.

"I think I already have it. My head hurts like a bitch."

She eased back in the chair and took her aspirin. She sipped the coffee and stared at the ceiling. Sunlight and shadows from the curtains played along the surface, like children in the surf. She closed her eyes and thought of Rory and Kylie.

"When will they be here?"

Nadine glanced at her watch and continued to dust the framed photos of Avery's two nieces on the grand piano.

"A half an hour."

"And what about now?"

"Bobby."

"Ah." She sat up. "Good. Send him to the veranda." She walked with her coffee to the floor-to-ceiling glass doors and stepped outside into the warm, misted shade. She sat in a lounge and lit a cigarette while enjoying the cool feeling of the misting system. She'd considered quitting smoking, but she didn't have any other vices…except women. And she was trying her best to control that, but so far, she'd had little success. Her sex drive was more than most, and she wasn't ashamed of it, she had just been thinking a lot about it. Everyone seemed to have someone special in their lives. And those that didn't, wanted her. She could settle down, date one woman, but she knew she'd be bored. She'd only end up cheating and moving on. It would cause pain, but more concerning to her was the fiasco it would likely cause. And she tried her best to be free from relationship drama.

She tapped her cigarette into the crystal ashtray and sipped her coffee. She was staring out at the valley of Las Brisas when Bobby came to the doorway.

"It's hot as hell out here," he said. "Can't we do this inside?"

She crossed her ankles and exhaled smoke. "The heat is good for you. Gets out the toxins." She pointed to a chair. "Sit."

He grumbled and moved his awkward, former boxer body across the veranda and into the chair. He shifted to get his weight right and then opened his leather satchel. She studied the sweat on his brow, watched it glisten back into his receding hairline. Watched it drip down his nose to where he had to remove his wire rim glasses and wipe his face before slipping them back on. She knew he was hot, but she craved the heat like a reptile craving a hot rock. She needed it to seep into her body to warm the cold hidden places she'd tried so hard to fill. It seemed to be the only thing that could fully penetrate and reach her, much to the dismay of her lovers.

"I, uh, got some of what you asked for," he said, handing over two files. "The man, Finley, was easy peasy, but the woman…she's either got very little in the way of a life or she's got some seriously hidden shit."

Avery opened Maria Diaz's file. "Maybe it's a combination of both." She studied the candid photos of her exiting what looked to be her home and her car. "How's her ankle?" She didn't appear to be wearing a boot or using crutches, yet her leg looked stiff.

"It's not her ankle that's the problem." He shoved on his glasses. "It's her leg. She's having some trouble with it."

"What kind of trouble?"

"That I don't yet know. Apparently, she's not one to go to the doctor. And when she's at work, she hides it pretty well."

"Stubborn."

"Yes."

"What else? Girlfriends?"

"No, none. She goes on blind dates, but they don't end well. She's alone, save for her time with Finley."

Avery felt her brow furrow at the mention of his name. "What's the deal there? Are they intimate?"

"No. But they are extremely close. She goes to his home for dinner, he checks on her frequently…they seem to really care about one another."

"So it would seem." She sifted through photo after photo and paused at one of Maria holding a baby. She was smiling and snuggling the baby to her cheek. "Who's the baby?"

"That would be Finley's youngest. Silas Junior."

She sifted through more photos. "What about her family?"

He sighed and rubbed his forehead with the back of his arm. "Well, she has quite a large family, but she doesn't see them all that often. Not enough time really. Right now, she's very busy with the Hale Medley case."

Avery grimaced and tossed the files onto the table. She reached for her coffee. "How are they doing on that?"

"Not great so far. From what I can tell you're still their number one suspect."

She closed her eyes. "Fuck."

"I can throw some chum in the water from somewhere else. Lead them away from you."

"No, don't. I don't want something like that leading back to me and biting me in the ass." She sipped her coffee and suddenly wanted more sugar. "Fucking Hale. How can he be dead and still be a pain in my ass?"

"You ask me, that murder was damn near perfect. Guys at the precinct, they're all up in arms. Talking about it day and night. I heard the guy was shaved of all body hair. Even his balls."

She rubbed her aching temple and did her best to ignore him. "You would think his death would help me not hurt me."

"You would think."

She met his gaze. "Keep digging. And try to find out what they know about Hale's death. I can't stand being in the dark."

"Of course." He stood. "Uh, what about the detectives? They are pretty good at their jobs you know. They've got a really good track record."

She waved him off. "Don't get in their way or hinder their progress, but continue to look into Diaz. I want to know her every move."

"You got it."

He moved hurriedly to the door.

"And, Bobby?"

He turned. "If she goes on another date, I want to know immediately."

He nodded and then walked through the open glass doors, closing them behind him. She reached for her Prada sunglasses and slid them on as she once again stared out at Las Brisas. Tiny flecks of light shimmered like diamonds in the sunlight, windows reflecting the sun. She watched it hypnotically, trying not to think of Hale or of Diaz. She knew she was playing a dangerous game with her hands in both pies, but she knew she wouldn't or couldn't stop. Both were too important to her, and she always was good at playing dangerous games.

A soft bang came from the door and Avery turned to see her nieces, Rory and Kylie, spill out into the misted shade.

"Auntie Avery!" They ran into her arms, already dressed for a swim in bathing suits and bathrobes and flip-flops.

"I want to go off the diving board today," Rory, the older one said. She was eight going on thirty-five, and she was bouncing up and down with excitement.

"Me too, me too!" Kylie said with a big toothless grin.

Rory elbowed her. "You're too little."

"Am not."

"Are so."

Avery held up her hands. "Okay, okay. Let's not argue. Let me go get changed and we'll go."

They jumped up and down. "Hurry!"

She stood, embraced them both, and headed for her bedroom. They ran after her, always on her heels, and flopped onto her bed as she dressed in the bathroom.

"Don't jump on the bed," she said as she stripped and pulled on her black bikini.

But it was too late; they were both giggling and jumping. At least they'd taken off their shoes first. And besides, who was she kidding? Rory and Kylie were her one and only soft spot and they could get away with anything. She adored them and often times they were the only thing that kept her going, to keep her fighting in the threatening darkness.

"Get off the bed," she said with a smile as she reentered the room. "You know the rules." She bent over and made her hands into opening and closing claws. "You know what happens when you break the rules."

"No, no!" Kylie hopped from the bed and took off. "Not the tickle monster."

Rory laughed and dropped to her bottom. "She's so silly."

Avery wrapped an arm around her. "Yeah. But so are you." They walked slowly from the bedroom and Rory held her hand. Avery's heart warmed as she looked down at the eight-year-old. Rory had Avery's younger sister's dark hair and gray eyes while Kylie looked more like her, long and slim with blond hair. But Rory had her demeanor while Kylie had her mother's. Night and day. Just like Avery and Monica had been and still were. She was just grateful Monica, despite their constant disagreements, still let her see the girls.

Nadine stood just inside the living room, already spraying sunscreen on Kylie. Rory stepped up to be next.

"Auntie Avery, I'm gonna spray you," Kylie said when she had finished.

"Okay."

When Nadine finished with Rory, she handed the spray to Kylie who began spraying Avery while giggling. Rory came to help, doing her upper body. Nadine smiled and Avery winked at her.

"All right, let's do it," Avery said, gathering her small herd. The girls bolted out of the penthouse and to the elevator. They bounced with excitement all the way down. Avery was smiling and laughing with them until the elevators stopped and the doors opened. Guests milled about the lobby as usual, but near the front desk were a small group of people with cameras. Reporters. One caught a glimpse of her.

"There she is," he said, and the group ran toward them as they stepped from the elevator. Avery threw up her arm to shield the girls, but it didn't stop the crazy chaos as they bit into her with questions.

"Ms. Ashland, how does it feel to be named the number one suspect in the Hale Medley murder case?"

"Are you a killer, Ms. Ashland?"

"How has this affected business? Will it affect business?"

"Word has it, you're still throwing your private parties despite the murder. Is this true?"

"Just what exactly is it that goes on here at Euphoria, Ms. Ashland?"

Cameras were shoved in her face, and Kylie began to cry. Avery did her best to hurry the children away and shield them, but the reporters followed them outside to the far pool. Avery yelled for her security and the guys struggled to hold them off. Avery cursed and told them to call the police as she escorted the girls inside the gate to the pool.

"Go on, it's okay, honey." Avery tried her best to calm the girls as the reporters were finally led away by her security. With anger still heating her cheeks, she threw the pool gear on an empty lounge chair and dialed her phone. She gave the head of security a good tongue lashing before hanging up and forcing a smile at the now timid girls.

"What were those people saying?" Rory asked. "Are you in trouble, Auntie Avery?"

"Did you hurt someone?"

Avery knelt and they fell into her arms. "Oh, no, baby. They were just trying to upset me is all. I haven't done anything."

"Then why are they here?" Kylie asked, rubbing her eyes.

"Because they think she did," Rory said. She took off her robe and put on her flippers. "They think Auntie Avery did something bad."

Avery straightened and Kylie clung to her. "That's enough, Rory. I haven't done anything wrong. And I promise you won't see them again, okay?"

How could her security be so lax? And since when did everyone know she was the main suspect in the case? She glanced around the sparsely crowded pool, and a man nearby looked away from her quickly. She caught the headline on his newspaper before he folded it up and left.

Euphoria Resort Owner Main Suspect in Medley Murder

Avery cringed and then seethed. She helped the girls into the pool and then she sat and retrieved her phone. She dialed the number she'd been staring at since the day she'd found the cards on the coffee table. The number she'd wanted to call but for totally different reasons.

The phone number to Detective Maria Diaz.

Chapter Eight

Maria did her best not to limp into the office of the medical examiner. She shoved her shaky hands into her pockets and slid inside the automatic doors. She flicked the tiny dog bobble heads on Nan's counter and watched them dance.

"How have you been, Maria?" Nan asked. She was a plump woman with bleached blond hair and too much lipstick. Her long nails always seemed to match whatever color painted her mouth. She had been at the medical examiner's office for years, longer than Maria had been detective, and Maria knew she was one hell of an investigator.

"I'm hanging in there. How about you?"

"Can't complain except for these blasted hot flashes. Feel like I'm in an oven one minute and the next I'm fine." She flicked open a small Chinese folding fan and cooled herself.

"Thankfully, I can't relate," Maria said.

Nan laughed. "Just wait. Your turn will come." She pressed the button below her desk and buzzed Maria in.

The stale smell of the industrial carpet turned to worn, bleached white flooring as Maria pushed through the door and entered the hallway. Her hip began to tinge with pain from favoring her leg, but she was determined not to react.

She hadn't told Finley, but she'd gone to see her doctor that morning. And while he had ruled out physical injury, he'd scared her more with the concerning look in his eyes. He'd asked her a lot of questions and some of them had led to her other symptoms, which she'd been hesitant to admit. He seemed to read her face though, because he'd examined her walk, her reflexes, her sensation in her hands and feet, and even her eyes. He requested she have an MRI and see a neurologist.

The suggestion had sent her mind racing, and she'd taken the paperwork and left quickly. So much for just a pinched nerve. What could possibly be wrong with her head? Finley would've no doubt joked about that, but he'd also insist she take it easy, which she wasn't about to do. She had a serious case to work and a suspect that stirred her in ways that terrified her. One moment, she was breathless with desire, and the next she was breathless with fear. It was a wonder she was thinking straight at all.

She pushed through the locker room door and found Finley suiting up in the protective gear they were required to wear when in the autopsy room. He tucked his paisley tie into the plastic suit and zipped it up. Then he tossed her a size small suit and snapped on a pair of blue gloves.

"Been trying to call you," he said, trying on a surgical mask.

She removed her thick-heeled boots and stepped into the suit to zip it up. "I told you, I had something to do."

"Like what?" He was used to knowing her every move. Just like a protective big brother. And that was her own fault really. She told him everything.

She ignored him, though it wasn't easy. She could feel his steely blue eyes on her. "Toss me some gloves will ya?" She caught the gloves, slid them on, and then stepped into her shoes to cover them with disposable booties. When she tied on her mask, they pushed out of the locker room and walked to exam room four and back inside.

Dr. Judy Haddock was waiting for them with her hands behind her back. She lowered her mask and smiled. Next to her, a pathologist they'd rarely worked with before was near the back counter, talking into a recorder. He was bent in concentration, gloves off, scrubs a little messy. Maria eyed the body of Hale Medley and breathed a small sigh of relief. The autopsy appeared to be finished. An assistant in yellow garb breezed past them and peeled off her gloves and suit to dispose of in the biohazard bin by the door.

"Detective Diaz," Haddock said. "Please, join me."

Maria crossed to stand next to her. Finley followed but chose to stand across from them. He knelt and took a closer looked at the wounds on the body. Maria chose to focus on Haddock for the time being.

"You look pale," Haddock said. "Are you feeling queasy?"

Maria shook her head. "No. I'm fine."

Haddock glanced at Hale Medley. "Even so, this is brutal."

Maria stared at the gaping gash in his torn throat. He'd been cut deeply, and from what she could see, all the way back to his spine. She grew a little dizzy and waned. She could still smell remnants of the liquid decay that had been drained from him.

"You sure you're okay?" Haddock asked as she steadied her.

"Mm, fine. Just didn't eat much this morning."

Finley eyed her. He knew that excuse was bullshit.

Maria forced herself to focus on the body. It was pale with some discoloration and reflected the fluorescent light in a way that made the white in his skin almost look like marble. The body hair, as they'd noted before, had been removed everywhere, even on his fingers and toes. She'd never seen anything like it.

The other pathologist pushed away from the counter and came to stand next to them. Haddock spoke.

"Detectives Diaz and Finley, you remember Dr. Gregory."

They mumbled hellos, and Dr. Gregory began, encouraging Haddock to jump in when she felt it necessary. He switched on the camera overhead, and a high-definition image of Hale lit the television screen hanging at the head of the table. Maria preferred to stare at the body itself as Dr. Gregory continued.

"This is Hale Jalbert Medley the Third. Thirty-nine-year-old Caucasian male, approximately five foot ten inches tall and one hundred and sixty-five pounds. He exhibited no former injuries prior to the wounds that caused his death. No broken bones, implants, or plates or screws. He appears to have been a well-nourished and an otherwise healthy male for his age. Exterior examination showed a deep incision to Mr. Medley's throat, approximately four inches in length. Incision penetrated through the larynx and nearly serrated the spine. From the incision, we can estimate that the knife used was most likely a hunting knife at least five inches in length with a serrated tip."

"And the killer or killers had to take more than one try to cut him so deeply and thoroughly," Haddock said. "We noted several trial cuts as I mentioned at the crime scene."

"Jesus," Finley said.

"And he was…awake and alive?" Maria asked.

Dr. Gregory sighed. "We believe so. You can see here where the cuts are in a scattered pattern as if the victim was trying to move or was moving while the murderer attempted to cut.

Maria closed her eyes. What a death. Horrible. "This was cause of death?" she asked.

"Yes."

"He bled out."

She opened her eyes. "What about the marks on his forehead?"

Haddock spoke. "Those were also made while he was conscious. You can see the small scattered cuts where the killer tried to cut a moving target. There is also scabbing where the blood clotted."

"The cuts on the forehead were made with a smaller, more precise instrument. More like a pen knife," Dr. Gregory said.

"Could the killer just be really shitty at carving?" Finley asked. "I mean it's not every day you cut on a live human being."

"I would say they were no artist, no. But I believe Mr. Medley was aware when this was happening," Haddock said. "I think eventually he was restrained so they could execute both tasks of cutting. But this killer or killers, it seems to me they wanted him alive and aware for the cutting."

Maria locked eyes with Finley. Sadistic. Cunning.

Dr. Haddock cleared her throat and continued. "Stomach contents show his last meal was cocktail shrimp and champagne. We also found traces of the muscle relaxer Tizanidine. We have to wait for toxicology to be sure, but it would render him somewhat defenseless depending upon how much was in his system."

"Explains how the killer got and maintained control of him," Maria said.

"What else have you got?" Finley asked.

Maria studied the alabaster body, the thick sewing of the y incision, and the drawn look to his face. He almost looked alien like with his bald head and sunken cheeks.

Dr. Gregory continued. "Abrasions and ligature marks on the wrists and ankles. Also on the upper chest and along the chin. At one point the ligature used penetrated the skin of his wrists and he would've bled. Most likely caused from the struggle to free himself."

Maria's phone rang and she struggled with the suit to reach it. When she retrieved it, she didn't recognize the number so she sent it to voice mail. She refocused on Dr. Gregory.

"Something else interesting," he said and pointed to the eyes. "He was strangled before his throat was cut. See the petechial hemorrhaging? My guess is it was a form of torture."

"Strangle him until he neared passing out and then releasing," Haddock said. "We've seen it before."

Maria nodded. Many killers loved the game and the torture. They enjoyed bringing their victims close to death and then stopping, only to do it again.

The ringing sounded again, and Maria grimaced as she saw the same number on the screen. "I better see who this is." She stepped away, and instead of taking the call, she listened to her voice mail. Her skin crawled as she heard the deep, angry voice coming from the other end. The woman sounded so angry, so wounded, she almost didn't recognize who it was. She ended the call and returned to the body where Dr. Gregory was going on about the toenail and fingernail removal.

Finley eyed her. "You won't believe who that was," Maria said, still a bit shocked at the language that had been used.

"Who?" Finley asked.

"Our main suspect."

"Ashland?" He looked incredulous.

"And she's beyond pissed. I guess the press showed up today."

Finley led her away from the doctors. His eyes were bright and halo like under the light. "She called you?"

"Apparently, she wants me to take care of it."

He laughed.

"The gall."

"We did release her name to the press." They'd done it purposely, to turn the heat up on her. But now, in hearing her, she wasn't sure it had been such a good idea. She'd said her nieces had been traumatized by the slew of reporters.

"This can work to our advantage," Finley said. "Call her back—"

"Finley. I know what to do."

"What?"

"I'm going to Euphoria."

He blinked. "Alone?"

"I'll be fine."

He sighed. "I don't know. I should go with you."

"She hates you. She'll give you nothing."

He eventually nodded. "All right."

"Go see if forensics has anything on that wallet or anything else they may have found. I won't be long."

"How are you going to handle Ashland?"

Maria pulled off her gloves and tossed them in the biohazard bin. "Pretend like I care."

CHAPTER NINE

A very paced the length of her living room. With every step
she took her anger grew. She glanced at her watch. It had
been hours since she'd called Detective Diaz. Where the hell was
she? Did cops not have any sense of time?

She sank onto her sofa and stared into her empty glass tumbler.
She was warm and her skin flushed with a heavy buzz, but instead of
it making her feel better, it only seemed to light her fire even more.
She blinked long and slow and began cursing aloud. Her nieces had
left hours ago, so distraught by the reporters and what they'd said,
that they'd cried off and on the rest of the time they'd had with her.
She'd done her best to comfort and reassure them, but they were too
upset, and the guests staring at them as they'd walked back through
the resort after their swim hadn't helped. It seemed she was famous
now and not just for her private parties and great wealth. Now she
was a murder suspect.

She startled when Nadine approached from behind with a fresh
glass of bourbon. She gave her a tired smile and took a hearty sip.

"You should go to bed," Nadine said, folding a throw blanket.

"I can't. I'm waiting for the detective."

"I think it's obvious she's not going to come."

"She'll come. She better. I need to give her a piece of my mind."

Nadine placed the blanket on the end of the couch. The soft
fleece reminded Avery of Rory, who used to cling to the blanket
when she came to stay the night. She missed those early days.

"Do you really think that will help?"

"I don't really care. I just know it will make me feel better."

Nadine grew quiet. "Remember what I've always told you about things that make you feel better. They aren't always good for you no matter how good they feel."

Avery fought rolling her eyes. The alcohol had shortened her fuse, and she didn't want to bite into Nadine. Especially since she knew she was right. Whether she would listen or not, that had always been debatable. "I need to yell at someone tonight." She met her eyes. "After what the girls experienced…I can't rest easy until I tear into someone."

"I thought you liked Detective Diaz."

Avery took another few large sips of her bourbon. She embraced the burn of it as it coated her throat on the way down. "I thought we were building a rapport. But now, after what they did and she didn't even warn me…now I don't know."

"Perhaps she had nothing to do with it."

"She's a part of them. She's responsible."

Nadine straightened the magazines and the remaining coloring books on the coffee table. She put away the crayons and wiped down the glass. "The way you spoke to her on the phone, maybe she got the message loud and clear."

Avery scoffed. "I actually held back on the phone."

Nadine straightened. Her soft, kind eyes scanned Avery's face. "You should go to bed. Start anew tomorrow."

Nadine had always been more like a mother figure to her than housekeeper. She'd been there for her through thick and thin and rarely did she agree with Avery's behavior. But she stayed and cared for her regardless. Avery loved her for that.

The phone rang, and Nadine hurried to the wet bar and answered while studying the security monitor. Avery nursed her bourbon and blinked sleep away. She wasn't up for visitors, even if it was Lana or one of her other lovers. She wasn't in the mood. She'd probably sit and drink until she passed out on the couch. She'd awake in the morning with that fleece throw covering her, Nadine's doing.

"Tell Lana I'm not in the mood." The ice in her glass clinked as she swirled her drink.

Nadine rounded the sofa and hurried from the room. When she returned moments later, a figure shadowed her.

"Avery, Detective Diaz is here to see you."

Avery sat up straighter as Diaz came into view. She was wearing dark jeans and a form-fitting collared shirt. Her hair was down in shiny chestnut waves.

"May I get you a drink, Detective?" Nadine asked. She gave Avery a look to let her know she was being rude by not welcoming her.

"No, thank you," Maria said. She pointed to the sofa across from Avery. "May I?"

Avery forced herself to speak. "Of course, please."

"I'll say good night then." Nadine touched Avery's shoulder. Avery thanked her and bid her good night with the squeeze of her hand. When they were alone, Avery had to pull her eyes away from Maria in order to remind herself that she was upset.

"You're late," she said, crossing her legs. "Hours I've been waiting."

Maria didn't look fazed. "I apologize. I've been caught up in the investigation."

"Could've called to let me know. That would've been the polite thing to do."

Maria cocked her head. "Why exactly am I here, Ms. Ashland? You said something about the press disrupting you today?"

Avery deposited her glass on the coffee table. "They ambushed me and scared the hell out of my nieces."

"I'm sorry to hear that."

Avery laughed. "I don't think you understand. They referred to me as a murderer. In front of children."

Maria threaded her fingers together and remained poised. "What exactly would you like me to do about it?"

Avery began to shout but bit her tongue. When she spoke, she shook with barely harbored control. "For starters, I'd like to know why my name was leaked to the press to begin with. Secondly, I'd like an apology. And finally, I'd like reassurance that it won't happen again."

Maria chuckled with what seemed like amusement. "You are considered a suspect, Ms. Ashland. And until you further cooperate or we clear you, you will remain as such. As for an apology, I'm not sure what I'd be apologizing for. And as far as reassurance…I don't control the press. They're going to go where the story is, and right now that seems to be you."

"Me?" She threw up her hands. "Don't you have any other people you're looking into? I mean, my God, Hale Medley was an asshole times two. Surely there are more people out there that wanted him dead." She clamped her mouth shut as she realized what she'd said. Frustrated, she rose to go to the wet bar where she made herself another drink.

"So you admit you wanted him dead."

Avery drank and squeezed the tumbler so hard she thought it would shatter. "I'm sure I'm not the only one."

"You never did tell me your whereabouts on the night of the thirteenth. Care to share that information now?"

"My God. You're really playing the cold bitch tonight, aren't you?"

Maria smiled, but it wasn't friendly. "I've tried to be nice. It hasn't gotten me very far."

"I see. Can I get you a drink? Scotch? Surely you drink. You can't always be such a tight-ass."

"Your alibi, Ms. Ashland. That is, if you have one."

"She was with me," a voice came from the shadow of the entryway. Avery swallowed hard as Lana Gold stepped into the light. She offered Maria a sarcastic smile, and then crossed to Avery.

"Hey, baby." She leaned across the bar and kissed Avery on the lips. When she lingered, Avery let her, hoping Maria was getting an eye full.

"And you are?"

Lana crossed back to the sofa. "Lana Gold."

"Lana's an old friend," Avery said, following her. She and Lana sat across from Maria and Lana placed her hand on Avery's thigh. Avery grinned and sipped her drink as Maria rubbed her palms on her jeans. "We go way back. Don't we, darling?"

"Mm."

"And where were you on the night in question?" Maria sounded short, irritated.

Lana answered. "We were at my place. All night."

Maria looked to Avery and Avery nodded.

"We'll have to look into that," Maria said.

"I'm sure you'll do a thorough job, Detective Diaz," Avery said. "After all, I know you won't waste any time having any actual fun between now and then."

Maria shook her head and laughed softly. "Not when there is a killer on the loose. But like you say, you wouldn't know anything about that now, would you?" She looked to Lana. "Ms. Gold, did you know our victim. Hale Medley?"

Lana shifted slightly. "I'd met him once or twice."

"Once or twice? Where?"

"Here. At Euphoria."

"What did you think of him?"

She laughed, but Avery could tell she was growing uncomfortable. "I'm sorry, am I a suspect or something?"

"I'm just doing my job, Ms. Gold."

Lana took a deep breath and brushed her hair back. "Well, I think I have to insist that you speak to my attorney if you have any further questions for me."

"I just might do that," Maria said. "Especially if I found out that you despised Mr. Medley as much as your friend here."

"I hardly knew the man. Just in passing really."

"Then I'm sure you'll cooperate fully at another time." She stood and tossed her card on the table. "The quicker we can clear you, the quicker we can move on. And I know you want us to move on." She aimed a look at Avery.

"I'll see you out," Avery said, crossing to her. She led her back down the hallway to the elevator. "As always, it was a pleasure to see you, Detective."

"Likewise." She turned before she pushed the button. "I'll send a car for you tomorrow so you can come to the station to finish with our questions."

Avery stared at her in disbelief. "Excuse me?"

"I'm not playing games, Ms. Ashland."

Avery saw the deep seriousness in her dark eyes. The fiery spark of determination. It caused her skin to heat and her bones to turn to concrete. She stepped toward her.

"Watch your step, Detective. I'm not always so nice." She smiled and leaned into her, inches away from placing her lips on hers. "I can play rough. Just ask Hale."

Maria didn't flinch, didn't move. "I can't exactly do that, now can I?"

Avery laughed. "Good night, Detective."

Maria stared into her eyes for another moment. "I am sorry yours was so...disturbing." She turned and pressed the button and Avery stood steaming. She wanted to tell her to fuck off, to go to hell, but it would get her nowhere and Maria would win getting to her like that.

Instead she watched her step in the elevator and face off. Avery smiled as the doors closed, then she stomped back down the hall and into her penthouse. She slammed the door and locked it and found Lana waiting for her by the sofa.

"Relax, she doesn't know anything."

Avery continued on into her bedroom. Lana followed. "No, then why am I their number one suspect?"

She tore off her clothes, not caring when a couple of buttons popped.

"Because they don't know anything, that's why. They're reaching in the dark."

"They need to stop." She turned on the bath and stripped out of her bra and matching panties.

"They will."

"When?"

She crossed her arms and waited for her bath. Lana came up behind her and wrapped her arms around her. "Give them what they want and they'll leave you alone." She kissed her shoulder.

"I don't think I can. And what if they find out you lied tonight? Then what?"

"They won't." She kissed her other shoulder. "Now relax."

"I can't."

"Then let me help you." She turned her and lowered to her knees. She placed delicate kisses along her upper thighs, and then traced her hot tongue up into her folds. Avery sighed and gripped her head as Lana swirled her tongue and focused on her growing clit.

"Oh, God." Avery craned her neck and moaned toward the ceiling. The room filled with steam, and she held fast to Lana and widened her stance, allowing her more access to her aching flesh. "That's it, baby. Yes, lick me. Lick me so good." She came in silence, her body straining and writhing against Lana. When the last of the spasms left her, she cried out as if her voice were already spent. She breathed heavily into the steam and closed her eyes. When she opened them, she saw Maria walking toward her, untying a robe. She smiled and reached out for her. But it was Lana who fell into her arms.

Maria Diaz was still unattainable.

CHAPTER TEN

Maria threw down her chopsticks and ran a hand through her hair.

"What?" Finley's mouth was full and a grease stain marked his chin. If he knew, he didn't seem to care.

"These pot stickers."

"They gross?"

She pushed the Chinese take away carton away. "Yes."

Finley swallowed. "They're your favorite."

She sipped her Diet Dew. "I know. I don't know what's wrong with me."

Finley pushed his Mongolian beef her way. "Here, try mine."

She pinched a piece and chewed. She cocked her head and grabbed her chopsticks. When they shook in her hand, she threw them down again and reached for a plastic fork. Finley chewed on and she took a bite, knowing he'd seen her shake.

"You ever gonna do anything about that?"

Maria lifted a shoulder. She didn't look at him.

"I'll tell the sarge."

"No, you won't." She lifted her gaze. "Because it would fuck up this case, and we can't afford to fuck up this case."

"Just tell me, is it something bad? Is it serious?"

"I don't know, Fins."

He smacked the table. "Damn it, Diaz, you've got to see someone."

When she didn't respond, he took her fork from her.

"I did, okay? I saw my doctor."

His eyes widened. "And?"

"He's wants to run some tests."

Finley swallowed some more, then dug around in another carton for rice. "What kind of tests?"

"An MRI."

"Let me guess. You have yet to get it done."

Maria didn't answer; she just pushed the beef away and finished half her drink. She'd been running on caffeine for two days straight.

"Take the morning off and get it done."

"I have to make an appointment."

"Then do it. And take time off."

He was searching her eyes as if desperate to get through to her. She finally caved.

"I'll do it."

He smiled. "Thanks." He sat back and belched softly, then bit into an overdone egg roll. He chewed loudly, took another bite, and then tossed the remainder in the rice carton.

"That hit the spot."

"Wish I could say the same."

He held up the remaining egg roll and raised an eyebrow at her. She waved it off.

"I give up for this evening."

He shrugged and stuffed the entire egg roll in his mouth. She stared at him in disbelief.

"It's a wonder your wife lets you out of the house." She handed him a slew of paper napkins and watched as he finished and cleaned himself.

"You done now? Or do you want to inhale what's left of the pot stickers?"

He shook his head but tossed her a fortune cookie instead. She didn't open it, just pushed it aside, preferring to focus on the case rather than her so-called future or any corny advice the cookie was sure to give her.

She preferred to make her own way, depend on herself. But truth be told, she was a little anxious in thinking about the near future so much so that she couldn't even take looking at a damn fortune in a cookie.

Finley, however, read his own in a loud, announcer-like voice.

"Distant lands await you." He threw it aside. "Sounds good to me. I could go for escaping this hellhole for a while."

"Please, you wouldn't leave this case if you were offered a free trip to paradise."

"True. There's just something about unfinished business."

They cleared the desks of trash and retrieved their tablets and files. Maria rolled her chair closer to her desk and rubbed her eyes from the strain of the harsh fluorescent lights. She'd long ago replaced her contact lenses with her glasses, but her eyes still begged for mercy.

"Why don't you go on home and get some rest?" Finley said, rolling his chair back up to face her at his own desk. "I got this."

"Not with the way the sarge is riding us. No time to take a break." They'd been tiptoeing around him, trying to avoid his nasty temper and unwavering impatience. They were responsible for Ashland, and he wanted her in custody yesterday. He didn't like to play footsie with suspects because he was old school and didn't like the whole behavioral science approach to things. He wanted her dragged in and questioned for hours upon hours until she confessed. He believed she was guilty, and once he believed that, very little could give him pause and force him to reevaluate. His way got things done, yes, but on the off chance he was wrong, they were screwed.

"I told Ashland I was sending a car for her. I think we should do it."

"Yeah? She shit her pants?"

"Pretty much."

He swiped his tablet awake and focused. "Lana Gold." He whistled. "She's a looker." He rubbed his chin.

"We need to get her in here, run some prints off a soda can just to see what pops up."

"What about the footage from the night of the murder? We get that yet?" They had subpoenaed surveillance footage from both Euphoria and Lana Gold's condo complex. So far, the Euphoria tapes were mysteriously screwed up, but they had their fingers crossed on the ones from Lana's place.

"Not yet."

"There's no way Ashland was at Lana's. She prefers to stay on her own turf when visiting with her lovers."

"She still calling you?" Finley asked.

"Yes. At least four times a day."

He laughed. "I think you finally figured out how to play her."

"I know and I think it's driving her insane. Which is why when I do call her, I think I should ask her to come down here if she wants to talk. Keep my edge."

"Genius."

She had no idea what Ashland wanted with her, but she wasn't about to continue to react to her every qualm. Ashland was used to people doing so, but Maria wasn't one of her lovestruck women or wannabe suitors.

"The sarge would seriously have a coronary if he knew you were putting her off like this."

"Yes, well what the sarge doesn't know won't hurt him. Besides we both know as soon as we get that footage she's toast."

Finley switched over to his laptop and chewed on the straw from his soda. Maria checked her email, hoping to have a forensics report on the wallet they'd been waiting patiently for. Finley had been riding them so hard about it they'd begun to call him "Jockey." She opened an urgent email from Ken Sing in forensics. She scanned it quickly.

"Fins."

"Hm?"

"We got something." She stood and rounded his desk with her tablet. "Kenny found a photo in Hale's wallet." She zoomed on the photo of Hale and Ashland arm in arm in their younger years at what appeared to be a ball.

"There's a target drawn on his face."

"Yes, and look at what's written on the back." She zoomed in once again. It was a phrase in Latin along with the dark dusting of a fingerprint. "The phrase means *To the depths of Hell I will send you.* And the fingerprint belongs to Avery Ashland, along with traces of Hale's blood and an unknown female. Dollars to donuts it's Ashland's."

Finley grabbed her tablet and stared as if it had physically struck him. "Holy Christ. This is a fucking calling card."

"I know."

"Even if it was planted, we get to use it to our advantage. We get to use it to get her ass in here."

She smiled. "God, if I wasn't so tired, I'd do a damn dance."

He smacked the desk and tore off his eyeglasses. "We got her ass now, Maria. She has no choice but to answer to this."

"Her prints weren't on the wallet, but…" She took her tablet and shut it off for the evening. "Kenny said he's still waiting on the DNA results from her cigarette butt to compare to the blood on the photo."

"Thank God I thought to take that little ol' cigarette," Finley said.

"And…guess who studied Latin in boarding school and college?" Maria had spent the past three days delving into Ashland's past. She'd been fascinated and caught up in it as if it were a best-selling novel.

"Ashland."

"The one and only." She rounded her desk and began packing up to go home. "Why she would leave the photo in the wallet is beyond me. But like you said, we've got to run with it."

"Maybe she didn't know it was in there. Maybe she'd given it to him as a threat and he'd kept it in there."

She pointed a finger at him. "You got a point."

Finley killed their desk lights and they both gathered their things and walked to the wall to kill the overhead lights. Homicide was empty and it was nearing three in the morning. They had a lot to do tomorrow.

"I'll call Kenny in the morning to get more info on the wallet and the photo."

"And I'll call in our girl," Finley said.

"Oh, she'll just love hearing from you."

Finley bounced on the balls of his feet. "I know. I absolutely can't wait."

Maria shook her head, grateful for the evidence and the fact that she could go home and get a few hours' rest. But something deep down inside her churned with dread. It was looking like Avery Ashland was involved after all. And that didn't leave her totally happy, for reasons she didn't want to admit.

CHAPTER ELEVEN

Avery rolled over and groaned as her cell phone vibrated again. She opened her eyes wide enough to read the number and then powered it off and threw it across the room. She'd already unplugged her house phone because it hadn't stopped ringing. Whoever it was could fuck off. She'd had a handful of sleepless nights thanks to Detective Diaz's disastrous visit, and she was just now able to drift off.

She snuggled down into her Egyptian cotton sheets and down pillows. The room was blissfully cool and quiet. Her eyes drifted closed and Maria's face floated to her mind. Why hadn't she called her back?

No.

She refused to think of her any longer. It was obvious that Maria had drawn the line and now she was trying to get her goat. But she wouldn't let her.

She sighed and turned over. Maria's face wouldn't leave her mind and her words, the last time she'd seen her, kept replaying.

"No!" She sat up and grabbed her temples. Why was this woman getting to her so? She was just a cop. A detective doing her job. Why couldn't she get her out of her head?

She threw back her covers and sat on the edge of her bed. She was just about to get in the shower when Nadine knocked and called from her door.

"In."

Nadine came in with an apologetic and worried look on her face. She had a house phone in her hand.

"Oh, fuck me." Avery rubbed her forehead. She held out her hand for the phone. "Who is it?"

"Detective Finley."

She narrowed her eyes. "Finley?" What did that asshat want? She studied Nadine for answers, but she shook her head, clueless in her bathrobe. "What time is it?"

"It's just after seven."

Avery eyed the phone. Where was Maria? Her eyes widened. Where the hell was Maria?

She took the phone.

"Where's Detective Diaz? Is she okay? Is she hurt?" It would explain why she hadn't returned her calls.

"She's just fine," Finley said, sounding like the smartass he was turning out to be.

Of course, she was fine. Bobby Luca was supposed to be watching her closely. He would've called if she'd been hurt.

"Then why hasn't she returned my calls?"

"You will have to ask her that question."

"What do you want?"

"I'm calling to ask you to come down to the station to answer some questions for us."

"What?"

"We can send a car if you like. Or I can come and escort you."

"In your dreams."

"No, in reality."

She stood and stalked to the bathroom where she frowned into the mirror. "You've got some nerve."

"So they tell me. Be here by nine."

"I won't speak to anyone but Maria."

She heard a click and then the dial tone. The jerk had hung up. She squeezed the phone and considered throwing it.

Nadine came to the entrance of the bathroom. She folded her arms with obvious concern.

"Is everything okay?"

"No."

"What did he want?"

"I have to go to the station. They want to talk."

"We have to call Bruce. You can't go down there without him."

"No. No lawyers. Not yet. I'm just going to go down there, answer their damn questions, and lay into them."

"That's not a good idea," Nadine said.

"It may not be, but I have to do it. I don't want that Finley asshole coming here asking me more questions. Besides," she ran a hand through her hair, "I need to see Detective Diaz. I need to see what's going on there."

Nadine pressed her lips together. "I like her, but you're going to have to give up on her."

Avery held up a hand to stop her. "It's not going to be a friendly conversation, trust me."

"You like her. I know you well."

"Nadine." She looked away. "Please. Don't."

Nadine sighed. "Okay. I'll make you breakfast."

"Don't. I can't eat a thing."

Nadine walked away quietly and Avery switched on the shower. As she stepped into the double-headed spray, she closed her eyes and thought about just what she'd say to Maria when she saw her. She didn't have to think hard.

❖

"Like I said an hour ago," Avery said. "I'll only speak to Detective Diaz." She groaned and held her head in her hands. The interrogation room was tiny and suffocating with a small stainless steel table and stool. She'd kill for a fan and cushion for her ass. A damn Diet Coke sounded good as well. But she said nothing. They wanted her discomfort. That much she knew. So she didn't complain.

Finley smiled and slapped his palm on the table. "You want Diaz?"

"Yes."

He smiled.

"Okay." He stood, adjusted his tie, and left the room.

"Finally." She sat back and stretched. Finley had nearly exhausted her with questions about Hale, their relationship, and her own past. She'd tried desperately to figure out what he was trying to get from her and to figure out how much he knew. But she hadn't been able to grasp anything important. And now, after having heard all his questions, she knew exactly how she wanted to answer them.

The door opened and Maria entered with her thick dark hair down, wearing a plain white tee and black jeans and boots. Avery fought licking her lips.

Maria smiled but only slightly and placed a frosted can of Diet Coke in front of her. Avery cracked it open and drank, unable to hide her thirst. When she finished, she set it down and stared at Maria, waiting for her to speak. But she didn't.

"Aren't you going to say hello?" Avery asked.

"I think we're a little past greetings."

"What about just being polite?"

Maria didn't look amused. She sat, placing her elbows on the table. "I hear you want to speak to me," she said.

"I'll only speak to you, yes."

The door opened and Finley entered and handed her files and a legal pad. Maria placed it on the table, mouthed thank you, and then riffled through the files, stopping at the legal pad.

Avery rolled her eyes. More questions. Were they really going to ask the same ones over again?

Finley left the room and Maria cleared her throat.

"How difficult was it to cut Hale's throat, Avery?"

Avery looked up in complete shock. "What?"

Maria looked at her coolly. "It must have been difficult, because we can see all the attempts." She opened a file and slid a photo of a dead, pale Hale across the table to her. Avery reared back and covered her mouth.

"You bitch."

"I'm guessing you'd never done it before. Or maybe, by your reaction, Lana had never done it before. Or…maybe you were the one who originally tried, but Lana had to finish him off."

"You animal," she whispered. "Get that away from me." She couldn't look at it. Couldn't look at his bulging eyes.

"Oh, well, maybe you'll like this one better." She slid another over, but Avery turned her head.

Maria didn't stop. "Or how about this one? Or this one? You know the forehead carving is original, I'll give you that. And the word horny. Very funny and quite true. He liked his women didn't he, Avery? And he sure liked you. Probably hit on you a thousand times. Probably drove you nuts."

Avery clenched her teeth and stared at the wall. "You're wrong. He didn't dare hit on me. He knew better."

"Is that right? Because you see, we've heard differently. We've heard that Hale has always wanted you, Avery."

"He knew better," she said.

Maria made a clicking sound. "I see. Maybe that's what happened. He hit on you one last time after you'd warned him not to. That's it, isn't it? You had to put him in his place. This time, forever."

Avery swallowed and tried to slow her heart rate. Something was wrong here. Very wrong. This wasn't the Maria she'd expected.

"No," she said.

"No?"

Avery turned and looked at her. "No. I did not kill Hale."

"Well now, you see that's funny. Because everything we've got points to you. Not to mention what Hale left behind. He told us you did it. Did you know that?"

"What the fuck are you talking about?" It was a trick. It had to be. Maria was in here seriously fucking with her.

"You didn't bother to check his wallet, did you?" Maria asked.

Avery just stared at her.

Maria smiled. "Recognize this?" She pulled a plastic protected photo from a file and slid it toward her.

Avery glanced at it and then looked harder. She recognized it all right. It was a photo she'd given to Hale months ago, threatening him to back off. She clenched her jaw and tried to control her breathing. His wallet? It had been in his wallet? Jesus Christ.

Maria slid the photo back toward her. "I think you've answered my question."

"I haven't answered a damn thing." She was angry now. Maria had shown her up. She had the photo, the fucking photo. She fought for steady breath, but it was difficult to maintain. What she really wanted to do was tear up the photo and flip over the table and scream. The madness of the overbearing walls was getting to her and the photo, Hale smiling, it was making her blood pound. And Maria sitting there smirking like she had her now, infuriated her. She was just about to stand and tell her so when the door opened and Bruce Milo, her long-time attorney, strolled in. He motioned for her to stand.

"This interview is over."

Avery stood and rushed from the room. She trembled as she turned to wait for Bruce. Maria followed her after gathering her things. She was still smirking. Bruce cupped Avery's elbow.

"The next time you want to speak to my client, you'll have to go through me."

Maria shrugged. "I wouldn't go far from your phone then."

Avery squeezed her fists and forced herself to stop trembling. She shook her arm away from Bruce and hurried with him from the station. When they stepped out into the bright sun, Bruce loosened his tie in obvious anger.

"When are you going to grow a brain?"

She turned on him, opened her mouth to speak, but stopped cold. What could she say? The interview had been a disaster. A total complete disaster.

"I handled it just fine." She wasn't about to admit fault or defeat, even if it was obvious. The brilliant but pompous Bruce would no doubt gloat like he'd done a dozen or so other times throughout her life when he'd had to save her ass. If he hadn't been such a good friend of her father, she would've tossed his ass to the curb. But Bruce was fiercely loyal to the Ashland family. And loyal was what she needed right now.

He scoffed and slid on his black Gargoyle sunglasses. They went well with his perfectly shaped flattop haircut. He'd been trying for the Terminator look since the eighties. It seemed some dreams died hard.

"You're lucky Nadine called. Lucky someone cares about you like that."

Avery slid on her shades. She pushed back her shoulders and took in a deep breath. She stared at him while she dug in her small purse for her car key.

"What can I say? She's an angel."

Bruce eased his hands into his pockets and stood with her next to her Jaguar. "Like it or not we're going to have to discuss this before it gets nasty. I tried to tell you this the day they found Hale. I knew they'd come for you, at the very least to sniff around. You can't fuck with these people, Avery. They aren't like the disgruntled husbands of your lovers, upset over the seduction of their wives. They're cops. The law. And if you don't play your cards right, they can send you away for a very, very long time.

Avery fought off a chill. She unlocked her car, climbed in, and lowered the window. "Okay," she finally said, her shoulders sagging a bit as she gripped the wheel. "What do I do?"

"You need to bring me up to speed on that interview."

"I didn't say anything they could use against me."

"What do they have? Anything?"

"A photo I gave Hale some months ago. I wrote a threat to him on the back and drew a target on his face."

"Jesus," he breathed. He tapped the top of her car. "We can handle it."

She sighed, wrung her hands on the wheel, and looked at him. "I didn't do it, in case you were wondering."

He held up a hand to silence her. "Save it for later. In the meantime," he bent and aimed the comment directly at her, "stay out of trouble, will ya?"

She powered up the window and peeled out, giving him the finger as she sped away.

Chapter Twelve

Maria stared out the window of the popular breakfast and lunch diner. She stared beyond Finley, beyond the other patrons, to the darkening sky. Finley continued speaking, oblivious.

"I'm telling you, her face said it all. She's guilty as hell." He held a finger up for the waitress. "Can I get an iced tea to go, please?" He swished what was left in his glass with a straw and then leaned in to suck it down.

Maria stared at the variety of syrups on the table and considered his words. The look of pure shock on Ashland's face when she'd seen the photo, it had truly surprised her. She'd expected more practiced ambivalence from Avery. Avery had tried to recover quickly, as if she, too, knew she'd given herself away. But it had been too late. They'd all seen it, and if Maria wasn't mistaken, it had also scared the hell out of Avery. What that meant, she wasn't sure. Was it because she knew she was caught? Or was it fear of something else?

"I don't know. I'm not quite ready to jump to that conclusion yet. I'll wait for the surveillance and the cell phone records." Something about the way Avery had looked. Horrified, shock, fear. It didn't jibe with guilt. With what she knew of Avery, she knew the woman would try her best to play coy, to tease them for the sheer fun of it. But this, this had played out so far from that, Maria was beginning to wonder just how many depths there were to Avery Ashland. Could one of those depths really harbor a killer? Still, the satisfaction she'd felt in that moment when Avery had shown her cards, had yet to leave her gut. It was warm and pleasant. Sheer satisfaction. What she felt each time she nailed a perp. Avery was squirming now, there was no doubt. What she would do about it remained to be seen. But there would most definitely be a reaction. Maria expected nothing less from the infamous Avery Ashland. In fact, she was surprised her phone hadn't rung with an angry Avery on the other end, demanding a meeting. Perhaps her lawyer had killed her spirit. What a shame that would be. Her stubborn confidence was what had given them the best insight to her so far.

They stood and both fished money out and onto the table to cover the bill and tip. Finley took his iced tea and they headed into an overcast sky. Lightning split the dark sky in the near distance and the wind had awakened, whipping the smell of dust and rain around their faces. She opened the passenger door to their unmarked Dodge sedan.

"How's that tree in your front yard?"

The car was stifling, oven hot. She carefully buckled her seat belt, careful not to burn her fingers, and adjusted the air as Finley started the engine.

He groaned. "Not good. One more batch of strong wind and she's done for."

"Looks like I'll be helping you pull that down after all." Her old Jeep had a winch and they'd had to use it more than once to help people with their fallen or dead trees.

Finley leaned forward and stared at the churning, blackening sky. "Guess so."

He pulled onto the road and sped toward the east side of Las Brisas, where the wealthy huddled together in various elite, connected neighborhoods, cuddled up to brown and purple mountains, as if the rest of the population were planning to attack.

"That saves me from having to go to Mama's for dinner on Saturday." She aimed the air vents toward them both and tried to relax.

"Oh, well, in that case I'll get someone else to help. You need to go see your family."

She fought rolling her eyes. "No, I don't. I don't need any more talk of me settling down or dating or any such nonsense."

"They mean well, Maria. They worry about you."

"Yeah, well, they can just stop. I'm fine."

"You're alone."

"I have Horace and we are fine."

He laughed.

"Besides, my tia still tries to set me up with men. It's seriously awkward."

"Yikes, is she still doing that?"

"Yes." She crossed her arms over her chest remembering the last time. They'd had a big family get-together at her mama's and in walked Tia Rosita with a man way too young for herself. Maria had known at once that he was intended for her. The entire evening he'd followed her around and tried to make small talk. She'd ended up leaving early.

"I take it telling her you're a lesbian doesn't work?"

"No. She says she's trying to find me the right man."

He shook his head. "I would tell your parents. Just say you aren't coming if she's planning on bringing a man for you. Tell them it makes you feel uncomfortable. Maybe then they'd understand why you avoid coming around."

They sped past towering palms blowing in the breeze. Golf course after golf course. When they reached a cluster of low-lying mountains serrated against the dark blue sky, they slowed and crawled up to a residential gate. Finley eased down the window and pressed the call button to announce their presence. A woman responded and the gate slowly swung open. They drove on and wound through the wealthy neighborhood playing host to large homes with circular drives and long flanking driveways leading to multiple car garages. The homes were all mostly lightly stuccoed with contrasting Spanish tiled roofs. It reminded Maria of the song, "Pink Houses." She inhaled the freshly cut grass as yard workers manicured lawns with loud mowers, leaf blowers, and weed whackers. Middle-aged women in sun visors power walked along the sidewalks, women on a mission. Everyone was tan, coated with sweat, and eagerly moving with purpose. Even the dogs being led on leashes seemed determined and ambitious. All of them out to beat the storm.

"Nice neighborhood," she said. "What do you think these homes go for?"

"I don't know. Probably a few mil, easy."

"I can see how this would impress the ladies," Maria said. From what they knew, Hale was all about impressing, no matter who he was entertaining.

"Got that right."

Finley slowed and they pulled onto an elaborate cobblestoned drive, rounding to the front of a vast, two-story home. The walls were stuccoed a light beige and topped with dark brown tiled roofing. A large ceramic sun matching the roof hung above the front entryway. Finley put the vehicle in park, and Maria tried to breathe easy, enjoying the darker shade from the numerous trees. The clouds were thick with rain now. Ready to pop. The heat was only encouraging a downfall.

"I'm pretty sure I'm stuck to this seat," she said, crawling from the car.

Finley stood too and plucked at the back of his golf polo style shirt. She could see the dark stain running down the center, and she knew her own light colored blouse probably looked similar.

They stepped up to the front door. "Hope she's nice," Finley said, bouncing on his feet.

"She sounded very nice on the phone."

Maria rang the bell and Finley peeled off his sunglasses. The door opened almost immediately, showing them a young looking middle-aged woman in a white skirt, navy blouse, and matching short white jacket.

"Hello, please come in." She ran a nervous looking hand through her raven hair and pressed her lips together for a smile.

They entered and exchanged handshakes.

"Melanie Prague, pleased to meet you."

Her smile looked warm, and Maria felt her own frame relax as they moved into the house. Finley seemed to drop his guard too as they walked into a sunken sitting room where they found tea on a silver tray.

"Tea?" She motioned for them to sit.

Maria waved her off politely, but Finley sat and awaited a cup.

"First of all, let me tell you how sorry we are for your loss," Maria said.

"Yes, please forgive us for our delay in seeing you," Finley said. "We've been so busy with the case…and you weren't here the day our team came to go over his things…"

She held up a hand and sat across from Finley. "Please, I know how busy you've been. I've been equally as busy with closing out all his affairs. Hale lived a very busy life as you can imagine."

"Yes, of course." Maria glanced around and saw stacks of boxes marked "kitchen" and several stacks of garment bags with what she assumed to be suits in them. It seemed as though Melanie was packing up his home as well as getting his affairs in order. And so soon after their own team had been through it. She wondered what the rush was. She crossed slowly to peek in the other rooms. Boxes filled those rooms as well, leaving only furniture. Was this because of Hale's family or was this all Melanie's doing?

"He was quite the businessman," Maria added as she reentered the room.

Melanie smiled, but it didn't reach her eyes.

"And…we hear he was quite the ladies' man as well," Finley said.

Maria studied her for a reaction, but Melanie remained poised. "I don't really feel it's my place to discuss Hale's private life."

"How long did you work for Hale?"

Melanie looked to Maria. "Ten years."

Finley slurped his tea. "Now that Hale's dead, there's no need for secrecy."

Melanie cleared her throat. "It's out of respect, sir. He paid me well to keep such matters behind closed doors."

"He ever put the moves on you?" Finley asked.

Melanie straightened. "No, he did not."

Maria smiled in return. "Mrs. Prague."

"Miss. I divorced last year."

"Ms. Prague, we understand the delicateness of your job as Hale's personal assistant, but Hale was murdered, and frankly, we have no time for secrets or respect, as you call it. We need to know about his private life. And we need to know about it now."

She shifted but did not speak.

"A beautiful woman like you and he never made a move? Not even a suggestion?"

She shot Finley a dangerous look. "I've already answered that question."

"Who was he last seeing?" Maria asked.

Melanie stood. "I'm not sure. But I have his appointment book." She left the room, and Finley made a whistle between his teeth.

"She's ice."

"She's professional," Maria said. "But yes."

Melanie reentered carrying a leather-bound book. "He refused to keep an electronic schedule. Said he needed things written down. He carried it everywhere during the day. "I've had it with me, calling everyone, closing things out."

She handed it to Maria who opened an evidence bag for her to drop it into.

"The last entry before his death is highlighted. The entry is handwritten by me, and then he made some notes next to it. I don't know what they mean."

"What was the entry?"

"Anniversary party at the country club."

Maria sealed the bag. "Were you there that evening? At the country club?"

"No."

"Where were you?" Finley asked.

"At home."

"Can anyone collaborate that?"

She returned to her seat. "Yes. A…lover. If it's necessary."

"Name?" Maria asked.

"I…I'm not sure. It was a one-night thing."

Finley's eyebrows shot up. "We're going to need it."

"I don't know how to find it. We both had had a lot to drink."

"Where did you meet?" Maria asked.

"At a lounge. We met over drinks. Is this really necessary? I mean I can't possibly be a suspect. With Hale gone, I've lost my income, my important contacts." She laughed a little as if they were being ridiculous.

"We'll still have to check that out," Finley said. "Procedure."

She eventually nodded. "I'll see what I can get you."

"Please do." Maria knew almost all they needed to know about Melanie, but they had to be sure and cover their bases. Most of Hale's close associates were hesitant about their private affairs so it didn't surprise her that Melanie seemed to be as well. What was surprising was the drop in temperature from her. Maria swore she could almost see her breath in her icy wake.

"Do you know of anyone who wanted to hurt Hale? An ex? A husband of a sex partner, something like that?"

"I would say no. I mean I'd like to say no, but Hale had enemies." She met Maria's gaze. "Most of them women. He...put them off you see."

"Yeah, we know," Finley said.

"Anyone specific you can think of?"

She cocked her head. "Like I said, I tried to stay out of his private affairs, but he did have strong hate for Avery Ashland. How she felt about him...well, I don't think that's any secret."

Finley set down his tea mug. "What do you think? Could Ashland murder Hale?"

"I-I never met the woman. But from what I do know...I wouldn't put anything past her."

Maria made a note and looked to Finley.

"Really? You do know how brutally he was murdered don't you?"

She stared at the tea set on the table. "Yes, unfortunately, I had to identify the body. His mother...couldn't handle it."

They waited to see if she would continue. "Ms. Prague?"

She blinked. "Ms. Ashland has threatened Hale on numerous occasions. Once, when I answered the phone. Her hate for him was venomous, and I'll never forget how her voice seethed through the line when she said she'd see him dead. When she promised she'd see him dead." She hugged herself. "It unnerved me."

"So you're going by a verbal threat?" Finley asked.

She looked at him as if he were stupid. "Yes. Isn't that enough?"

He stood. "And you can think of no one else?"

She shook her head. "Who wanted to kill him? No, not fresh off the top of my mind." She stood along with him. "I'm sorry. I don't hear a person's life being threatened every day, Detective."

"Didn't mean to upset you," he said, moving toward the door. "Thank you for your time."

Maria followed and handed over her business card. "We'll be in touch. Please remember to call us with that name if you can find it. Or even a receipt from the lounge will do." She offered a warm smile, but Melanie did not return it.

She took the card and walked them to the door.

Maria turned. "One last thing." She waved at their surroundings. "All this packing up of his home. Your idea?"

She seemed to stumble for words. "I don't see what that has to do with anything."

"You didn't answer the question."

"It was my idea, yes. I—if you must know I can't stand being here. Gives me the creeps."

"You could have someone else do it."

Again, she fought for words. "I know where everything is, and—he was a private person."

Maria nodded slowly, looked around one last time, and then stepped outside with Finley.

This time Melanie spoke.

"After I give you my alibi...will I have to speak to you again?"

Maria allowed her eyebrows to raise. "If it checks out, we may not have to, no—"

"Good." She slammed and locked the door in their face.

Maria turned to Finley. "I guess we just bring out the best in everyone," she said, shaking her head.

He slung an arm around her. "That we do, my friend, that we do." He wagged a finger at her. "Know who else seems to bring out the best in folks?"

"Who?"

"Avery Ashland."

She laughed in agreement.

"Seems like everyone loves her."

They climbed in the car just as fat drops of rain began to fall. Maria breathed deeply and glanced at the house to see Melanie Prague watching them from the window. They drove off without offering a wave.

CHAPTER THIRTEEN

Maria pulled into the medical examiner's office at precisely ten o'clock at night. She lowered her visor, touched up her lipstick, and frowned at her hair. She swept it up into a manageable bun and exited her Jeep Cherokee. She jogged in the rain to the front door, stepped inside, and waited for George, the night security, to let her in. When he came down the hallway, he moved slowly, keys on his large hook dangling. He gave her a wave and buzzed her on through. She smiled at his gray scruffy beard and dark kind eyes.

"Doc's in her office," he said, returning to his seat near the front window.

"Thanks, George."

She hurried down the hall to where the offices were held. She found Dr. Judith Haddock sitting at her desk, dictating. She waved Maria in and encouraged her to sit. Maria did so and waited patiently. She skimmed Dr. Haddock's bookshelves as she'd done many times and again searched for family photos. She found none.

Dr. Haddock stopped her recorder and put it away along with a file. Then she plucked out another file and flipped it open.

"And how are we this evening, Detective?" she asked without looking up. Her reading glasses teetered on the tip of her nose, and Maria smiled inwardly, wanting so badly to push them back a little just as she always did.

"I'm fine, thanks for asking. How are you?"

"I'm tired as hell, are you kidding? Ready to go home."

Maria laughed. "Well, now that you mention it…"

"Yeah, I thought so." She set down the file and whipped off her glasses. "I have a confession to make. I didn't call you out here strictly for business purposes."

Maria heated a little with surprise.

"Oh?"

"We've known each other for a few years now, correct?"

"Yes."

"And I've known Finley for, God, seems like forever. Anyway, I consider you both friends."

Maria waited.

"He called me the other day. Seems he's concerned about your health. And I have to admit, I've noticed some changes in you as well."

"I—"

But Dr. Haddock continued. "You look off. Weak even. And I've noticed the trembling and the change in your gait."

"It's just my hip. I—"

"Please don't make excuses, Maria."

Maria clamped her mouth shut.

"Have you seen someone?"

"Yes."

"Good."

"I just need to schedule a test."

"So Finley says. I'm going to jump on board with him and insist that you get that done."

Maria laughed and shook her head. While her own concern had been mounting, she'd thought she'd done a pretty good job at hiding her issues.

"This is so ridiculous. I'm sure I'm fine. Probably just a vitamin deficiency—"

"Who are you kidding, Maria? I'm a physician."

"Yes, but you don't know everything about me."

"No, I don't. But I know what Finley told me, and I know that if you've seen a doctor, then he or she has probably already done blood work, which would've ruled out a vitamin deficiency." She raised an eyebrow.

Maria looked away.

"I'll get the test done."

"Beautiful." She smiled. "And don't be too hard on Finley. He cares. As do I."

Maria sighed. "Thank you."

Dr. Haddock tapped her desk.

"Well, since I didn't call you out here strictly for a lecture or simply for the mere shits and giggles of it, I'll get to the main point." She tapped the file. "I've got some lab results on our guy. On Mr. Medley."

Maria leaned forward.

"His toxicology came back, and he had a hell of a lot of that muscle relaxer in him. I mean a lot."

"Enough to what, kill him?"

"Well, yes, he would've fallen into cardiac arrest eventually. But he was killed before that. This, though. This amount. It would've rendered him nearly unconscious for most of the duration of his eventual homicide."

Maria shook her head. "What are you saying?"

"Mr. Medley was completely out of it during his torture and murder." She stood. "Maria, his killer wasn't fighting a moving body like we originally thought. His killer was unskilled, hesitant, and, well…scared."

She waved Maria up. "Come. I'll show you what I mean." She shoved her way into the swinging doors of the locker room and they suited up in silence. When they finished, they double gloved, careful to pull the ends over their wrist cuffs, and headed into the main examination room. The lights came to life as they entered and Dr. Haddock headed to the large stainless steel drawers and slid out Hale Medley. She unzipped his black body bag and tucked it away from his head and chest. "Come here."

Maria was waiting by the door, but she moved quickly to stand across from her. Hale was as pale as ever with his mouth still agape in a terrified yawn. His eyes were like milky blue marbles, boring into her soul.

She shuddered.

"You all right, Detective?"

"Fine."

"Don't faint on me."

"I wouldn't dream of it."

Dr. Haddock met her gaze. Seemingly satisfied, she moved on. "I want you to look at his wounds on his forehead. "See how sloppy the cuts are? Two to three right next to each other? Some start and just stop? Some deep, some shallow?"

Maria nodded.

"We originally thought this was because Mr. Medley was alive and moving some. That he was difficult to cut. But now that we know he was most likely unconscious…it leaves only one possibility. The killer was having a difficult time all right. But not because of Hale. But because they were scared."

Maria straightened from her slight bend. "Oh, my God."

"Precisely."

"Our killer is a novice."

"That's my bet."

"Not so cold-blooded after all."

"Nope. I'd say they were most cowardly and almost took the easy way out by killing him with the muscle relaxer. This, these cuts…they didn't want to do them. They had a hard time in doing them. So my question is, why do them at all?"

"Because they had to. It was part of the plan. They had to make their point. Like it or not."

"Now look at the throat." She touched the flesh with her gloved fingertips. "It's the same here. See these hesitant cuts? Mark after mark. And the way they only cut four inches? If a killer wants to kill by cutting the throat, most try to go ear-to-ear, or at least cut long enough to be sure the job is done. This looks as though they couldn't go through with it all the way."

"But they severed down to the spine."

"True, but that took more than one cut as well. I can show you the slides from under the scope." She zipped the bag back up and slid Hale's body back into the cooler. Maria stood looking at the closed drawer while Dr. Haddock powered up the large television screen.

"Detective?"

Maria shook herself out of her trance and crossed to her. Though her body had been still, her mind had been racing. She had to call Finley first thing in the morning. They had to go over everything again. She would start on most of it tonight.

She focused on the shots of the slides showing several cuts into the tissue and bone.

"You don't understand," Maria said. "This could change everything."

Dr. Haddock nodded.

"I thought it might."

Maria thanked her profusely, asked for copies of all the new information, and headed for the door to go change.

"Uh, Detective?"

"Yes?"

"Mr. Medley's assistant called today. She said the family wants him cremated as soon as possible."

"Is that so?" Maria tore off her gloves and disposed of them, wondering why the rush on burning the remains. Funny how Melanie Prague hadn't mentioned it during their meeting. "She calls again, let me know."

Dr. Haddock nodded and Maria pushed through the doors with all the new information pushing in on her mind.

Maria and Finley stared through the fence at two scantily clad women playing a heated game of tennis.

"This case can't get any hotter," Finley said, folding in a stick of gum on his tongue. Maria didn't bother to answer; she just stared at the fast volley of the ball and the two women grunting each time it was their turn to hit. Both women were in incredible shape, but Maria's eyes were on the redhead on the far side. Her legs were powerful, and she seemed to shimmer in the sun as if her pinkish skin were covered in tiny glitter particles. She was beautiful in an old-fashioned way, in a Ginger Rogers kind of way, and Maria could see why Avery was drawn to her physically.

"We both agree now more than ever that a woman killed Hale, right?" Finley asked clicking his gum.

"Yes."

"Think this could be her?"

"I don't see why not. We've now got new info that points right to her."

"Then let's go get her."

They pushed through the gate and strolled parallel to the net flashing their badges.

"Lana Gold."

The woman in the short tennis skirt stopped her advance and the ball whizzed by her. She grimaced.

"Yeah?" She placed her hand on her hip and gawked at them with obvious frustration. When she recognized Maria, she scoffed. "Christ, you again. What do you want?"

"Answers," Finley said.

"I'm afraid we didn't get to talk very long the other evening," Maria said. She pointed to a nearby table with an umbrella. "Shall we?"

Lana waved off her partner who walked away eyeing them with disgust rather than curiosity. Lana crossed to a bench and placed her racket in a cover and grabbed a towel. Maria sat at the table carefully, afraid it would be hot to the touch. But thankfully, the umbrella had done its job. Finley joined her, and they watched as Lana dried her face and neck and then slid out of her tight polo to reveal a sweat-soaked torso and white sports bra. Then she paraded to them as if on a catwalk, a sly smirk on her face.

Finley laughed, amused, and Maria countered her previous thought and wondered why Ashland was so intrigued with her. Her body was tiptop, sure, but she was so...conceited and the way she flaunted herself was almost sickening. Did Avery consider that attractive?

"Are you done amusing yourself?" Maria asked as a bit of jealousy tried to spark inside her. She had no reason to be jealous over Lana Gold even if the woman did share Ashland's bed. Maria had no business thinking of either woman as more than suspects. She bit her lower lip as punishment for the feeling and grounded herself.

Lana eased into a chair and wrapped the towel around her neck. "I'm just having a little fun."

"Yeah, well, he's married and I'm far from interested."

"Not according to Avery. She says you're more than a little interested in her and in women in general."

Maria laughed out loud. "Did she? Well, she would, wouldn't she?"

"Are you?" Lana asked, relaxing in her chair and crossing her thick, toned legs. "Interested in Avery?"

"The only interest I have in Ms. Ashland is whether or not she killed Hale Medley."

Lana gave a wave. "Oh, that. How boring."

"Boring?" Finley asked. He grinned at Maria in what she recognized as disbelief.

"I thought if you two came all this way then something of dire importance needed to be discussed."

"And Hale's murder is not important?" Maria asked.

"Not to me. Why should it be? I hardly knew the man."

"I don't believe you," Finley said. "You see we've recently learned that you were a guest here at the Valle Sol Country Club the night of the fundraising ball. That just so happens to be the last night Hale was seen alive."

"So? There were a lot of people here. Very important people."

"Yes. But none fit the description of the woman Hale left with except you."

"Oh, bullshit. There were plenty of redheads there, hanging off rich arms or looking to hang off a rich arm."

"We have the surveillance tapes, Lana. Why you didn't think to cover that little loose end speaks to your intelligence. We also have

Hale's day planner with your initials penciled in next to the country club event. Coincidence? We think not."

She blinked and appeared deeply offended. "My intelligence? Pardon me, Detective, but fuck you."

She pushed back her chair and stood.

"Where did you go with Hale that evening, Lana?"

"I'm sorry. You'll have to refer to my attorney for any other questions."

"Don't jerk us around, Ms. Gold. Your neck is at stake here. Where did you go? Did Ashland pay you to kill him? Or did she help right alongside you?"

Maria stood as Lana turned to walk away from them. "Whose idea was the carving? Ashland's? Was she finally fed up with his wandering eyes and perhaps his hands? Had he made advances toward you as well, Lana? Did you two finally shut him up for good?"

But Lana only grabbed her athletic bag and racket and walked away. Maria turned to find Finley still sitting with his fingers in a steeple at his mouth.

Maria kicked the chair Lana had been in. "We've got to get those surveillance tapes from her condo."

"Mm."

Maria sank into the chair and stared at the blue-black sky. An announcement came over the speakers closing the courts for the storm. People began hurrying inside.

They had been lucky to get the recordings from the country club early that morning. They'd about fallen out of their chairs as they'd seen Lana Gold lead Hale into a limousine. None of the other witnesses at the country club that night had been able to pinpoint which woman he'd left with. There had been a storm, and it had been a big distraction.

"This is a huge lead. It puts Lana as one of the last people to see Hale alive. If not the last person."

"Melanie swears Hale didn't bring her to his place," Finley said.

"And his alarm company confirms it."

The wind kicked up, and they sat in it for a while until lightning chased them off. As they exited the country club, they saw Lana Gold on the phone, pacing back and forth.

Maria wondered if she was dumb enough to have used her personal cell phone to talk to Ashland around the time of the murder. Hopefully, they'd find out soon enough.

CHAPTER FOURTEEN

"Who the fuck do they think they are?" Avery said, tossing the phone onto the couch. She ran a hand through her hair and looked out the vast window. "My God, are they going to question everyone I know?" She burned with embarrassment at the thought, a feeling she wasn't used to. It ate at her insides and she could hardly bear to think about it. She liked to pride herself on not caring what people thought, but in reality, she cared very much.

"Who's bothering you, darling? Another rude idiot? Don't tell me it's another Hale. I should think one of him on this earth was quite enough." Bryce Daniels uncrossed her stocking covered legs and leaned forward for a delicate taste of her scotch on ice. "Whatever higher power there is surely knows we couldn't handle another one like him. Or at the very least not so soon." She sipped her drink and closed her eyes as she sat back to relax.

The back doors to Avery's penthouse were open, letting in the cool breeze brought on by an impending storm. Avery couldn't let herself enjoy it though. She paced and held her phone pressed to her lower lip.

"It's these goddamned detectives. They are adamant in ruining my reputation."

Bryce let out a hearty laugh. "Which reputation would that be, love?"

Avery aimed a sinister glance at her. "Funny."

Bryce threw an arm across the back of the couch and tapped the cushion. "Come sit, love. Let's chat."

Avery sighed and pocketed her phone. She crossed the room to join her old friend and former lover. It had been years since they were lovers, but Avery still held a strong affection for her, and Bryce flirted with her no end.

Avery snuggled up next to her and rested her head on her shoulder. "I hate Hale," she said. "Even in death he's mocking me, causing me hell."

Bryce laughed. "Did you expect anything less?"

"Yes, I had actually hoped with him being gone that I could have some peace. But, damn it, no."

"Darling, what have I always told you? Keep your friends close and your enemies closer. Hale being dead…well, he's not close any more is he? He's out of your control completely now."

"Yes, but he's dead. He can't do anything, yet it feels like he is somehow."

"Because he is. You have no idea what he did before he passed, what he said or what he left behind for these detectives to find. None whatsoever."

Avery turned to look her in her magnificent blue eyes. "It's funny you say that. Hale…he…kept that damn photo I gave him months back. The one I'd found in my old things of Hale and me in school together? I'd drawn a target on his face and written to him in Latin, knowing he'd understand, and I'd given it to him at a benefit when he let his hand slip to rest on my ass. He's really lucky I didn't knock him out." She stared off in thought. "He was always pushing it. Always."

"Well, he obviously pushed it a little too far."

"Yes, but more than that, he had that photo in his wallet when he was found dead. He'd kept it. As if it were a memento."

"It probably was. He probably jerked off to it nightly."

Avery elbowed her. "Bitch."

"You know I'm probably right."

"The cops think otherwise. They think it was him letting them know who killed him."

"Oh, hogwash. They're just trying to get your goat. Don't let them. Be the Avery Ashland I know and love. The 'Fuck you all, I'll do as I please,' Avery Ashland."

"I am. I mean, I will." But inside, she had deflated a little. She could feel it. Her dragon fire wasn't as strong. She was less likely to strike out. Now she was actually thinking before she breathed fire. It unnerved her. Had she lost her edge? Were the cops quelling her somehow?

"You're frightened," Bryce said as she tilted her chin to look at her once again.

Avery pulled away and stood. "Don't be ridiculous." She strode to the window and allowed the wind to blow through her hair. She searched nervously for a cigarette, and when she placed it between her lips and lit up, Bryce protested as usual.

"You know how I feel about the smoking," she said. "You're much too beautiful to ruin yourself."

Avery narrowed her eyes and exhaled long and slow, blowing smoke into the cool air. "I'll take my chances." Bryce shook her head, and Avery studied her light brown hair, perfectly made up and set, her exquisite creamy skin accented with smoky eye shadow and deep red lips. She could still model, even in her early seventies. Her classic features were ageless and her friendship was priceless. Even so, her vocal opinions of late seemed to rub Avery the wrong way.

"How about a little massage then? To ease the pain?" Bryce stood and crossed to her. She downed the rest of her scotch and set the glass aside. She held her shoulders. "Remember my famous massages?"

Avery looked away. "How could I forget? You seduced me with one."

"Mm-hmm, so I did. Not that long ago I might add."

Avery hugged herself with one arm and continued to smoke. "We're long past dalliances, Bryce. Besides, you have more than one lover to choose from if I recall."

"What can I say? I want the best." She touched her face, but Avery felt nothing other than cool fingertips.

"The best isn't good enough for you. At least it didn't used to be."

Bryce laughed. "Are you still hurt from all that? I always thought you couldn't be hurt. That my secret goings on couldn't possibly bother you."

"You were wrong."

"So I was."

Bryce stared deeply into her eyes and placed a delicate kiss upon her lips.

Avery stared back, unaffected. Bryce had been her first all those years ago. First to seduce her, first to love her, first…and last to betray her. Avery swore she'd never let it happen again. Instead she'd turned into what had torn her apart. A lover who had no bounds, no rules, and no cares. She'd turned into Bryce, only stronger, fiercer, and more passionate than anyone could've imagined. Including Bryce herself, who had turned around and begged to bed her once again. But Avery would never give in, even if it was just for spite.

Bryce dropped her hands. "It's all just as well. I'm seeing someone new anyhow."

"Oh?" Avery knew she was trying to make her jealous. But jealousy, where Bryce was concerned, had long ago faded.

"Yes. She's very…special. And the sex…my God."

"That's nice. I'm happy for you."

Bryce was silent for a long moment, and when Avery said nothing else, she said, "Very well. I can show myself out."

Avery kept smoking, kept looking out the window. She forced back the pain of the present, of the cops and their questions, of Maria and her unattainability. She pushed it all away and watched as the woman she'd once called the woman of her life walked out the door.

She approached the door, ready to dead bolt it when she heard mumbled voices. She pulled it open to find Bryce and Lana conversing. Lana jolted a little at being caught. Bryce merely smiled and walked toward the elevator.

"What's going on?"

Lana took her by the hands and led her back inside. "Just being polite," Lana said. "She's very attractive. Who is she?"

Avery closed the door and locked it. "Someone I used to care about."

Lana seemed surprised. "Really? I must hear this."

Avery extinguished her cigarette, not much wanting it anymore. She collapsed into her chaise lounge and stared out the windows. "Nothing to hear. It was years ago. Back when I was...young."

"Don't tell me she's your first?"

"Don't worry, I won't. I don't want to talk about it." She never shared her private feelings or past with her lovers. Rarely did she do so with Bryce. But she'd been feeling a little vulnerable as of late, and she knew she needed to toughen up and steel herself once more. Even Bryce could use her vulnerability against her. She had before.

Avery changed the subject as Lana scooted in to cuddle with her. "Tell me what the cops wanted." Lana had called her not long ago complaining about them ruining her tennis match. Not to mention embarrassing her at the country club.

Lana snuggled into her, and Avery could smell her mint shampoo and body wash. It used to stir her, but now it did nothing.

"They know Hale left with me the night of the murder."

Avery stiffened. "What do you mean by 'know?'"

Lana held her tighter. "They have surveillance."

Avery pushed her away. "Lana, how could you've been so stupid?"

She groaned like a playful child. "It doesn't matter. Doesn't prove anything."

Avery used to think her childish games were somewhat fun, especially when it came to teasing and foreplay, but lately she'd grown tired of her blatant irresponsibility.

"It doesn't matter to you how devastating this could be?" She wondered what the police thought and of how the knowledge must've led them to think of her too. She thought of Maria and what she must think. She couldn't take it.

She pushed away from Lana and stood.

"Baby, come on. It's nothing."

"I don't understand you," Avery said. "I don't understand you at all."

"What's to understand? I had a lot to drink and so did Hale. I got in his limo. So what?"

"So what?" She tapped her finger to her head. "Think about it, Lana. The cops must know how you felt about him. How all women feel about him. It's called motive. And now they can place you with him? Jesus, Lana. Jesus."

She lit a cigarette, sucked on it, and then smashed it out in an ashtray. "Not to mention how this makes me look."

Lana rolled her eyes. "Right, because it's all about you."

"It's about you too, but you don't seem to be concerned."

"I told them to talk to my lawyer. In the meantime, I'm not going to worry. You shouldn't either." She began unbuttoning her blouse and licking her lips. "Come here," she whispered.

Avery stood with her arms crossed.

"Avery. Come here." She held out her hand with her dark purple bra exposed against the milky white flesh of her abdomen.

Avery sighed and walked to her. She took her hand.

"Are you afraid?" Lana asked.

Avery hardened her jaw. "I don't get afraid." But inside, she was beyond worried. Lana was careless and clueless, and it was leading them both down a very dangerous path.

"Let me make you feel better," she said, lifting her bra to show off her rose-colored nipples. She played with them and grinned. "Don't you want to feel better, baby? Don't you want to taste them? Make me feel better?"

Avery lay down next to her and swallowed against the angry lump in her throat. Her feelings were surfacing and she didn't like it. And she didn't like being asked if she was afraid.

She pinned Lana's hand over her head and kissed her. Lana squealed and then moaned at her power.

"Yes, Avery. Take me. Fucking make me yours."

Avery bit into her neck and lowered herself to nibble her nipples until she cried out with both pleasure and pain.

"Mm. God, baby. That's it, I want to be yours. Make me so. Make me so."

Avery looked up at her with hunger and dominance the only feelings remaining.

"You'll never be mine, Lana. Never."

And with that, she tore down her tight-fitting jeans and attached herself to her bare center, causing Lana to forget any remaining demands.

CHAPTER FIFTEEN

Maria sat at her parents' backyard picnic table and downed a Dos Equis as quickly as she could. It was Friday night, a little past nine, and she was still anxious over the MRI she'd had a few hours earlier. The results, she'd learned, would have to be told to her by her doctor. She'd seen the neurologist once, at the suggestion of her doctor, and he'd promptly ordered the MRI after examining her and going over her symptoms.

Her rational mind had told her not to search her symptoms on the web, that whatever she found would only cause her to go insane with worry and speculation. But she'd done so anyway, while fidgeting in her seat at the radiology center waiting for her MRI. What she'd found had beyond worried her and even caused her to break out in a cold sweat. She'd tried to talk about it with her technician, but she'd only told her she'd have to discuss it with her doctor, leaving her anxious as hell with nowhere to turn but the bottle.

"Thought you might could use another," a woman, one she didn't recognize, said as she slid in across from her. She placed the icy bottle near her hand and smiled. Maria returned it, easy and relaxed, though her insides were still in turmoil. The woman was attractive and nice to look at with short, bleached blond hair and sparkling green-gray eyes. She had a small tattoo on her neck, which normally would've turned Maria and her Goody Two-shoes way off, but she found herself staring at it, amused.

"What's it say?" She pointed with her pinky as she drank from the new bottle.

"Breathe."

"Ah, as in don't forget to breathe. Got it."

"Something like that." She tipped her own beer and rubbed her toned arm up near the tight sleeve of her T-shirt. She looked up at the dark sky and the slowly moving silver clouds.

"Thought for sure we'd get a monsoon," Maria said.

"Me too."

"I was counting on it." Maria laughed a little.

"Why? So you wouldn't have to be here tonight?"

Maria met her gaze. "Maybe."

The woman smiled. "Then you wouldn't have met me." She stuck out her hand. "Samantha."

Maria shook her hand. "Maria."

"I know. Your brother told me all about you."

"Oh no, not another one." She shook her head when Samantha looked confused. "Sorry, that was rude. It's just...my family...they try to set me up all the time and it gets to be frustrating."

"I guess so. I think I'd kill my family if they did that to me."

Maria smiled. "Thank you!"

"I'm serious, that must be awful. Thank God, my folks let me figure it out on my own. I think I'd die if they got involved."

"It's maddening," Maria confessed. "And embarrassing."

"Sounds like a nightmare."

"It can be." They both drank in silence.

Samantha sat back and tipped her beer at her. "You'll be glad to know your brother didn't set us up. He just told me who you were when I asked about the pretty lady in the corner."

Maria fought a blush and pretended to be interested in her beer. Samantha seemed nice, funny even. But she didn't want to read into it, and she reminded herself of all the others that had crashed and burned.

"So are you the sister who's the detective?" Samantha asked, appearing to be genuinely interested.

"I am."

"That must be exciting."

"It can be."

"What are you working on now? Can you tell me?"

"No, not really. It's a high-profile case. And it's taking up most of my time."

Samantha nodded. "I get it. No time to date, huh?"

"Afraid not."

They turned as voices grew closer and Maria's mother slid in next to her. She set a bowl of freshly made salsa on the table along with some tortilla chips, and then she leaned in and planted a wet kiss on Maria's cheek.

"Mija is here!" She held her arms up. "Everyone, Maria is here!"

Friends and family cheered and someone turned the music up. Maria's nieces and nephews began chasing each other around the yard, and her father began to dance in his tight Wranglers and cowboy boots.

"Why do you not come?" her mother, Cecelia asked, looking upset. "I cook all of this and you don't come. The only one. My baby, my youngest."

"Mama, I'm busy. I told you."

"Always too busy for us."

"No, not true. I'm just busy. It's my job."

Her mother scoffed. "I don't like the job. It's dangerous, mija. It's so…masculine."

"Mama, don't please. And if you want me to come more tell Tia to stop setting me up with men."

Her mother reared back. "She still does that? Aye, Dios mio. I tell her no more a long time ago."

"She's still doing it." Maria dipped a chip in salsa and took a bite. It was an explosion of heaven in her mouth. "Oh, Mama. So good."

She smiled and looked to Samantha. "Go ahead, please."

Samantha ate some and grinned. "Wow. That's incredible."

"That's my mama for you. Nothing but the best."

"All homemade?"

Her mother balked. "Of course, who do you think I am? Old El Paso?"

They laughed and her mother gave Maria another kiss and stood. "I bring your new friend some enchiladas. She's cute."

She left them alone, and Maria finished her second beer, which, thankfully, was helping her to relax. She continued to eat the chips and salsa, not realizing just how hungry she was until that moment.

"Your mother is adorable," Samantha said.

"Yes. She's pretty amazing."

"Seems like it. Seems like she really loves you too."

"She does. I'm very lucky I guess."

Samantha slid over an unopened beer and tilted her own at her. "That makes two of us." She took a hearty sip. "Only my mother's specialty isn't enchiladas, it's goulash."

Maria laughed. "No kidding? That sounds good too."

"It is. You'll have to try it sometime. An old Hungarian recipe."

"I just might do that."

"I could bring it by one night. When you're ready."

Maria cocked her head. "You'd really do that?"

"Sure. Beats the same old same old first dinner date."

"Yes, lounging on my own couch does sound much better than staring over at you at a stuffy restaurant."

"Yep, you can stare at me in your own comfort. It will be groundbreaking as far as first dates go."

"Sounds like it." Maria opened the third beer. "And I kind of like…"

"What?"

"Nothing."

Maria smiled and it felt sloppy. She was such a lightweight. She was about to flirt with Samantha, a near stranger. She stood and excused herself, claiming the restroom. She weaved in and out of people to the Arcadian door where she met her brother, Gabriel, head-on.

"Hey, Gabe, Samantha seems great."

He smiled and placed his hands on her shoulders. "Haven't seen you in a while." He leaned down, kissed her, and then whispered in her ear. "Heads up, Tia has a man for you. A real Poindexter looking dude. Better run."

"Nah, I'm okay. I'll just hang with Samantha."

He looked up. "Yeah, who's that?"

Maria laughed. "Your friend, silly. Over there."

He looked toward the picnic table and then smiled. "Oh, Sammie. Yeah, she's great. Very…. capable."

"What?"

"She's strong, keeps up with the guys, you know."

"She's a mechanic?"

"Yeah. And smart. But watch out. I think she's a heartbreaker." He winked and left her alone. She walked slowly down the hallway to the bathroom where she closed herself in and locked the door. She sat on the edge of the tub and rubbed her temples. Despite fatigue she felt good. The best she'd felt in a while. And if Finley didn't call tonight, she might actually get some good sleep. She stood and rinsed her face and walked back out to join the party. A few relatives said hello along with a few long-time friends. It felt good to see everyone, and she reminded herself that she needed to show up more often.

She turned into the kitchen and saw her tia Rosita and she froze. Her tia came at her quickly, tugging a tall, gangly man along with her.

"Maria, Maria. This is Donald. He's dying to meet you."

Donald smiled and seemed pleased. He held out his hand.

Maria took it. "Hi, I'm Maria and I'm gay. As in lesbian. I will never be interested, ever. I keep telling my aunt this, but she ignores me. So you can blame her for wasting your time." She gave him a brief smile and then walked back out the Arcadian door. She took a deep breath and rejoined Samantha at the table where she was digging into what used to be enchiladas.

"Oh, my God, these are so good. Your mother is not only adorable, she's evil."

Maria laughed and sat down. Her own plate was steaming in front of her. She dug in and took hearty swigs of her new beer. They talked until they finished, and then for an hour after that. After five beers, Maria was laughing loudly and slurring her words a bit. She felt warm, relaxed, free. It felt stupendous.

More people were dancing now, and she knew they'd go well into the night. As badly as she wanted to join, she knew she needed to rest more.

"I'd better get going." She stood and braced herself against the table. "Whoa. I feel a little too good."

Samantha stood with her. "You okay?"

"I'm not sure."

Samantha rounded the table and cupped her elbow. "You should let me drive you home."

"No. No, really, I can manage."

"Well, you won't be managing behind the wheel. I'll call a ride for you."

But the last thing Maria wanted was to ride home with a stranger when she felt so good. She realized she didn't want the night to end. If only she had more time in her life. She always found herself bargaining for time in one way or another. She never won.

"I just want a night to myself. One night where I can have fun and sleep peacefully." She'd said the words to herself, but Samantha had heard.

"You've had fun, now let's get you home to sleep peacefully."

"Right. I'll get a phone call. Dollars to dimes I'll get a phone call."

"Turn it off."

"I can't."

She palmed her forehead, and Samantha led her out the back gate to the front sidewalk. She started thumbing her phone, but Maria stopped her.

"It's okay. You drive me."

Samantha stared at her for a moment as if she was waiting for Maria to be sure. "Okay. I'm over here." Samantha drove a black classic two-door Impala. Maria wasn't sure what year it was, but it was very impressive and when Samantha started the engine, it vibrated Maria's entire body.

"Holy shit."

Samantha grinned. "Yeah, she's got some power. You better buckle up."

Maria fastened her seat belt and rolled down her window. She smiled into the wind as they drove, closing her eyes, allowing it to blow away her worries, her fears, the case. She was in such blissful peace when they arrived at her place, she had to be shaken back to reality.

"Which one is yours?" Samantha had slowed on her street, and they were crawling toward her house.

"Here."

Samantha pulled in the drive behind the Jeep Wrangler. She killed the engine and stepped out of the car. She helped Maria out and walked her to the door. Maria leaned into her and held her hand. She found it strong, sure, powerful. It stroked her down deep, and she moaned. They reached the front door and faced one another. Samantha brushed her face with the backs of her fingers.

"You're incredibly beautiful," she said. "I'd really like to bring you dinner sometime."

But Maria stopped her with a pressing kiss. Samantha pulled away, obviously surprised.

Maria laughed. "I don't want you to leave." Her insides were swirling with heat, pushing out against her aching flesh. She knew what was happening and she didn't dare stop it. She needed touch. Passion. Sex. It had been too long, and now it was taking over like a starved beast.

She unlocked the door and tugged Samantha inside. And when Samantha tried to speak again, she drowned her out with another kiss, this one fierce and dominant. She sought with her hungry tongue, and Samantha answered just as fierce and turned her against the wall. Maria tried to turn back, but Samantha stopped her by pressing her hands over hers, holding her to the wall.

"Don't move," she said.

Maria heard her unzip her jeans and then fumble with what sounded like a wrapper. And just as Maria was about to ask, Samantha unfastened and tugged down her pants and underwear. She ran her hands over her ass and smacked her.

"Yes," Maria said. "This is what I want. What I need."

Samantha laughed.

"God, you are curved in all the right places."

Maria moaned again and she felt Samantha search for her opening. Head pounding with desire, she pressed back toward her and spread her legs farther apart. "This is what I want, what I need," she said. She had to have it, now.

"Here I come, baby." Samantha found her and Maria felt a cool moist tip a split second before it slid inside her and filled her with pressing fire.

She arched her back and called out, clenching her eyes. "Ah, fuck yes."

"Feel good?"

"Mm. God yes."

Samantha grabbed her hips and began to thrust slowly in and out. The hot sword of ecstasy slid in and up again and again and Maria collapsed against the wall, sweat coating her brow, teeth biting her lower lip as Samantha pounded her fast and hard.

"Dear God..." Maria could barely form words, and when she could, her throat threatened to cave in on them before she could get them out. "I—Oh fuck. Fuck me—yes. Please. Don't—ever—stop." She now understood why no one else had interested her. They were too soft, too slow. There had been no passion, no excitement, no fucking real, hard pleasure.

Samantha gripped her harder and moved her hips in a circular motion. "I'm fucking you, baby. So good. So good and deep. Getting you way in deep, making you feel oh so good."

Maria closed her eyes as her cheek slid against the wall in sweat. She pushed back in rhythm to Samantha's thrusting, and soon Maria was clenching fists and mouthing unintelligible words. She was riding crest after crest of beautiful pleasure waves all the while thinking of Avery Ashland and her seductive voice and walk. The thoughts brought her climax closer and closer, and by the time she went she was begging Samantha for sweet release, begging her to never stop, to fucking fill her up all the way, fuck her like she'd never been fucked before.

Samantha obliged with a deep laugh and tugged her back into her for five long, deep pulls, and Maria went over in a loud, animalistic voice so deep and dark she hardly recognized herself. When she stilled, she breathed heavily into the wall and realized she had her hand back around gripping Samantha's loose jeans.

"Ah, my God," Maria said. "I can't stand." Her legs trembled and her body shook from residual fireworks. Samantha eased out of her, refastened her pants, and wrapped her arms around her, but Maria pushed her away. Images of Avery Ashland were still shooting off like fireworks in her mind, causing crazy, mixed emotions. The last thing she wanted was to be held, restrained.

"Here, let me help you." Samantha tried to pull up Maria's underwear and pants, but Maria stopped her and did it herself. Then she stumbled to the nearby couch and collapsed to brush her hair away from her face.

"I think I really needed that," she said. She'd just been fucked long and hard and she'd loved every second of it. The only thing that would've made it better was if Avery had done the fucking.

"I think so."

Samantha sat across from her, and Maria tried to smile but failed. Samantha looked way too cozy. Like she wanted to hang out. Or worse, spend the night. And just as she was about to reach out and touch her hand, Maria's phone rang.

"Oh no, not now." She could hardly walk, how could she possibly rush out the door to meet Finley? She dug the phone out of her back pocket and her face flooded with alarm. She sent it to voice mail only to have it ring again. "How can she know? How can she possibly know?" Jesus, had she somehow read her mind? Was she psychic?

"Who? An ex?"

Maria shook her head. "I really need to take this, and I really need some sleep."

Samantha stood. "Say no more." She lightly kissed her on the lips. The kiss was warm and lingering. It felt nice, despite Maria's feelings, as if Samantha were tying a final bow on a nicely wrapped gift. "I'll call you?"

Maria nodded, but she couldn't think of anything else but the phone call. When Samantha closed the door behind her, Maria answered the phone, which was ringing again.

"Ms. Ashland. To what do I owe the pleasure?" Her heart thudded in her ears. In her mind, Avery had just fucked the hell out of her. It was difficult to sound calm.

But there was only silence to her question and then a long exhale that Maria assumed was Avery blowing out smoke.

"Looks like she was pretty good," she finally said. "If you're into the more masculine type."

Maria looked out her living room window and saw only grays and blacks. Her curtains were mostly shut. She and Samantha had been in virtual darkness. How could she have known?

A chill ran through her, followed closely by embarrassment and anger. She had been watching her somehow.

"What do you want, Ashland?"

"Isn't it obvious? Come now, Detective, you're better than this. Surely you know what I want by now. No?"

Maria tried to come back with something clever, something powerful, but her mind was mush and words couldn't be found, no matter how hard she tried to concentrate.

"Cat got your tongue? Or did that handsome butch take it with her?" Avery laughed and made the sound of exhaling once again. "I'm having another engagement in a few days. Be sure to bring that beard of a partner of yours. I look forward to seeing you, Detective."

The call ended, leaving Maria completely spent, mentally and physically. She rose and locked her doors and closed her curtains tight. Then she collapsed once again on the couch and slept the hardest she'd ever slept.

Chapter Sixteen

Avery moved so hard and fast she just about ran right off the elliptical machine. Her pace was insane along with her calories burned. She'd been pushing it for close to two hours, going in spurts of intense pressure and speed, yet she still couldn't get the blond butch out of her mind.

Samantha. Sammie. Samantha Rogue. Was that really what Maria wanted? A strapping, strong, butch who knew how to fix engines? She wiped her face with a sweat soaked towel and then threw it across the room.

"Goddamn it!" She jumped off the machine and nearly buckled to the floor her legs were so spent. She stumbled to the mirror and leaned against it. A sheen of sweat coated her face and soaked into her hairline. Her breathing was labored and she had a stitch in her side, but she didn't care. It wasn't near enough to numb her. It just wasn't enough.

She reached up and snagged the photo of Samantha Rogue and Maria Diaz off the mirror and crumpled it to the ground. Then she turned and tore the one off the screen of the elliptical. She threw that one to the ground. She forced herself to move to every single spot in her personal gym where she'd hung the photos. She tore and trashed every single one and then finally fell to the floor, her back pressed to the wall. She held her head in her hands and fought screaming.

How could she compete? How could she be better? Samantha Rogue was everything she wasn't. And at the moment, she'd had what Avery wanted most. Maria. She moaned in anguish as she mentally replayed the video Bobby had sent her of Samantha Rogue fucking Maria from behind. It had caused her stomach to clench with a rage and jealousy she'd never felt before. Not even with Bryce. Not even the first time she'd caught her in bed with that young model.

No, nothing compared to this physical and emotional hell.

Why did she want her so badly? Why was she feeling this way? It wasn't just Maria's looks; it went far beyond that. It was her aching innocence hiding her darker desires, the way she desperately wanted to do right, her stubborn attitude, her ability to act fearless when Avery knew she was anything but. She wasn't like the other women in her life with their caked-on makeup and confidence. Maria was real. And Maria wanted what none of the other women did. Love. Passion. Loyalty. She would accept no less, and though she'd never said it, Avery knew it. Maria deserved a life, a love, an honest partner, a passionate partner who would know how to awaken her deepest desires and one who knew how to put feelings into words.

"Fucking shit." Avery knew it wasn't her. Could it ever be? She didn't know. But she wasn't going down without a fight. She knew Maria had some attraction to her, and it was time to step it up a level. If Maria wanted to assume her guilt and treat her like a criminal, then she'd play the game right back. Why make it easy for them? The way they'd behaved around her at the station, the way they'd looked at her. Like she was filth. A madwoman. A murderer.

Well, maybe a madwoman wouldn't be so hard to play. After all, she'd done it before.

"Don't even bother. I'm not in the mood." Avery pushed past Lana and walked into her bedroom where she threw the towel around her neck onto the floor and began to peel off her workout clothes.

"Believe it or not, sex is the last thing on my mind," Lana said, arms crossed tightly across her chest. She sat on the side of the bed, staring at the pile of damp clothes Avery left in her wake.

"Well, what is it? I've got guests arriving in an hour." Avery stopped, completely nude, and placed her hand on her hip. Lana was quiet and she wasn't dressed for the evening's proclivities. "You're not staying to play?"

Lana shook her head. "I'm not much in the mood."

Avery laughed. "Since when?"

Lana met her gaze and Avery swallowed hard, not liking the look she was giving her.

"Lana?"

"The cops are after me," Lana said. "They asked for my DNA."

"I thought you weren't worried?"

Lana squeezed herself as if she were cold. "I don't know, Avery. I think they are looking into my past. The questioning, now this DNA request, not to mention my lawyer, it's all getting to me."

Avery grew unnerved, but she shrugged with indifference. It was nice Lana was finally caring, but at the moment, she had no words of comfort for her.

"Just listen to your attorney. Give them nothing."

Avery turned, crossed to the shower, and switched it on. Seeing Lana so scared and worried was beginning to get to her. It made their predicament seem all too real.

"We'll cross it all when we come to it." She stepped inside the steamy cavern and closed the door. As she soaked her hair, she saw Lana enter the bathroom and rest up against the counter.

"What will we say?"

Avery sighed. "I don't know." Panic started to creep up her throat, but she pushed it back down. Not tonight. She couldn't do this tonight.

"If we don't give them real answers, pretty soon they'll have enough to search our property, even arrest us. I'm surprised they haven't done so already."

Avery shampooed her hair and rinsed. "Damn it, Lana, I don't want to deal with this tonight. When I wanted to talk about it you weren't interested."

Silence.

"I'm going to give them my alibi, Avery."

Avery wiped water from her face. "Lana, you can't."

"I have to. My lawyer is suggesting it."

"He's a fool. A scared fool."

"They know I left with Hale that night," she said, raising her voice. "What am I supposed to do?"

Avery stepped back under the spray and conditioned her hair. Her heart pounded, and for a few seconds, she forgot about how badly her muscles ached from her rigorous exercise.

"Just tell them you saw him home." She didn't know what else to say, what else to do.

"Somehow I think they know he didn't go home."

"Well, whatever. They can't prove you were the very last one last with him." But she didn't believe her own words.

"I think you're wrong about that, Avery. I think maybe if you'd close your legs long enough to pay careful attention to this, you'd know more."

Avery stepped forward and popped open the door. "What the hell do you mean by that?"

Lana pushed off from the counter. "I mean that instead of trying to seduce the damn detective in the case, maybe you should be busy trying to find out what all she knows."

"Whoa, where the hell is this coming from? You go from not caring to this?"

"I'm scared." She tossed Avery a towel and began to walk away. "It's up to you to save our asses, Avery. Don't fuck it up by chasing tail."

Avery watched her walk away and then reclosed the door. She leaned back into the spray and soaped herself. She was so angry, she stopped, rinsed, and then pushed against the shower wall to let the water beat down on her. Lana was going to be a problem. She should've known. But what could she do about it?

But more importantly, how was she going to handle things tonight?

CHAPTER SEVENTEEN

A slight sweat broke out along the back of Maria's neck as she pulled up to the front entrance of Euphoria in her Grand Cherokee. Valets rushed to work two lanes of cars, and Maria noticed a cluster of press huddled near the front entrance. The announcement of Avery Ashland as a main suspect in the case seemed to bring more people in rather than scare them away. Curiosity often won out even when danger was involved.

Maria exited her vehicle with the help of a polite valet and walked slowly, wearing her kitten heels and silver sleek cocktail dress, hoping not to be recognized by the press. Her sergeant usually gave the press briefings, but she and Finley were often waiting in the wings and sometimes they were questioned. Thankfully, she looked much different this evening with her hair down, thick and wavy, face nicely made up, and dress skintight. She let out a breath when she made it through the small crowd of press and entered the resort to find it dimly lit and cool. Somehow it smelled like a tropical breeze, and the sound of the fountains to the right offered false promises of calm and serene when Maria knew anything but calm and serene was going on in the rooms upstairs.

"Pardon me, ma'am. May I see your invitation?" A woman, the one she'd seen before working the desk, was dressed in a white skirt and jacket and shining a black light on the invitations people were handing her.

"I'm afraid I don't have a paper invitation."

"Oh?" Kelly asked.

"No, I received a verbal one from Ms. Ashland herself."

The woman shifted and picked up a clipboard. She eyed the board and then Maria. She smiled.

"I see. Please go ahead, Detective Diaz. Ms. Ashland expects you on the fourth floor."

Maria nodded politely and began to walk away.

"Oh, will your partner be joining us this evening?" Kelly asked.

Maria was caught by surprise. "No, he won't."

Kelly appeared surprised, but she said nothing, just waved her through.

Maria wove between dozens of guests and sidestepped several waiters carrying hors d'oeuvres. By the time she reached the elevators, her muscles twitched and a Charley horse cramped her calf. She had to stand on her tiptoes to release the knot. The twitching and the knots were becoming more frequent, so much so that she knew Finley would never let her come tonight alone if he'd known. Which was why she hadn't told him about the invitation. She wanted to do a little investigating on her own, and Finley rubbed Avery the wrong way. And truth be told, her insides had been doing flips ever since the moment she'd decided to come alone. Something about being alone with Avery again made her skin feel electric and charged. So much so that she wondered if, when they touched, if she'd be able to see an actual spark ignite between them.

If so, what would she do? How would she react? Would she be able to hide her heated attraction?

She boarded the elevator with two other couples and rode to the third floor where the couples, who had been talking softly with sly smirks, exited. Maria attempted to adjust her hair as she rode alone to the next floor. She wondered why the couples hadn't ridden to her floor until the doors opened and she was greeted by more security. Gone was the friendly female in front. Instead there stood a giant of a man wearing an earpiece and what appeared to be a Taser on his waistband. He was dressed in white.

"Ma'am," he said with a nod.

"I'm here to see Ms. Ashland."

"Of course." He moved and waved her through. Her presence must've been relayed already. She nodded in return and walked down the poorly lit hallway. She recalled what she had seen before, the women having sex in a bedroom with Avery Ashland whispering in her ear from behind. Her skin came alive at the mere thought, and when she heard soft moans coming from the bedrooms, she nearly had to lean on the wall to keep her balance.

She forced herself to straighten and walk with purpose, careful to avoid looking into the open doors of some of the rooms. But when she came to the last one before a landing, she stopped, the moans too loud, the whips cracking like clapping thunder. Sheer ecstasy came at her like a wave as two women climaxed together, crying out into the night. A spark of animal desire slapped her in the face and she wanted desperately to turn, to look inside, but she clenched her jaw and made herself stare straight ahead.

"Just walk," she whispered to herself. She took four more steps and heard other voices coming from the landing. She looked to her right and saw two women binding a nude woman to a large leather cross. The nude woman looked serious, and the women adjusting her wrist cuffs were dressed in shiny black thongs, heels, and eye masks. The black tassels on their hidden nipples swayed as they worked. Then one moved to a rack where dozens of floggers were hung, and she pressed buttons on a remote control, causing music to play and the lights to turn from deep blue to a deep red. The music developed a thudding beat, an erotic thump, and Maria felt her throat tighten.

"Would you like a blindfold, Detective? Since you can't seem to make yourself look?" The voice was deep and melodious and teasing her ear from behind. Maria tried to turn, but strong lean hands on her hips halted her.

"No, no, no. What you need to see, it's no longer behind you. It's right there in front of you."

"Ms. Ashland, I don't think—"

"There's no thinking allowed. Only seeing and feeling." Avery pushed her gently, and they walked toward the cross, stopping a couple of feet away from the bound woman, who was now gagged and sweating.

"I don't—"

"What? Want to be here? Want to watch?" She tsked. "I find that very hard to believe. In fact, I think if I slid my hand deftly up your thigh, like this, I'd soon feel your heat and your slick juices." She traced her hand up her dress, and Maria had to squeeze her legs together and push her hand away in order not to succumb to her touch.

It caused Avery to laugh, and she finally stepped in front of her and led her by the hand. "I think you'll like what you see, Detective. You know, I too, can be a little rough around the edges if I or the one I'm with, so desires."

Avery was smiling devilishly wearing dark men's dress slacks and a white button-down dress shirt with a dark tie and hat. As Maria tried to calm herself and look away, Avery removed her fedora and tossed it aside. Maria noticed her slicked back hair and dark liner around her eyes. Avery stepped in and gently held Maria's chin, quietly ensuring she wouldn't look away.

"Can you help me with this shirt?" she asked. "It's a bit hot in here."

Avery unbuttoned the top few buttons of her white shirt and then reached for Maria's fingers.

"Come on now, I know you want to help me. And we mustn't keep our guests waiting."

As if on cue, the two women in thongs and tassels stepped up and tied an eye mask onto Avery. When they tried to help unbutton her shirt, she shoved them away.

"Come on, Detective. You came to play, after all. Merely watching will not be enough this time. You're already too turned on."

Maria's fingers shook as Avery held them close to her chest. "I am not." She knew she should run far and fast, but she was determined to spend time with Avery. Their case depended on an inside eye. She would just have to harden herself and remain detached. But at the moment, that seemed far from possible.

A grin spread across Avery's face as if she knew she wouldn't be able to turn her down. And as much as Maria wanted to meet her gaze head-on to show her resistance, she could no longer bear to keep looking at the angles of her jaw and the plump of her red lips. So she moved her gaze only to see how her high cheekbones slashed upward toward the outer edges of the mask.

Maria grew dizzy and squeezed her fists to fight it. But Avery's face kept coming at her, luring and dangerously appealing. And the music. The music was maddening.

"You know I never pegged you for a liar," Avery said. "But in knowing you a little better I know you will not hesitate to do so if it helps your case."

Maria tried to back away, but Avery held tight.

"Uh-uh-uh."

"I don't want to do this," Maria said. The loss of control that was threatening was as terrifying as it was tempting.

"Very well." Avery released her and snapped her fingers. The two scantily clad women hurried to her and nearly tore her shirt from her body, leaving the dark tie to snake down between her glistening bosom which was encased in a shiny leather low-cut bra. With her eyes trained on Maria, she unfastened her belt and whipped it from her waist, causing her lean, etched muscles to writhe beneath her skin.

Oh God.

Maria took a step back. Ashland smiled again and turned. She lashed out and slapped the bound woman lightly across the chest with the belt.

"Do you want this?" Ashland called out, tossing the belt aside. The bound woman heaved with breath and nodded.

A lightning slash of red plumed along her breasts. She jerked at her restraints as if she wanted to be freed but then demanded more.

"Remove her gag. I want to hear her beg."

The women did so quickly, and when the bound woman caught her breath, she said, "Give it to me. Please, Madam."

Ashland held out her hand, and one of the women placed a knotted flogger in her hand. She rotated her wrist, whipping the flogger around. She lashed out again and whipped the bound woman's breasts, causing her to call out.

"God yes! More."

Ashland lashed her again and again, and Maria watched in a trancelike state as the woman's nipples darkened and hardened with every single lash of the flogger.

"You like the pain?" Ashland asked, taking pause. Her own body was covered with sweat, sleek and writhing. She held out her hand toward Maria.

Maria didn't move.

Ashland looked at her. "Come."

Maria took a breath. Then another. Her chest shook. She was amazed that her heart was still beating even though she could feel it in her ears.

She thought again about leaving, about turning tail and running. But she'd come alone for a reason. This was what she needed to see. The real Avery Ashland.

Maria took a step forward. Then another. She took Ashland's hand and found it hot against her fingers. Ashland tugged her into her and turned to face the bound woman.

"Look at her," Ashland said. "See how much she's enjoying this? She loves this. The pain, then the pleasure. One nearly right on top of the other."

Ashland leaned into her and ran a hand down her bare arm. "She's had some pain. Let's give her some pleasure, shall we?"

Ashland snapped her fingers and then returned her hand to stroke Maria's arm.

The two other women hurried to the bound woman and lowered to their knees. Maria's breath hitched as she watched them lick and kiss their way up her inner legs. When they neared her wet, red center, they nibbled and sucked, and Ashland whipped the flogger next to Maria.

"You want to come?" she called out.

The bound woman struggled for breath. "Ye-es. Yes."

"How badly?"

"So bad. So bad. Please."

Maria stiffened and Ashland stopped to speak in her ear. "Give it to her, Detective. She's about to die for it."

Maria shook her head. "But what—" She felt the flogger handle press into her palm. She looked down. Ashland was hugging her from behind. She gently grabbed her wrist and pulled her arm back. Maria gasped as Ashland whipped her arm forward and the straps of knotted leather struck the bound woman across her chest. The woman cried out, and the women at her center attacked her delicate flesh with hungry mouths.

"Again," Ashland said. She pulled Maria's arm back, and they struck the bound woman again. Maria trembled. She shook. She vibrated from the inside out.

And then she got wet.

Again, they lashed her.

Again.

And again.

Maria let out a noise, and Ashland released her to lash on her own. The bound woman begged, pleaded, writhed, and struggled. Maria lashed her again, watching the heads bob at her center, the tongues sneak out and flick her red flesh. She lashed her again as she came and watched as she pulled her restraints so hard the veins in her neck bulged. Moaning so loud, Ashland laughed, and a deep grunt that came from somewhere guttural escaped Maria. The woman moaned and cried out and yanked and pulled, and then, with one last spasm, she went limp and hung like a wet sack of bones.

The other women rose and kissed her and sucked on her breasts. They began releasing her from her cuffs, and Maria blinked back into reality and dropped the flogger. She turned and pushed past Ashland and covered her mouth with her hand.

Her whole body was afire and she could feel her own wetness soaking through her panties.

"Enjoy yourself, Detective?" Ashland was at her ear again.

Maria shook, unable to move or voice words.

Ashland led her away from the landing to a nearby room with a locked door. She slid in the keycard and tugged her inside.

Maria walked zombie like to the luscious looking king-sized bed and stood eye to eye with Avery Ashland.

Ashland didn't smile, didn't grin. She slipped off her mask and touched Maria's face. Maria didn't speak, didn't move. She couldn't. All she could do was fight to breathe. And then it happened. Ashland cupped her jaw and pulled her in for a kiss. A long, sensual, seeking kiss. One that caused Maria to rise to her tiptoes and groan. And instead of pulling away, Maria kissed her back, this time seeking with her own tongue and sucking with her own lips.

Ashland responded by cupping Maria's ass and scratching up her dress to reveal her panties. She lowered them quickly and tossed them aside along with her kitten heels. Then she walked Maria to the floor-to-ceiling mirror and stood behind her.

"I want you to look at yourself," she said softly. "While I make you come."

Maria reached up and wrapped her arm around Ashland's neck. "Hurry."

Ashland inched up her dress once again and licked her ear as her fingers toyed around the edges of Maria's flesh.

"Hurry," Maria breathed. "Dear God, hurry. Before rationality comes rushing back to me." She was about to bolt and about to crumble. Which one remained up to Avery Ashland.

Ashland groaned in her ear and slid her fingers into her flesh, causing Maria to nearly jump out of her skin. "Ah, fuck!" She clung harder to Ashland and watched her hand circle around in her flesh in the mirror.

"Faster," Maria said.

Ashland moved faster, stronger, playing her like the most beautiful of instruments. She framed her engorged clit and moved up and down and then covered it in a circular motion. She played Maria as if she were her puppet, making her call out and rise to her tiptoes and then buckle down and groan as her knees shook.

"Fuck," Maria said. "Avery, fuck."

"Look at how beautiful you are," Avery kept saying. "Do you see it? Tell me you see it."

"I see it," Maria said. She clenched her eyes. The pleasure too great. "I'm coming."

"Open your eyes, lovely. Open."

Maria opened her eyes and then burst with orgasm, coming in Ashland's hand and against her strong body. Ashland stroked her like a magician and swirled her tongue in her ear. All the while whispering to her how beautiful she was.

Maria clung to her, head thrown back, feet pushing against the floor, knees trembling. She turned at last and held fast to her tie, then her pants as she sunk to the floor. Ashland knelt and scooped her up with relative ease and walked her to the bed. She placed her gently down and covered her with the duvet. Then Maria felt another kiss and opened her eyes.

Oh God, what had she just done?

Chapter Eighteen

A very backed away from the soft kiss and searched Maria's face. And just like that, in the flash of a split second, her look of spent desire was gone, replaced by what looked like fear sprinkled with regret.

Avery sighed and crossed the room. She pulled on a satin robe and made herself comfortable in a chair at the foot of the bed.

"Now is where you run, feeling shame and regret." Avery fumbled in the pocket of her robe for her cigarettes. When she found the case empty, she threw it across the room.

"It was a mistake," Maria said, rising to a sitting position. "I shouldn't have let it happen."

"Let what happen? Desire? Want? Need? Don't you ever give in to yourself, Detective?"

Maria swung her legs over the side of the bed. "That's really none of your business."

"You're right, it isn't. Only you give the answer away with every shuddering breath you take, every blink of your hungry eyes, every rise to your toes when we kiss. You aren't that difficult to read."

"Neither are you," she bit back. "This was obviously just a game. One played to conquer me after you found out about my last encounter. You were jealous."

"Jealous? Ha! I don't do jealous."

"Bullshit." Maria stood and gathered her clothes. Avery watched hungrily as she dressed.

"You don't have to leave," Avery said. "Don't you want to stay a while, relax in your sweet bliss?"

Maria slid her dress on and struggled to zip up the back.

"I don't have time to relax."

"And yet, you're here." Avery rose and zipped her dress for her. "Might as well stay."

"I have work to do."

"Isn't that what this is? Work? Because I know you didn't come to fuck."

Maria stiffened.

"Surely you came to investigate some more."

"So what if I did?"

Avery shrugged. "I don't have a problem with it."

"I thought you did. At the station, you seemed rather sure. And according to your lawyer—"

"Fuck Bruce. He's an idiot. I do as I please." Avery felt unnerved at the mention of Bruce and the case. It brought reality right back in, smacking her in the face. In her fantasy, she had Maria all to herself, the goddamn Hale Medley case blown away in the wind, never to re-form and reappear again. But she was a fool to fantasize. And Hale was far from gone. The bastard.

She moved to the door and opened it.

"Where are you going?" Maria asked.

"To my home. I need a drink." She took a step and paused. "You coming?"

Maria seemed to hesitate but then followed. Avery led the way and they bypassed more women in dark corners, in dark beds, moaning and laughing. Neither looked inside, and when they reached the elevator, they rode in silence.

"You seem uncomfortable," Avery finally said as they entered the penthouse. "I can give you a change of clothes."

"No, thank you."

"Please," Avery said, offering her a seat on the sofa. She flicked on a soft light and headed for the bar where she made them both a drink. She smiled sincerely when she handed Maria her glass and sat across from her. "Are you cold?"

Maria sat tightly, arms held to her body. Avery gave her the soft throw her nieces loved to use. Then she settled back down and sipped her drink. Maria toyed with hers as if she were afraid to take too big a sip.

"Do you mind if I smoke?" Avery asked, eyeing a case on the coffee table.

Maria glanced up at her with obvious surprise. "You mean you actually care if I do?"

Avery laughed softly. "I'm asking, aren't I?"

"What a surprise. And yes, I do mind. It bothers me. Gives me a headache."

Avery sighed. "I've got to find a new vice."

"You mean other than women?"

Avery raised an eyebrow. "Why don't you ask me what you really want to ask?"

"And now you're offering to talk about Hale. Are you feeling okay?" This time Maria raised an eyebrow.

"Somehow I was hoping Hale wasn't on your mind. Silly me."

"He is. He always is. I want to know who killed him and why. I won't stop until I do."

"I believe you."

"I wish I could believe you, Avery."

Avery paused, cool glass to her lips. She said nothing.

"I know you're lying. About a lot of things, in fact. And if you were innocent, I would think you would want to come clean about everything, so you could move on with your life. Free of the police."

Avery crossed her legs and caught the light scent of Maria's flesh on her hand as she sipped her drink. It shot straight to her core where it ignited and burned. She wanted her again, and she wondered if the hunger for her would ever die.

"Maybe I don't want to be free of you, Detective."

"So you would rather obstruct justice, just to keep me coming around?"

Avery laughed but shifted a little under her penetrating gaze. "There are things you don't understand."

"Try me."

Again, Avery shifted. She felt hot, stifled. "I can't."

"Tell me about Lana. She your lover?"

Avery forced a smile. "I think you know the answer."

"I want to hear you say it."

"Sometimes, yes."

"For how long?"

"Years."

"Why not settle down?"

Avery sipped her drink and played with the ice in the glass. "She's not what I'm looking for."

"So she's only good enough to fuck and commit murder with?"

Avery pegged her with a serious stare. "There she is. That little hellcat is back."

"Answer me."

Avery sighed and thought about her earlier encounter with Lana and the way she'd seemed so scared and cowardly. And how she'd said she was going to give them her alibi. She was caving and fast. And there was no doubt she was going to leave Avery in the dust behind her.

"To tell you the truth, Lana is a bit of a roller coaster. She's hot one minute, the next a cold, rambling fool. I can't trust her with anything important. She can't keep a secret. She's rather a shitty friend."

This time Maria shifted but remained silent. She wanted Avery to continue.

"She lies. Does whatever she can to save her own ass or to make sure she gets ahead."

"Some have said the same about you," Maria said.

Avery heated. "Really?" She wanted to know who, demand to know who, but it would only prove her point. "I guess I'm not surprised."

"We know Lana was with Hale the last night he was seen alive."

"Yes."

"So you knew?"

"Let's just say I'm not surprised."

"We know she left in a limousine, chartered by her and that no one saw Hale after he climbed into that vehicle. So if she was with

Hale and therefore not with you as she'd previously said…where, may I ask, were you, Ms. Ashland? Did you meet them somewhere?"

"That would make it all so easy, wouldn't it?" She set down her empty glass. "No, I did not meet up with them. I was here. All evening."

"Why not say so from the beginning?"

"Because Lana needed for me to say otherwise."

"I thought Lana was a shitty friend?"

"She is. I, however, am not."

"Oh, how noble. You lie to the police for someone you don't even respect."

Avery itched for a smoke. She reached for the case and fumbled with it, wanting desperately to inhale and exhale the pressure away.

"Can you prove you were here, Ms. Ashland?"

"My surveillance should prove it."

"Yes, well, we've had some issues with the recordings. They seem to be ruined."

"Ruined?"

"Yes."

She stood and crossed back to the bar where she made another drink. This one stronger.

"I know nothing about the recordings."

"What about the photo found in Hale's wallet? Why did you threaten him?"

"My threatening Hale has been no secret. Just as it's always been well known that he's threatened me as well. We went back and forth. Whenever his mouth or his hands got him in trouble. As for the photo. I don't know why he kept it." She took large sips of her drink and removed her robe, growing hot. She moved back to the couch and saw Maria glance away.

"Glad you like the outfit."

Maria cleared her throat. "You're going to have to prove your alibi."

"Why? I think Lana is in deeper than me." She sat, this time next to Maria who shifted. Avery placed a hand on her leg. "Why don't we stop talking for the evening and start enjoying each other once again?"

Maria stared at Avery's hand. "I don't think so. I think I should leave."

"Did you get the answers you wanted, then?"

Maria stood. "I'm afraid not."

"You can't possibly think me capable of murder." Avery searched her face, incredulous.

"I don't know what to think. And frankly, that scares me to death."

"You just gave yourself to me. You wouldn't do that if you thought I was a killer."

"I...haven't been thinking..." She shook her head. "It was a mistake. It went too far."

"So you still see me as a killer?" Avery stood in front of her.

Maria looked away. "I don't know."

"Jesus, Maria, look at me."

"I can't. I need to go."

"Will you ever see me as a normal human being?"

Maria stopped and stood very still. "No. Because you are anything but."

She straightened her shoulders and walked out of the room and through the main doors, leaving Avery all alone.

CHAPTER NINETEEN

Finley was fuming, hands on his hips, pacing Maria's living room. He grabbed his head with his hand and then pushed his hair back. He let out a breath.

"Tell me again why you thought this was such a good idea?"

Maria winced as she tried to get comfortable on the couch. Her abdomen and chest were killing her, like she was in a vice of some sort. She'd had to call in to work, which had led a concerned Finley right for her. That and the front page of the local newspaper, showing Maria at Euphoria in her sleek silver dress along with the headline:

Uncover Cop or Cop Under the Covers?

The article went on to suggest that Maria had been alone with Avery Ashland for some time and hinted that they had been engaged in sexual activity. Maria cringed again, not from pain, but from the headline as Finley tossed it down on the couch next to her.

"Do you realize how infuriated the sarge is? He can't even form the words to scream at me, Maria. Can't even form the words. I thought his head was going to explode."

"I had no idea the press saw me. They didn't call me out or shove the camera in my face. I was sure I was clear."

"Why in the hell did you go alone? Do you know how dangerous that was? You should've at least told me."

Maria shifted and grimaced. Every breath was agony. "I can take care of myself."

"Obviously not." He motioned toward her ailment.

"This is not from last night. I don't know what this is, but it hurts like hell."

"Well, what all happened? Did you...you know...engage?"

"Fins."

"Maria, for God's sake."

"You told me to play it up. You told me to engage."

"I did, but—fuck what happened?"

Maria shook her head. She didn't want to think back to picture Avery in her tie and dress slacks, muscles writhing as she moved. Not to mention her blond slicked back hair and the slash of her cheekbones. She shuddered with desire once again, but then cringed from pain and from the shame of the memory. She had acted completely irresponsibly and had let it go way too far. She'd never ever do such a thing, so why now? What was happening? Why had she lost total and complete control when she never had before? And with a possible murderer?

"We talked."

"And?"

"And I'm not sure what to think about her involvement. She seemed to think Lana—"

"She turned on Lana?"

"In a matter of speaking."

He sank down onto the ottoman and allowed Horace to jump in his lap. He stroked him but only for a moment before he moved him to the couch. "Lana's turning on Ashland."

Maria wasn't sure she heard correctly. "What?"

"She called this morning and gave her alibi. She's hired a lawyer and is willing to cooperate fully."

"What did she say?" Maria gripped a throw pillow. Her pulse raced. She thought of the look on Avery's face. The way she'd pleaded with her to believe her.

"She admitted to leaving with Hale." He stared into her. "She said they then picked up Ashland and drove to a nearby warehouse. She...she said they tied him up and toyed with him. But after that, Lana left, leaving him alone with Ashland. She claims she doesn't know what happened next."

Maria sat very still. The words stabbed her insides and she felt sick. Briefly, she shot back to her childhood and the ride she used to love to go on even though it made her stomach rise and drop. She imagined she was strapped in next to her brother and father, feet dangling, anticipation building. Then they would rise up and up, leaving the ground behind. And just when she thought they couldn't get any higher, the ride would stop and lean them forward to look at the ground far below. She'd say a prayer and close her eyes. Seconds would seem like minutes. The wind would whip her hair and face. Her feet would stop kicking and her body would go rigid. She'd open her eyes, thinking it wasn't ever going to drop, and then whoosh, they would fall, fall, fall straight down to the ground where the magnetic brakes would kick in and the ride would slow and they'd be hanging by restraint, hair whipped and faces red with excitement. It would always take her a while to recover, and she'd walk on shaky legs for a few minutes afterward with her stomach clenched tight, sitting right up against her throat. And she'd swear she'd never get on it again. But by the next visit, she'd be ready to go, the pain and fright forgotten somehow.

She felt like that now, like she'd just dropped from the sky and the brakes had stopped her, leaving her dangling in fear and shock. Could she walk? Could she think? Why had she gotten on in the first place?

Avery Ashland was like the ride. So alluring with its bright lights and loud music, people in awe of it and how it could make them feel. Others had climbed on, so why couldn't she?

"I—She almost had me convinced she was innocent." She spoke softly, almost to herself.

Finley stared at her with concern. "I don't know what happened between the two of you, but with your current condition, you definitely shouldn't have gone in alone. Damn it, you know better. What if she had been a male suspect? Would you have done it?"

She closed her eyes. "No."

Finley was about to reply when their phones both beeped with texts. Maria fished her phone out, saw it was from forensics, and tried to sit up. It took her a moment before she could, and she was wincing in pain. Finley replied to the text and helped her stand. "Wonder what they've got."

Maria slid into her shoes. "I don't know, but it must be big. Kenny sounded hyped up."

They crossed carefully to the door where Maria pushed him away. "I need to walk on my own or everyone will notice."

"I thought you were going to stay home. You should stay home. Mainly because you hurt but also because of the paper. It's all over the department."

She shrugged and regretted it. "I've got to face it sooner or later. And solving this case will hopefully shut everyone up."

He nodded.

Maria squared her shoulders and walked out the door with Finley hot on her heels.

Kenny Sing was sitting hunched at his computer at the front counter of the forensics lab when they entered. Finley tossed him a bag of fresh bagels from the deli he loved and he broke out into a smile.

"Fins, you're the man."

"Thank Maria. She's the one who insisted."

Kenny saluted her. "Pretty and thoughtful. Be still my heart."

"Quit flirting," Finley said, tapping the counter. "Don't leave us hanging, Sing. What've you got?"

"Wow, straight to the point." He winked at Maria. "Next time come alone so I can at least make pleasantries."

Maria tried to laugh, but it hurt. So she nodded instead. Kenny looked at her for a moment longer. "I won't say anything about the newspaper," he said.

She sighed. "Thank you." She already had a rampaging Sarge on her voice mail. Luckily, when she'd returned the call, she'd been put through to his voice mail where she'd left an apology and an explanation. She knew that probably wouldn't be the end of it, but she hoped it softened the blow a little. And the Sarge was the master at spinning things for the press. He'd handle it; he'd handled far worse before.

"Figured you're getting enough grief on that."

He refocused on a file in front of him. The forms he pulled out looked like graphs. Maria had seen them all before in going over forensic evidence for years. Even so, Kenny leaned in and explained.

"You guys tracked down the limo that Hale Medley had been in the last night he was seen alive. And as you know we examined it."

Finley cleared his throat and Kenny continued.

"We found a stain that registered as human blood. A small stain, about the size of a dime. We ran DNA."

He raised his eyebrows. "It's Medley's."

"No shit?" Finley said.

Ken pointed to the graphs with his pencil. "There's no doubt. It's his. And that's not all. We found a fiber that seemed a little odd. We ran it and it comes back as a fleece fiber, like those used on blankets. That was interesting, but what is even more so is what was on the fiber itself."

"What's that?" Maria asked.

"Sunscreen."

"Sunscreen?"

"Yep. Water Babies to be exact."

"What the hell?"

"So it's cross contaminated," Maria said. "From someone who was in the car before Hale, maybe weeks before."

Ken shook his head. "Could be. But I don't think so, Maria. That car had been professionally cleaned. When we climbed in, I didn't think we'd find much at all."

"Where was the blood?" she asked.

"That's what's also curious. The bloodstain was found on the very top back side of the seat. As if someone had maybe rested a hand there."

Maria couldn't make sense of it. Of any of it. She searched her mind with the Water Baby clue. Lana Gold had no children in her life. She went rigid and stared at Finley.

"Ashland. She has nieces."

Finley clicked with her, their minds in tandem. "Do they swim with her?"

Maria nodded, and her stomach clenched again. "Most likely."

"Did you pull DNA from the fleece fiber?"

Kenny was watching them closely. He nodded.

"Well?"

"We got mitochondrial. It's a match for Avery Ashland. So is the female profile we got from the back of the photo."

Maria took a step back, and then her world tunneled in on her. She registered falling to the ground and seeing Finley's face above her. She tried to speak but couldn't. Tried to hear his words but couldn't. A black blob appeared in the center of her vision. She reached out for Finley, felt his hand, and then closed her eyes.

CHAPTER TWENTY

A very knew what she was doing and why. But for the first time in her life, she wasn't totally sure about it. An irritating itch of rationality was trying to take hold and grow, along with something along the lines of a moral compass. She rejected both and stopped cold to grit her teeth and squeeze her palms, to make sure both rationality and morality knew they were not welcome inside her. As she exhaled and walked on, she found them still to be present, but their voices drowned out.

She forced a smile and tossed her hair back. Tiny strands of it were loose around her moist face and they were bothering her, more so than usual, as was the humid heat. She wiped her brow and smoothed her hair. Despite feeling unsettled and annoyed, she had the confidence of a woman that looked good. That alone helped her continue on in the noisy auto center, a place she'd never been before.

With her head held high, she waved off man after man in blue greasy jumpsuits coming at her offering help. The first two, she'd been polite, but now she simply scowled with a quick wave, like swatting an incoming fly. She had a mission and she was damn sure she was going to succeed, regardless of the new inward irritations. Doing things this way was how she'd always played the game. So why should she change now?

An image of Maria came to her. Beautiful, mesmerizing, alluring...good. The first three, she could deal with and even thrive on. But the last one, she was having trouble with. She knew she didn't fit that bill, but even so, she kept at her quest, determined more than ever to get Maria.

She came to the last garage where more men stopped and stared. She turned and motioned at the young man driving her car. He was easing along behind her, per her instructions. She pointed at a spot near the front of the garage where he parked. She then tipped him enough to make his jaw drop. He thanked her profusely, and she turned away from him, annoyed at his gratitude. She walked inside the garage, found the music and riveting loud, so she shouted at her target.

"Hi." Avery tugged her sunglasses down and eyed the blond butch working under the elevated car. "I was hoping maybe you could take a look at my car?" She smiled her best seductive smile and placed a hand on her hip. She'd made sure to wear her tightest designer skirt and satin tank, along with her stiletto heels. She wore enough lotion to make her legs shimmer and shine like the highest quality wheels on the market. She hoped like hell the hard-working mechanic would notice. The men had obviously approved. But there was only one mechanic on her radar, and she wasn't male.

Samantha Rogue lowered her arms and glanced at Avery. She stiffened and blinked and did a double take. The car, suddenly, she seemed to have forgotten. She faced Avery fully.

"I'd be glad to take a look." She returned the smile, and Avery perked up, pleased at having her attention. Samantha wasn't her type, but she was very handsome and well carved, and the grease marks on her skin seemed to accentuate her bone structure.

"What seems to be the trouble?"

Avery walked her to her Shelby Cobra and she watched as Samantha nearly dropped her tool and drooled.

"She sounds a little cranky." Avery gave her a pouty look.

Samantha rounded the car with her fingertips an inch away, as if she were lightly caressing it as she walked. "You're serious? You want me to look at her?"

"They said you're the best with the classics."

Samantha rubbed the back of her neck. "Okay, why don't you get in and start her up?"

Avery approached her and placed a hand on her upper arm. She felt the strength there, and she burned with jealousy. She'd seen the video Bobby had taken. She'd seen how easily Samantha had physically handled Maria. She swallowed with difficulty and tried to calm the monster that was clawing up her insides trying to escape.

"I don't actually have the time right now. Are you free later?"

Samantha looked confused.

"I'll pay you handsomely of course. My place? Say seven?" Avery handed her a Euphoria Resort business card and Samantha once again did a double take.

"Ah, sure. I think."

"You didn't have plans, did you?" Avery suspected she might be planning to see Maria.

"No. I'm free."

Avery grinned. "Very well, then. I'll see you soon." She climbed in her car and started the engine. Samantha backed away and waved as Avery pulled out of the parking lot. She pushed up her shades and watched as Samantha stared after her.

"Like taking candy from a baby," she said as she gunned it onto the main road. She was just about to blast the stereo when her phone rang. She knew by the ring tone that it was Bobby. She scooped it up quickly.

"Yeah?"

Static came and then the sound of chewing. She held the phone from her ear and grimaced.

"Bobby, swallow for God's sake."

He coughed a bit. "Sorry, I'm starved." More coughing. "Thought you might want to know something's up with your girl."

Avery pulled to the side of the road and slammed on her brakes. She didn't even bother to give a finger to those that honked at her.

"What is it?"

"Not sure. All I know is her partner and some guy helped her to an unmarked cruiser. Her partner is driving her toward the hospital now."

Avery hung up and did a U-turn as soon as she possibly could. She floored it and raced to the hospital. Bobby kept trying to call her back, but she ignored him. Instead she focused on Maria as her heart and mind raced with worst-case scenarios. She knew Maria had been going to a doctor. She knew about the MRI. As to what was wrong, she was clueless. All she knew was that she had to get there. She had to know. She had to see her.

She didn't bother to ask herself why. Or if it was some kind of obsession, or worse, something more. She couldn't handle those answers and realizations at the moment.

She peeled into a parking space at emergency and climbed out of the car to hurry inside. Just as she stepped inside the sliding doors, a rough hand grabbed her by the arm and yanked her back outside.

"What the hell are you doing?" Bobby Luca demanded. He was, as usual, covered in sweat. More so than usual. He scrubbed at his face as if frustrated and tugged her alongside the building. "You want Finley to see you?"

"I don't care who sees me."

"Since when?"

"You wanna get busted for having her followed?"

Avery rolled her eyes. "I'm pretty sure she knows."

He shook his head. "You tell her or something?"

"Might as well have."

He turned and cursed at the ground. "Jesus fucking Christ. Why am I doing this? Why am I even doing this?" He turned and pointed a finger at her. "I got my reputation you know. I'm helping you as a favor. This…the murder…Lana…this cop you have a boner for… it's all too much for me."

She laughed at his drama. "What are you saying, Bobby?"

He looked her square in the eye. "I quit."

"You what? You can't quit. We have a deal."

"No, we had a deal. Now I don't give a shit." He started to walk away. "Tell whomever you want I like to watch people get it on. I no longer care." He stormed past her and headed for his car still shaking his head.

Avery stared after him in disbelief. "Don't do this, Bobby! You know you don't want to do this." She clamped her mouth shut as people walked by and stared. She stared after him a moment with her mind reeling. Bobby, her go-to guy, had just quit, despite the blackmail she'd threatened him with. And he'd mentioned Lana.

He thought she was guilty. He thought she killed Hale.

She clenched her fists and paced. How could she convince him? How could she convince anyone? She'd never had trouble getting people to believe her before. Why had things changed?

She turned and looked toward the emergency room. Maria. That's what it was.

She was growing soft. Letting things slip. Her tight ship was unraveling because she was at the helm chasing a damn detective who was trying to put her away.

Lana was right.

She turned to walk away, but another rough hand grabbed her arm. This time she turned with a high elbow and caught Detective Finley in the upper lip. He stumbled backward, cursing.

"Motherfucker. What the fuck was that for?" He held a tissue to his bleeding lip.

"You really shouldn't make it a habit of grabbing women from behind, Detective."

"Duly noted." He winced and straightened, eyeing the bloody tissue he'd grabbed from his pocket to put to his nose. "Fuck." He then looked at her as if he remembered why he'd grabbed her. "What are you doing here?"

"I heard Maria was ill. I came to check on her."

He stared at her briefly and then laughed. "You're serious?"

She didn't answer.

His smile faded. "What the hell do you know about it? And what do you care?"

"I…" But she had no words.

"What? You care?"

She looked away.

He dropped his hand with the tissue. "You care, don't you? That's it." He stepped toward her and leaned into her face. "Listen to me, you crazy, conceited bitch. You leave Maria alone. You've got no business here, no reason to be here. She's not your friend, your little lover, your girlfriend. She's no one to you. Got that? She's just a cop doing a damn good job of pinning a murder on you."

Avery fought trembling with anger. She stared into his cold blue eyes. "Back off, Detective."

"Or what? They'll soon find me dead? What will you carve in my forehead, Avery? Horny?"

"How about Limp?"

He inched closer and spittle flew from his mouth. "How 'bout I lock you up real tight and cozy and throw you in with your kind. The real crazy bitches who eat Barbie dolls like you for breakfast?"

She wanted to counter, to knock him off his feet with either a brutal verbal comeback or a rock-hard fist. But she didn't feel like giving in to him and doing so would be giving him his way. He'd either continue to come at her or he'd get to arrest her for assault. He would get to gloat.

And she wouldn't be able to stand that. Not by any means.

She forced a smile. Pursed her lips and blew him an air kiss. He pulled back and his face grew red. She had won. She stepped off the curb and walked quickly to her car. When she reached it and climbed inside, she glanced at him and found him on the phone, hunched over and pacing. Then he raced back inside the emergency room.

She started the engine and steered toward home. Finley had not stopped her from finding out about Maria. He'd only agitated her more, and now she was convinced to find out what was wrong. Not only that, but she was convinced, now more than ever, to make Maria her own.

CHAPTER TWENTY-ONE

Maria awoke to muffled silence. She could hear movement and voices in the distance, but only quiet nearby. She opened her eyes and blinked with panic when the black spot in the center of her vision remained in her left eye. She raised her hand to rub it, but she was connected to wires and tubes. A quick glance at the small white room and monitors next to her told her what she needed to know. She was in the hospital.

She pushed herself up and felt groggy, but tried to free herself of the tubes and cords regardless. An alarm sounded as she did so, and a woman in scrubs rushed into the room.

"No, no, no, sweetie, those have to stay on."

"No, they don't. I'm leaving."

"No." She gently eased her back. "You need to stay to see the doctor."

"Don't worry, I can handle her," Finley said as he entered looking like death warmed over. His normally neat hair was askew and he had a day's worth of beard on his jaw. His shirt and pants were wrinkled, and she knew he hadn't been home in a while. He deposited two cups of coffee on the table next to her and then swung the tray toward her. The woman left the room and Finley closed the door behind her.

"How long?" Maria asked, dreading the answer.

"Over a day now."

"Jesus, Fins, we don't have time for this."

He grabbed his cup of coffee and sat in an uncomfortable looking chair. He slurped. "Doesn't matter."

"Doesn't matter?"

"Not right now, no. What matters is you."

"What matters is this case." Her mind reeled trying to make up for the lost time. "How's the sarge? He still pissed?"

Finley rubbed his palms on his thighs. "He's cooled off a bit. He blasted the press for interfering with an investigation. Said they very nearly cost us the case and outed an undercover investigation. That shut everyone up."

"He's a genius."

"Yes, he can be."

He stared off as if in thought. "Is there a reason why Avery Ashland would be coming to the hospital to check on you?"

Maria wasn't sure she heard correctly. "She knows I'm here?"

"Apparently."

"She…came?"

"Right after you arrived. I caught her outside, trying to come in. She was arguing with old Bobby Luca. Remember that jackass? Quit the force to go private some years back. I'm guessing he now does her dirty work."

"She does seem to know things about me. Private things."

"Such as?"

Maria shifted under his gaze. "She knew about a date I had. A few nights ago."

"I see." He grew quiet, but she knew more was coming. "If she had Luca to check on you to find out what was going on…why did she come herself?"

Maria heated although she had no idea. "I don't know."

"That's what's eating me."

"Well, I have no answers."

"I think you do."

She glared at him. "What? Jesus, Finley, I can't even hardly see you. I have a black blob in the center of my vision, I'm in the hospital though I don't know why, and now you're grilling me about the mind and motives of Avery Ashland? Cut me some slack here."

"I would if I could trust you."

"What the fuck does that mean?"

"It means I think there's more going on between the two of you than you're telling me."

She wanted to cross her arms in anger and defiance, but she couldn't. "Damn it." She fumbled with the cords again and an alarm went off. She furiously reattached them and it silenced.

Finley stared down at his coffee. "Did you sleep with her?"

Maria wanted to yell at him, to argue, to scream, but she saw the hurt and seriousness in his eyes. She said nothing.

There was a knock at the door, and a woman entered rubbing her hands together with what smelled like hand sanitizer.

"Hello, I'm Dr. Torres."

Maria tried to smile but couldn't make herself. "I'm Maria, and this is my partner, Detective Silas Finley."

"Detective, right, I remember reading that now. So, you are actively on the force then?" She directed the question to Maria.

"Yes."

Finley tried to stand to leave.

"Don't. I mean, please stay." She needed him now. She could sense it. The doctor, though mild mannered and attractive, carried with her bad news. Maria knew it.

Finley eased back down, and the doctor came to her bedside. "Ms. Diaz. Detective. I've got some answers for you."

She waited.

"Your partner told us you've been having strange symptoms lately."

"Yes. Very strange."

She nodded. "I also spoke to your family physician and neurologist, and the information they gave me concurs with what we've found."

She paused again, and Maria couldn't hold her gaze. It was too warm, too sincere. She felt pitied.

"I believe you have multiple sclerosis."

Maria took a deep breath. *MS. MS. MS.* She let out the breath and trembled. She inhaled and pushed out another breath, this one shook. She nodded.

"Okay. Okay. I can handle this. I can handle this."

Finley came to her side and took her hand. She saw the tears welling in his eyes, and she had to look away. She glanced back at the doctor who had the same look of empathy and she couldn't stand it. There was no safe place to look. She closed her eyes.

"Do you know what MS is?" the doctor asked.

"Yes. I, uh, researched it a bit." It had been one of the diseases to come up in her symptom search.

"Right now, you're having a flare-up. So you're symptomatic. But these should ease as the medication takes hold and does its job. Your vision should return to normal, and the pain and muscle problems should ease as well."

"Can I work?" The rest she could look up and read about and deal with later. Right now, she had the case. They had to finish the case. And she had to put Avery Ashland where she belonged. Whether that be prison or tucked away in her mind as a distant memory. Or perhaps…in her bed. She shook the thought away and tears formed just like Finley. Only they weren't for herself or because of the MS, they were over Ashland and the mess she was in with her. She didn't know how to think or feel or anything really.

"At the moment, I would advise against it. But it will ultimately be a decision between you, your doctor, and your employer."

"You okay?" Finley squeezed her hand.

"I don't know. I don't know anything right now."

"It's a perfectly normal reaction to have," the doctor said. "And we'll send you home with plenty of information. I'd like you to stay another night until we can stabilize your symptoms some more, and then I'll release you to the care of your neurologist."

She smiled softly and left them alone, closing the door behind her. Maria shifted, rubbed her eyes, and then pulled off the cords and slid out her IV. The alarm went off again, and she grew dizzy looking at the bloody IV, but she shook it off and swung her legs over the bed.

Finley flew up next to her with wild eyes.

"What are you doing?"

"Getting out of here."

"Didn't you hear the doctor?"

"Yes. She wants my symptoms to get better. Well, they can get better at home."

"Maria, Jesus." He caught her by the elbow as she stood and the same woman in scrubs rushed in and turned off the alarm.

"What's going on?"

Maria didn't look at her. "I'm going home."

"That's against doctor's orders."

"I don't care. Send me home with the medicine. I'll be fine."

"I'll go get the doctor."

"Don't bother. I'm leaving regardless."

The woman stopped, started to speak, then changed her mind. She turned on her heel and left the room.

Maria moved as best she could to the bathroom. Finley brought her her clothes. She dressed very carefully and tried to look at herself in the mirror. But she didn't like what little she could see. Deep-set eyes, pale complexion, thick hair a mess. She reentered the room and sat on the bed. Finley slid on her shoes.

"I want you to stay with me," he said.

She sighed. "I'm okay, Fins."

"Hardly."

"I'll be fine at home."

"That's fine as long as you let me call your mother to let her know what's going on."

He straightened. She pegged him with a look she was sure could start a fire.

"You wouldn't dare."

"I would and I have."

She closed her eyes. "Finley, what the hell?"

"They needed to know, Maria. You're...not well. You're going to need help. At least for now."

She stood without waiting for his help. "Take me home."

"Maria—"

"Don't even talk to me."

"When are you going to let someone help?"

"When I need it."

She heard him sigh, and when he tried to take her elbow, she pulled away. She walked in a slow trance past the woman in scrubs holding paperwork and past the doctor who tried her best to stop her. She stepped out into the sun, squinted, and thought of only one thing.

Why had Avery Ashland come to check on her?

CHAPTER TWENTY-TWO

A very watched as Bryce sat on her overstuffed chair and stirred the cream into her coffee. They were on the shaded veranda of Bryce's elegant home, enjoying the slight cool of early morning. The birds came alive in the surrounding trees, serenading, welcoming the day. But Avery couldn't enjoy it. Even her rich coffee tasted dull. But still, she hoped it would give her life and will her weary heart to beat.

She rubbed her forehead and crossed her legs beneath the satin robe Bryce had given her. She'd arrived unannounced the evening before, distraught and anxious. Bryce had taken her in and comforted her. She'd slept in her bed, and when she'd tried to offer herself to Bryce, Bryce had declined, shocking her.

"How are you feeling?" Bryce asked, curling her bare legs up under her. Her hair was perfectly set, and despite wearing little makeup, she looked stunning. Like the former cover model she was.

"The same."

"I don't understand. A few weeks ago, none of this would've caused you a second thought. Not Hale's demise, the investigation, and especially the detective. What's come over you?"

"I don't know. If I knew, I could handle it. I wouldn't be here."

Bryce laughed. "I see. Using me to feel better. Sorry I couldn't come through for you."

Avery sipped her coffee. "You know that's not what I meant. I just feel…lost."

"I think the cops are getting to you. You need to keep your mouth shut and let Bruce handle it. And stop the obsession with this detective. It's ridiculous. And it's pointless."

"That's just it. I can't stop. She's on my mind every waking second."

Bryce shifted and frowned. "Are you telling me she's done what no one else has managed to do?"

Avery saw the spark of jealousy in her eyes. And yet she'd turned her down last night. Why?

Avery sipped her coffee and evaded the question. She'd shared her thoughts and problems with Bryce the night before, but she was only willing to go so far. She'd learned long ago, in part thanks to Bryce herself, that some things, the deep things, needed to be kept hidden. For if you shared those, you might as well offer your bare neck to the one welding the knife.

"Who is the hickey from? You're obviously not lonely."

Avery adjusted her robe which had fallen loose around her breast. She'd hoped it had gone away, but apparently, it hadn't.

"It's nothing."

"Ha, tell her that. I bet she'd dying to leave you another one."

"It was a one-time thing." She'd called on Samantha Rogue with the hopes of seducing her, conquering her. She'd thought at the time that it would make her feel better in regard to Maria. But when the time came, she'd pushed her away after a brief make out session. She just hadn't been able to go through with it. She'd only wanted one person, and that was Maria. Still, though, it hadn't stopped her from warning Samantha to stay away from the detective. Samantha had taken instant offense, realizing that that was why she was there to begin with. She'd promised no such thing and then cursed Avery out as she'd left. Things had not ended on good terms, leaving Avery in an unusual emotional turmoil. She just didn't understand what was happening to her.

"Does she know that?"

"Yes."

Bryce laughed. "Oh, maybe you haven't changed so much after all, Avery."

"Maybe I haven't. Maybe I still act just like you."

"Me? Oh, darling, don't even."

The French doors opened, and Bryce's housekeeper emerged with a tray of muffins. Avery could smell their fresh aroma, and she knew they were banana nut, right out of the oven. The housekeeper busied herself applying butter to one and then handed it to Bryce, who blew on it before taking a small bite.

"Mm. Glorious. Mimi, you've outdone yourself once again."

Mimi smiled and turned to Avery. "I remembered how much you liked them, Ms. Ashland. Would you like me to butter yours?"

Avery leaned forward to take one carefully. "No, thank you, Mimi. You've done plenty just by the smell of them." She peeled down the cover and took a bite. Heaven.

Mimi seemed pleased and left them to enjoy.

"She misses me," Avery said, amused.

"So it seems."

"I think I'm still her favorite."

"Probably."

"I lasted the longest didn't I?"

Bryce stared at her, the corner of her mouth lifting. "You know you did."

Avery took another bite and allowed the spices to melt in her mouth. "Why did you turn me down last night? Surely you aren't seeing someone. Even if you were, it never stopped you in the past."

Bryce set down her muffin and rubbed the crumbs from her hands. "You were distraught. I didn't want to take advantage."

"Oh, come on." Avery wasn't buying it. Bryce was a woman hell-bent on serving her needs, consequences be damned.

Bryce stood suddenly and tightened the belt on her robe. "I'm expecting company shortly. I assume you can show yourself out?"

Avery stopped chewing. "You're kicking me out?"

"Of course not. I just have things to do. The day is flying away already. I'm sure you have plans as well."

Avery stood and tossed her muffin on the tray. She crossed to her and cupped her face. Then she kissed her hungrily, but Bryce didn't return it. Avery pulled away, disturbed.

Bryce stared into her with cold eyes.

"A person can only want for so long, Avery. You ought to have learned that by now."

She turned and left Avery on the veranda.

Avery sat outside the modest house in the quiet neighborhood watching a small group of children run through a sprinkler. They jumped and shrieked and ran through with their arms open wide, slipping in the wet grass as they stopped to turn. She wanted to smile at their joy, but she realized she'd never had times like that. There was no fun and games with her sister. It was always school studies, dressage, ballet, and business. A game to her father was chess, where he purposely outplayed her from a very young age until her early teens when she began to beat him, causing him to lose the will to play.

She watched the children a little while longer and then started the car to drive away. But just as she put the car in gear, the front door to the modest house opened and Maria stepped out. Avery gasped at her appearance and the way she struggled to walk. She looked pale and weak, and she was using a cane to carefully maneuver to the mailbox. Avery sank lower in her seat. Maria made it to the mailbox wearing a worn terrycloth robe and slippers. She unlocked her mailbox and retrieved her mail. She dropped a few envelopes and struggled to pick them up. Avery had the urge to jump out and help her, but she remained in her vehicle. What was wrong? She was dying to know. Dying to help. Damn Bobby.

She watched as Maria made her way back to the door. A lone envelope fell from her stack as she closed the door behind her. Avery waited a few moments to see if she'd return. When she didn't, Avery crawled from her car and hurried up the walkway. She picked up the letter and read the return address. It was from a neurologist. Quietly, she slid it under the door and retreated. She climbed in her car and sped away, just as the door was reopening.

Chapter Twenty-three

*S*he was walking down a dim hallway. Music was playing, thumping. She felt hot, very hot, and her heart was pounding as if she'd been running. She came to a corner and her leg began to tingle. She cursed it, knowing somehow that danger was just beyond. She pulled her weapon and held it in front of her with both hands. Quietly, she eased around the corner, first with her extended weapon, then with her body. She blinked sweat from her eyes and focused. A dark figure was at the end of the hall, its back to her. She called out, but her throat was hoarse. She tried again and again, but nothing came. She kept walking, agonizing step after agonizing step. At last, the figure turned, whipping around in a long black leather coat. She registered the face yet couldn't place it.

The face grinned and raised a serrated knife. Maria yelled again, but the figure charged her, and Maria pulled the trigger, but the pop and the bullets did nothing to stop the figure from advancing. She tried to scream and emptied her chamber while stumbling backward. The figure continued, and Maria felt the whoosh of air as the figure swung with the knife and missed.

Maria turned fully and tried to run, but her leg was numb and she felt as if she were running in lava. She just couldn't run fast enough. She cried out as she felt a slice to her back. Another slash and she felt the tearing of her shirt. Onward she moved, as slow as a snail. She closed her eyes and willed with all her might to move. But she couldn't, and at last she cringed and jerked as she felt the figure tackle her and push the air from her lungs.

Maria sat up in bed with her hand to her chest. Her heart was careening, and she was struggling for breath. She glanced at the clock. Six thirty in the morning. She threw back her covers and placed her feet on the floor. Thankfully, she could see clearly, but her left leg was tingling and numb just as it had been in her dream. Regardless, she stood and walked unaided into the living room. Horace followed, prancing in front of her with his tail held high. He jumped onto the couch as if he knew where she was headed. Finley was sitting under her corner lamp, engrossed in paperwork.

"When did you get here?" He'd been keeping a near constant eye on her since she'd left the hospital. If she didn't make him leave at night, she was sure he'd insist on sleeping on the couch as well.

"About ten minutes ago." His hair was slicked back and clean; she could smell his spicy, freshly showered scent. He'd shaved and left a bit of tissue on a small cut on his right cheek. She sat on the opposite end of her sectional and yawned.

"What've you got?"

"We got the phone records on Ashland."

Maria's spine straightened on its own accord. "Oh?" She could've sworn she saw Avery Ashland driving away from her home two days before. Had it been her imagination? Someone had definitely slid an envelope under the door. Could it have been her? If so, why?

"Yes." He handed them over and removed his readers to rub his eyes. "There are a few we still need to look into, but it looks like a whole lotta nothing to me."

Maria took the pages and switched on the lamp next to her. She scanned the list of numbers, some of them highlighted with names by them, some of them not. She didn't recognize any of them. One thing was fishy.

"Lana's number isn't on here?" She knew he'd have checked that first.

He shook his head.

Maria tossed the papers aside. "She's got another phone. Probably a burner."

"Yep."

She pushed out a sigh. "And Lana's phone?"

He dug in his leather satchel and handed her a similar stack. She unclipped the holder and scanned through them. Lana's phone list wasn't as lengthy as Ashland's and it harbored little information.

"She didn't call Ashland, ever?"

"Seems not."

"Bullshit. They've got other phones."

"We need a search warrant," Finley said. "We put in for it."

"The DNA on the fiber we found should be enough to get us in her place."

"Yes."

"What's the holdup?"

Finley rubbed his jaw. "Not sure. We should get the go-ahead today."

"I'm coming with."

He made a noise like a grunt. "I'm not going to argue with you."

"Good."

"But the sarge might say different."

Maria inwardly cringed. She had a meeting scheduled with him as soon as she felt well enough. She knew he'd want answers about her health. Answers she couldn't yet give.

"What he doesn't know won't hurt him."

Finley merely shook his head. They'd argued a lot the past few days, and she'd always won with the last word. She was determined to work the case and he was determined to baby her.

"I thought you might say that." He flipped through another file. "Why don't you go shower and get ready?"

She stared at him with surprise. "I think I just might do that. In case that warrant comes in."

She walked to the bathroom. She stripped out of her pajamas and grabbed the stabilizing bars Finley had installed for her. He'd also brought her a shower chair, but she had refused to use it. She could still stand.

She stepped in and soaped herself slowly, rinsed, and killed the water. Dressing took her a little longer than usual, and by the time she returned to the living room, her hip on her left side hurt from favoring her leg. She stopped in her tracks when she heard Finley speak to someone other than her.

"See, she's hanging in there, doing quite well."

Her sarge stood and towered over her. He held out his hand.

"Maria."

She placed her hand in his large one and felt hers get swallowed whole as he squeezed.

"Sarge." She eyed Finley, but he raised his shoulders in innocence.

"Finley said it would be easier if I stopped by early this morning."

"He did, did he."

The sarge sat and encouraged Maria to do the same.

"We need to discuss your condition. I understand you may need some more time off?"

"I—I'm on the mend, sir. The medication is helping a great deal."

"Do you mind if I ask what's wrong?"

She felt her eyes close. This was the moment she'd been dreading. Everything rode on this very moment.

"They think I have MS."

His eyebrows rose. "I'm very sorry to hear that."

"But—my symptoms are clearing and I'm ready and willing to work."

"I noticed you're limping a bit."

"That's no big deal. Just some residual hip pain."

"Can you run?"

She looked to Finley.

"I haven't tried."

The sarge cleared his throat. "I understand you've had a vision problem as well?"

She swallowed the rising lump in her throat. "Yes, sir. But it's cleared up."

"There's no way to know if and when it might return though, correct?"

"Correct."

"I'm not quite sure what to do here, Maria. We obviously need to get a professional opinion."

She thought fast, sensing his hesitation. "For now, I'll take it easy, let Finley handle the physical stuff. I really would like to go if we get a warrant on Ashland's place though."

He rubbed his heavy looking jaw and looked to Finley. "You're with her the most, what do you think?"

"She's not going to stop until she gets her way. Trust me on that."

He nodded. "I thought as much. After the whole newspaper disaster and all. We didn't get a chance to discuss that. Things have been so crazy. Why did you go in alone?"

"Ashland doesn't care for Finley."

He glanced at him. "But you didn't even tell anyone you were going in."

"No, sir."

"You know how I feel about that."

"Yes, sir."

He sighed. "Maria, you're one of my best detectives. You're damn good, have excellent instincts. I'd hate to have to reprimand you on something stupid. Or worse, lose you completely because you played fast and loose with a murder suspect."

"Yes, sir."

"We're a team. Treat us as such. Finley and I only have your best interest at heart."

"I understand, sir."

He stood. "Okay, you can go if we get a warrant, and you can do desk work. That's it until we get a doctor's professional opinion. Got it?"

"Got it."

She smiled at the small victory, but she knew she had to try harder to prove to him she could handle the fieldwork. Her dream, however, resonated, and she panicked a little at the thought of not being able to run.

She walked her sarge to the door, thanked him for coming, and closed the door. She turned to find Finley stroking Horace.

"That was sneaky as shit, Fins." She stalked as best she could to the kitchen and turned on the coffee maker. She stood shaking out her tingling leg, trying to force feeling. Finley approached and leaned against the doorframe. He crossed his arms.

"It might have been, I'll give you that. But it might've just saved your life."

CHAPTER TWENTY-FOUR

The large bell clock in the lobby struck eight, and Avery maneuvered through the crowd feeling like a queen among her subjects. She felt especially elegant in her ivory silk dress and matching heels, expensive pearls tied in a loose knot cascading down the center of her chest. She'd lain in her tanning bed for thirty minutes earlier, and after her shower she'd applied a rich moisturizer, causing her skin to glow. She felt magnificent, and she only wished Maria were there to see it.

But as things were she didn't invite her, mainly because she knew she was ill, but also because she was trying to follow Bryce's advice. The whole idea was ridiculous and pointless, and she didn't like the jealousy she felt when it came to Maria. The only other lover she'd ever felt anything close to that with had been Bryce. And that had ended in catastrophe with Bryce cheating on her. Completely wrecked, Avery had left her and they'd been playing cat and mouse ever since. Until now where it seemed Bryce had turned her down for good. And she couldn't lie, that had pinpricked her ego just enough to cause a blood flow. And while she'd avoided thinking about it as best she could, the blood flow continued, leading into the evening where she knew she had to find a way to stop the leak.

She walked her best seductive walk up to a small group of familiar women, with her eye on a petite brunette, one she hadn't seen since Hale's death.

"Melanie, hello." She leaned in and said it from behind while lightly stroking her outer arm with her fingertips.

Melanie Prague, Hale's long-time assistant, turned with a sly smile. "Avery, so good to see you."

"Where on earth have you been?" Avery asked. "I thought I'd see much more of you after, you know, Hale."

She turned, and Avery led them away from the others.

"I've been busy," she said. "Closing up his affairs and, you know, relaxing." She brushed her raven hair away from her fiery green eyes.

"Sounds nice. Maybe we could pick up where we left off?"

"Perhaps."

"Perhaps?" Melanie had been eager, even begging before.

"Things have changed, Avery. I've changed. Hale's death…oh, never mind. I don't expect anyone to understand."

"Are you seeing someone?"

"Mm. Off and on."

Avery took two glasses of champagne and handed one to Melanie. She walked her to the elevator. "My place? To catch up?"

"Sure."

"You look fantastic," Avery said, sizing up her red mini dress and black heels. Her hair was short, shaved in back, and longer on top, resting at a sharp angle on her left side. Her lips, though thin, looked edible in matching red lipstick.

"Thank you, so do you."

They exited the elevator and walked the hall to Avery's main door. She pressed her finger to the keypad on the door and it clicked open. Melanie walked in ahead of her, and they settled near the grand piano in the front room.

"So tell me. Have the cops been all over you since Hale's death?"

Melanie seemed surprised. "Mm, I don't think anything more than they usually would. They came by sometime after with questions, but I simply handed them Hale's planner and itinerary. Things have been a mess, with me scrambling to answer phone calls and trying to get a funeral arranged."

Avery glanced away. "I wish I could say the same. They haven't left me alone yet."

Melanie sipped her drink and raised her eyebrows. She lit a long brown cigarette. "You? Why?"

"I guess because everyone knows I hate Hale."

She laughed. "Yes, everyone does know that, don't they?"

"God, I wish I'd never met the bastard."

"Mm, hear hear. I'll drink to that."

They clinked glasses and smiled.

Melanie set down her glass. "Do you mind if I use your restroom?"

"Of course not. You know where it is."

She rose and left the room, and Avery sat back to relax, trying to find a way to convince her to stay the night. They'd had a tumultuous affair before Hale's death, and while it had exhausted Avery, it had also kept her ravenous libido fed. Avery had been Melanie's first experience with a woman, and she'd wanted more from her. A relationship, something meaningful. She'd even left her husband. But Avery had refused, and they had gone back and forth between fucking and fighting. And then, one day, Melanie had just stopped calling. She'd sent her a letter saying she understood and that she had no hard feelings, that they just weren't right for each other. Avery had been grateful and she'd left it alone. But now, with her confusing feelings for Maria, she thought it might be good to have someone in her bed again. Maybe this time Melanie could agree to a casual affair. But as she set her glass down, she knew deep inside she'd still think of Maria. How could she ever stop?

She rose to fetch more champagne when her alarm chimed letting her know someone had stepped off the elevator. She crossed to the security monitors and saw both Detectives Finley and Maria step into the hallway. One of her employees had escorted them up. She swallowed the anger trying to rise and instead wondered about the well-being of Maria. She hurried to the door and pulled it open before they could ring the bell.

"Detectives. You came despite having no invitation. How delightful." She forced a smile and focused on Maria who was staring at her coldly. "Detective." Avery nodded toward her. "How are you feeling?"

Maria ignored her and showed her badge as if Avery didn't know they were cops. "We'd like to have a word if possible."

Avery cocked her head. So it was more harassment. She wasn't going to give them the satisfaction.

"Actually, I'm entertaining a guest at the moment."

"Who? Lana Gold?" Maria asked with bitterness dripping off the words.

"Noooo."

Maria tsked. "Oh, that's right. You've turned on each other. How interesting."

"Excuse me?"

"Oh, you didn't know? Lana says she left you alone with Hale the night of his death, which places you as the last one to be with him before he died."

Avery reared back. "She's lying." She felt her face redden and she squeezed the doorknob still in her hand.

"Can we take this inside?" Finley asked. "We'd like to discuss it with you."

Avery wanted to tell them to fuck off, to slam the door in their face, but she couldn't. She had to defend herself. She couldn't let Maria think she killed Hale. Even if there was to be nothing between them, it sickened her to think that Maria might always wonder.

Avery pulled open the door and allowed them to enter. She motioned toward the couch where both detectives sat. She watched Finley smooth down his tie over and over, and she wondered why he seemed nervous. Then she saw him glance at his watch.

"Am I keeping you, Detective?"

She sat across from them without offering them a drink.

He sat straighter and again smoothed his tie. "Not at all."

"What's the deal then? Why are you so nervous?"

He smiled. "Just a little excited. In seeing you again, you know?" He winked and she wanted to vomit. She looked away from his shit eating grin and focused on Maria who appeared calm and collected. Yet the chill coming off her could almost be seen.

Avery decided to save them the trouble of asking. "I wasn't with Hale the night he died. I was here."

"Not with Lana?"

"No."

"Not at all?"

"No."

"Yet you once agreed that you were with her."

"I was not. I was here. All night."

"And your surveillance could prove it. Right. Only the tape you so graciously gave us shows static. How could that be?"

"I don't know." Avery was about to light into them when Finley looked beyond her and stood. Avery turned and saw Melanie walking back in from the restroom. She was moving slowly and she paused at the grand piano.

"I should see myself out."

Avery rose and crossed to her. "No. Please stay. I'll get rid of them." She leaned in and lightly kissed her neck. Melanie pulled away.

"Detectives, nice to see you again," Melanie said. She grabbed her clasp purse.

"And you," Finley said. "I didn't know you two were... friends," he said.

Melanie stiffened. "We know each other through Hale of course," she said.

"Yes, yes. You being his assistant and all. Still...interesting that you two are tight." He looked to Maria who was boring her gaze into Avery. Avery crossed her arms, suddenly cold.

"Especially since you told us before that you didn't know Ms. Ashland," Maria said.

Avery tried to control the chill that went through her. Why would Melanie say such a thing? Was she really that over her? She forced a smile and shoved away rising thoughts of Bryce and her cold treatment of her as well.

"Our relationship should mean nothing to you, Detective," Avery said.

Melanie turned slightly. "You can trust her on that one. It meant nothing to her too." She smiled at the detectives. "I'll show myself out." She left before Avery could think of something to say. Instead she watched helplessly as the door closed behind her.

"Wow, rough night," Finley said.

"Fuck you." Avery returned to her seat.

"We'd like access to all your surveillance videos as well as your home and business," Maria said suddenly.

Avery laughed. "I gave you the tape you asked for. As for anything else, you'll need a warrant."

Maria didn't flinch. "We've got one."

Avery stood and her bones turned to steel beneath her skin. "Like hell."

Finley pulled out the warrant. "It's all right here for your reading enjoyment."

"You can't do this."

Maria stood and Finley followed. "We will need you to vacate the property while we search."

Avery clenched her jaw so tight she thought it would shatter. "Please don't do this."

Finley stepped aside and called someone on his phone. "Yeah, we're clear."

Avery shook in her shoes. Squeezed her fists. The world seemed to swirl around her. She was totally out of control. She. Had. No. Control. She swayed and then flinched as Maria cupped her elbow.

"I'll see you out."

Avery walked zombie like with her. Tears nipped at her throat, but she swallowed them down. She straightened her back and tore her arm away. She didn't need a goddamned escort. This was still her resort, her home.

"I can't believe you're doing this," Avery seethed. They stood and waited for the elevator. "You of all people."

"I have a job to do. You know that."

"Do you not believe me? How can I convince you?"

"I have a feeling this search will tell me all I need to know."

"There's nothing. I have nothing. I didn't kill Hale."

Maria looked at her. "Then why is it that every which way we turn, all signs point to you?"

Avery struggled to find words. "Because I hated him. That's no lie. I did."

"Seems you lie more often than you like to admit to, Ms. Ashland."

The doors opened and they stepped inside. "I lied about my alibi with Lana, yes. But honestly, this whole thing is so ridiculous, and I don't like being accused of something I didn't do."

"Maybe you've finally learned that this is not a game, Ms. Ashland. This isn't one of your parties. This is murder."

The doors opened again and a group of cops stood waiting to ride up. Avery wanted to scream, but she controlled herself. Her guests were milling in the background.

"I'll sue," she said. "You're ruining my name. My reputation."

They exited, walked through the crowd, and stepped outside. A storm-brewing breeze blew through, and Avery felt it ignite the thunder she felt inside.

Maria looked at her. "If you are innocent, then perhaps I just saved your life."

Avery shot her a glance.

"If we find nothing…"

"Don't placate me, Detective."

"What are you so worried about?"

"I'm not worried. I'm furious. And where the hell am I supposed to go?"

"Why don't you call Melanie Prague? Oh, that's right, she seems to want nothing to do with you either."

Maria left her on the front steps, leaving her alone with the wind.

CHAPTER TWENTY-FIVE

Maria left Avery out in front of the resort and hurried with more police back inside. Guests were being escorted out, many of them angry and all of them concerned. Though this wasn't one of Avery's sex parties, the guests were still rich and elite and they liked their privacy. She overheard several of them refer to the murder as they made their way to the front exit. While they'd showed up and remained Avery's friends to her face, they were beginning to question her innocence. And more than a few had concerns about surveillance.

Maria burned as her own concerns began to surface. She could only pray she wasn't on the tapes. She rode the elevator in silence with several other officers carrying evidence bags. And when the doors opened, she heard her sarge's voice booming down the hall. She followed it back to Avery's penthouse.

"I want everything. Anything and everything that looks like it could be something." He was pacing and pointing. He focused on the security monitors behind the bar. "Finley, find the tapes. We already looked downstairs; they aren't there. She must keep them up here."

"On it," Finley said.

Maria bypassed Nadine who was being gently led out. She had tears in her eyes, and she was already ready for bed and wrapped in her bathrobe. She gave Maria a pleading look, but Maria looked away, having no comfort to offer her.

Maria came to Avery's bedroom and entered. A bedside light came on as it sensed her movement. She walked to her nightstand, pulled on gloves, and opened the drawer. She found books, which somewhat surprised her, though she knew Avery was highly educated and articulate. She just hadn't pegged her for a reader. And surprisingly, some were self-help books on how to better yourself or how to get along well with others. Avery seemed so secure with herself, Maria never would've guessed she'd read such topics.

She settled down on the bed and flipped through them. Then she tossed aside two sex toys and a small bottle of lube. Then she opened the other drawer. A stack of photos of two small girls was on the top, and Maria recognized them as her nieces. She flipped through photo after photo of Avery with the girls all smiles. They seemed to travel a lot, and Avery appeared completely relaxed and truly very happy. Her face glowed and her eyes sparkled. She wasn't even wearing makeup in most of the photos. Maria wished she could see her like that; it showed a whole new Avery and she wondered again if she really could've killed Hale.

She set the photos aside and removed hand lotions and scented candles. Then she hit bottom, but the drawer seemed shorter than the other. Maria repositioned herself and dropped to her knees. She took out her Swiss Army knife and found the small blade. She inched it into the seam of the bottom and popped it lose. A stack of eight by ten photos was inside. She lifted them carefully and paged through them. They were black-and-whites, and all of them were of Hale Medley and various women. And in every single photo, Hale Medley was groping the woman he was with. Photo after photo, woman after woman.

Maria rose, placed the photos in evidence bags, and returned to Finley and her sarge.

"I think I've got something," she said as she came into the room.

But the room was silent and everyone was gathered around the security monitors. She edged her way through and stopped, frozen. On the center screen, the largest screen, was an image of her and Avery in the hallway. Avery was up against her back and whispering in her ear. Maria was looking in on the threesome. Thankfully, they couldn't see what she was watching, but the way Avery was moving against her and the way she was nearly melting back into her was more than obvious. And then as Maria turned, she'd hurt her ankle. She burned with embarrassment as everyone watched Avery lead her away to the penthouse.

Finley killed the tape and rubbed the back of his neck. Somewhere behind her, her sarge cleared his throat.

"Get back to work, people."

Her colleagues turned, caught sight of her, and lowered their gaze as if they were embarrassed as well. She wanted to bury herself somewhere deep and never come out.

"Maria?" her sarge boomed.

"Yes, sir?"

She was oozing red right through her skin. She could feel it. He cupped her elbow and walked her to the veranda where they stepped outside. He turned as the rain-scented wind caressed them.

"Is there anything else we're going to find on those tapes?"

She closed her eyes. "I'm not sure, sir."

"Not sure."

"Yes, sir."

His large eyes bored into her. "Have you had inappropriate contact with this suspect, Maria?"

Her breath hitched. She couldn't bring herself to speak. He took it as a yes.

"Jesus H. Christ." He threw up his hands.

"I felt some of it was necessary, sir. To get close."

"Well, I'd say you did a damn good job, then. What were you thinking? There's getting close and then there's I don't know. Whatever the hell you did. Tell me it's not on tape."

"I don't believe so, sir. She's not known to tape her escapades. It's why her friends trust her and come here to participate."

"Yes, but you're a cop. She would've had a field day recording you."

She cringed. "I don't think she did, sir." But had she? Had she really been playing Maria all along?"

He sighed and placed his hands on the railing to look down over the resort and out over the valley. Maria stared into the distant lights of Las Brisas and wished she could take it all back. Take it all back and then some. But she couldn't. And truth be told, she just hadn't been able to resist Avery Ashland.

"This is not good, Maria," he said so low she could hardly hear him.

"Sir?"

"You're going to end up suspended."

"Sir, please. I've found something of interest in Avery's false bottom drawer. I can finish this case. Nail her to the wall. I'm closer than anyone—"

"That's what scares me. You're too close. What you've done—it could cost us this case."

He turned and looked as though he'd been slapped.

"You know it ultimately isn't up to me. I have my superiors, and with the newspaper article and now the tape with what you've just told me…I'm afraid they will want you off the case."

"Sir—"

"With your condition…it's probably only a matter of time before—"

"Don't. Don't predict my future like that. I can't have you being biased against me based on my condition. No one knows my future, and if I can still work, I damn well expect to be allowed."

He didn't respond, just looked at her with sad eyes and held out his hand. She handed over the photos, knowing her presence there was no longer welcome. The sarge had to cover his ass or they'd all go down. She knew that, yet she hated being the cause.

She walked back inside and found Finley staring back at the security monitor. She focused and saw Avery Ashland seductively leading Samantha Rogue into her penthouse. Someone let out a whistle.

Maria let out a noise of shock and surprise and then lowered her head and hurried as best she could from the penthouse. And she didn't stop until she arrived home.

Chapter Twenty-six

A very was curled in a ball on her bed, resisting the urge to rock back and forth like a child needing comfort. It had been a long forty-eight hours and she knew she should be exhausted, but she was too keyed up emotionally to relax and sleep. She glanced to her left and took in the comforting sight of her nieces snuggled down into the covers. They were both breathing softly, and she wiped a stray tear from her eye as she watched them.

After she and Nadine had put the house back together, Nadine had suggested she have them over. Nadine knew their presence would help her, to calm her. Because as it stood, she wanted to yell and scream and curse at everyone and everything. Her privacy, her home, her innermost sanctum, had been not only invaded but torn apart. Savages. The whole lot of them. How could they do this? How had she lost total control?

She looked to her right at the nightstand. She'd found the drawers open and the contents strewn on her bed. Someone had found the photos of Hale. The photos she'd had Bobby Luca take. They'd all been in agreement then. They'd all said Hale needed to be stopped, that he needed to be taught a lesson. Now she could hardly find anyone to talk to her. They were all glad to be rid of Hale, but she was left hanging in the wind, taking the fall.

Maybe she should've given the photos to Maria. Maybe she should've told her about Hale and how he'd sexually harassed dozens of women, many of them her personal friends. Maybe she should've told her about the agreement. She still could. She could call right now. But it was too little too late. And she wasn't a rat. No matter what was happening to her, she was no rat. She wouldn't do what someone was obviously doing to her.

Lana.

She blamed Lana.

If Maria had told the truth, then it was Lana setting her up. Lana telling the police all they wanted to hear. Which was why she'd tried to pay her a visit. But Lana hadn't been home and she wasn't answering her phone. Avery knew she was probably avoiding her. She had to find a way to her. To shut her up somehow. She was only squealing to save herself. But did she really know what she was doing? Did she really realize she was setting Avery up for murder?

She doubted it. Lana just needed to be talked to. Reasoned with. And if that didn't work...

She pushed off from the bed, extinguished the light, and pulled the door closed partway. She knew Nadine was asleep, so she quietly made her way into the living room to pour herself a drink. Earlier that day, it had looked like a tornado had ripped through the room and she fought wincing at the memory. She poured herself some scotch over ice and walked to the veranda. She slid open the doors and stepped outside. Warm rain flecked her skin. She stared out at the lights of the city and made her mind up. She knew if she didn't do it, she'd never be able to sleep again.

She turned and walked back inside, determined more than ever, to fix things once and for all.

❖

"I want hearts!" Avery's niece Rory said.

"I want stars!" her other niece Kylie said.

Avery, who stood behind the kitchen counter, held up her hands in defeat. "All right, all right. Hearts and stars, it is."

She smiled at Nadine and began cutting the pancakes they'd just made into the appropriate shapes. She worked happily while the girls giggled on the bar stools.

"That doesn't look like a star, Auntie Avery," Rory said. "It looks like a deformed Christmas tree."

"You don't like my stars?" She held one up and the girls laughed. "What's wrong with my stars?"

"They're not stars!"

"Are too. They're special stars." She handed over the plates and then passed the butter and syrup. Both girls lowered from their knees to their bottoms and dug in. Avery took her coffee and sat at the table, watching with amusement.

"Mm. I don't care if it doesn't look like a star. Auntie Avery makes the bestest pancakes in the whole wide world!"

"Yeah!"

"She does make good pancakes," Nadine said, sipping her own cup of coffee.

"And she's the best hide-and-go-seeker," Kylie said.

"Uh-huh, yep." Rory said, nodding with her mouth full.

Avery smiled, feeling very warm and safe. It was quite a contradiction to yesterday's feelings. But she pushed them from her mind and focused on the girls.

"Well, you know…you guys are the best nieces anyone could ask for."

They both nodded. "We know."

Nadine laughed and Avery shook her head, chuckling.

"Can we swim today?" Kylie asked.

"I don't think so. I thought maybe we would go paint ceramics."

"Yeah!"

"I love that!"

They grew excited and bounced up and down.

"Okay, take it easy. Sit still and eat your breakfast. We have plenty of time."

Avery cocked her head as she heard the alarm to the elevator. She looked to Nadine who shrugged. Avery rose, annoyed that whomever it was hadn't called up with her staff first.

"I think I've got to fire a couple of security guys. I can't have people coming up unannounced."

She left the kitchen and went to the front door. She stopped dead in her tracks as she caught sight of the security monitor.

"Nadine, keep the girls in there."

Her heart sank to her stomach as she opened the door to Detective Finley and a larger man she'd seen on the night of her warrant. Her blood rose to her face when she saw Finley's satisfied look and the big man's dead one. She knew something was desperately wrong.

"I really don't appreciate you coming now. My nieces are here," she said.

The cops looked at one another and began to speak, but Avery only heard the commotion of her nieces as they ran into the room.

"Who is it, Auntie Avery?"

"Yeah, who's here?"

They ran up and hugged her legs. Nadine followed them in with an apologetic look.

"I'm sorry, but they heard you and took off."

Avery smoothed down their hair and tried to remain calm. "These nice people were just leaving," Avery said. She looked back to the cops.

The big man spoke. "I'm afraid we can't do that."

Avery steeled her jaw. "I insist."

"You can insist all you want," Finley said. "We're not leaving."

"You need to step outside with us," the big man said.

Avery felt a chill go up her spine. "Why?"

"Just trust me. For their sake."

Avery patted the girls on the back. "I'll be right back, okay?"

"I wouldn't say that," Finley said.

Avery stared into him.

"Please come with us," the big man said.

The girls looked up at her. "Why do you have to go?"

"Can we come?"

"Where are you going, Auntie Avery?"

"Where are they taking you?"

She managed to quiet them down, and Nadine came to take them by the hand. Concern marked her face, and Avery whispered for her to take them to the back bedrooms. Nadine led them away, and the girls continued to ask questions. They looked back at her with worried eyes and Rory began to cry.

Avery forced herself to look away. She glared at Finley.

"We need you to come with us, please," the big one said.

Avery closed the door behind her and followed the cops halfway down the hall.

"Where's Maria?"

"That's none of your concern," Finley said.

"Is this about more questions, Detectives?"

"Not quite," the big man said. "And my name is Sergeant O'Connell."

Avery stopped. Waited. They turned.

"Avery Ashland," Finley said. "You're under arrest for the murder of Hale Medley." He walked behind her and wrenched her arms up behind her back.

"What? You can't be serious."

"I'm afraid so."

He clicked on the cuffs and they pinched into her wrists.

She looked to the sergeant. "You can't do this. I didn't kill Hale."

"How about Lana Gold then?" He stepped up and grabbed her arm. "You're also under arrest for the murder of Lana Gold."

Avery's knees buckled. "What? Lana?"

Sergeant O'Connell tugged on her, forcing her to walk while Finley pushed on her lower back from behind.

Avery thought about begging, pleading, but her body went heavy and numb and she felt herself disassociate as if she were floating away. There were just no words. There was…nothing. She lowered her head and tried to control her rampaging heart. It couldn't be happening. It just couldn't be.

They put her in the elevator and she faced the wall, refusing to turn around. Her shoulders went slack and she began to tremble.

"Please take the cuffs off when you walk me out. These people count on me, work for me." Her voice was raspy, almost a whisper. Not at all like herself.

"Not on your life," Finley said.

Avery closed her eyes, then heard the elevator ding as the door opened. She turned and took a step out into what could only be her own future hell.

Chapter Twenty-seven

S he looks rigid," Finley said. "Closed off. I bet she tells us to go to hell."

Maria looked through the two-way mirror at Avery Ashland who sat handcuffed to the small table. Her eyes were wide, and she was pale. Her body was straight and stiff. With every breath she took, she seemed ready to completely cave, but then she'd straighten and grit her teeth. She looked terrified despite her best efforts to hide it.

"No. She'll talk. She's too scared not to."

"Scared? Right. She has no conscience, doesn't feel fear." He was tired yet hell-bent on getting Ashland to squeal. His wrinkled clothes and two days' growth on his jaw made him look like a drunk just home from a two-day bender. She was doing her best to keep him levelheaded.

"I don't know about that, Fins."

"You gonna lay it out for her?"

"Before her attorney gets here, yes. And she'll talk. Trust me on that."

He crossed his arms over his chest. "If you say so."

"It has to work." Ashland had already insisted she'd only talk to Maria. It was the only reason why her sarge was even letting her anywhere near her. He entered as if on cue, looking equally as tired as Finley. A few other higher-ups followed him in. She gave them a nod.

"It's up to you, Maria," he said.

"I know, sir. Thank you for giving me the chance."

He nodded and looked beyond her at their suspect.

"You better get in there."

Maria left them and entered the small interrogation room. She brought with her a cup of coffee and set it down in front of Avery. Avery eyed her and hesitated to take it.

"Wait, let me get the cuffs."

Maria released her and sat across from her. She pushed the coffee and Avery took it. When her hands trembled, she set it down and hid her hands in her lap.

Maria smiled. "I do that all the time. Hide my hands when they shake."

Avery looked at her curiously, and Maria continued.

"It happens a lot, or at least it did. And I'd freak out, afraid for anyone to see. I felt like it made me look weak."

Avery held her gaze but said nothing. Finally, she spoke.

"How are you feeling, Detective?"

Maria shrugged. "Better. But it's going to be a long road."

"I'm sorry." She stared into her eyes, and Maria saw the hard edges soften. "I was never informed about what was wrong. I just assumed it was bad."

Maria fell silent. "I'll be fine."

"From what my detective told me and based on your symptoms…"

Maria cleared her throat, feeling exposed.

"Is it serious?"

Maria glanced away.

"I'm sorry. For whatever it is."

"Don't be." Maria forced a smile. "I'll be fine. Question is, will you?"

Avery looked away. "I didn't kill anyone."

Maria expected as much. "You know, I didn't think you were guilty for a long while. Even now, it's difficult for me to believe. But, Avery, all the evidence points to you."

She whipped her head and stared into her with wild eyes. "What evidence? Tell me, so I can explain it or whatever. I swear to God I didn't kill anyone. I didn't even know Lana was dead." Her whole body trembled and she stopped to breathe. When she calmed, she spoke in a low voice. "I swear on my nieces I didn't kill anyone."

Maria sat back and took a deep breath. Swearing on her beloved nieces. She was serious. Or at least doing a damn good job pretending to be.

"Just tell me what you've got on me. It has to be bullshit because I didn't do it."

Maria saw the desperation in her face, heard it in her voice. She was surprised when she felt a pang of empathy. She'd heard the same from many a perp, but never before had she physically reacted. She pushed the feeling away.

"Let's start with Hale. We have the photo of you and Hale on which you've written a verbal threat. We have your DNA from that same photo. We also have a fiber with your DNA on it in the limo he was last seen in. That fiber matches a blanket we took from your home."

"But—"

"Let me finish. We have Lana's statement which we took before she died, that puts you with Hale on the night he died. We have surveillance photos of Hale that we found in your home. And we have surveillance tape of you and him arguing at one of your parties that we also found during our search. Not to mention, that you can't seem to prove your whereabouts on the night of his death. And finally, we have numerous witnesses that claim they've heard you threaten Hale's life on more than one occasion."

"A fiber? That's impossible." She shook her head. "I was never in a limo with Hale. Someone had to have planted it. Someone is setting me up here. Framing me."

"That's your answer?"

Avery looked incredulous. "Yes!"

"That's all you've got?"

"I'm telling the truth."

"See, we think Lana baited Hale that night. Maybe drugged him at the country club and got him in the limousine. You were either in there waiting or they soon picked you up. From there you took him to this mysterious warehouse she mentioned where you tortured and killed him."

"No. No. Impossible." She stared into Maria, and Maria swore she could almost hear her mind reeling for explanation. She jerked as if she'd found one and then spoke. "The fiber. It could've come from Lana herself. She was a frequent visitor to my home. You know this. She could've transferred it."

Maria nodded and shrugged. "Possible, but not likely."

"What do you mean? Of course it's likely. It has to be likely. Because I wasn't in any damn limousine."

"Was Lana at your home the day of Hale's death?"

"Well, I don't know. Because I'm not exactly sure what day he was killed. No one has ever told me."

Maria smiled. Good answer. Avery was coy, she'd give her that.

Maria continued. "Let's talk about Lana. Lana was found in her bed early this morning by a friend. She was tied to the bed with an empty bottle of pills nearby and a letter in which she confesses to her part in the murder of Hale."

"I don't believe it," Avery said. "Lana couldn't kill. It's not in her nature."

"As opposed to what? Your nature?"

"I'm just saying I don't believe it. Someone is setting this whole thing up. You assholes are just too dumb to see it."

"Why would she point the finger at you, Avery?"

Avery shifted as if uncomfortable. She sipped her coffee again this time with steadier hands.

"Lana and I have had our problems. She always wanted more than I was willing to give, yes. But nothing that would result in any of this. Not murder. She was squeamish."

"Did she love you? Was that the issue?"

"Even if she did…it proves nothing." She shook her head. "What makes you think I could possibly kill her?"

"For starters, the way she was killed. She was tied up and force-fed the same muscle relaxers that were found in Hale."

"So? I had nothing to do with Hale, so how does that tie in to me?"

Maria drummed her fingers along the tabletop. "You're really going to play it like this?" Was she that stupid? She highly doubted it. But she obviously thought they were.

"Ms. Ashland, we found the same medication in your home during our search."

Avery tried to stand, but Maria stood first and waved her down as a warning.

"That's crazy. There's no way."

"We found them hidden in the tank of your toilet in an unmarked prescription type bottle."

"Bullshit!" She slammed her fists on the table. "I've never had anything like that in my home. I never needed it."

"You're insinuating someone planted that as well? To frame you?"

"Yes!"

"Who? Lana? Would she do such a thing? Could that be why you killed her? To stop her and to shut her up?"

Avery shook her head. A tear formed and fell. She wiped it away quickly and steeled her jaw once again.

"I would never hurt her. Not like that. I've known her for years. She's…she was…a friend."

"A friend who killed Hale and tried to blame you? I'm sure glad I don't have friends like that."

Avery closed her eyes. "I'm telling you, she couldn't kill. Not Lana. As for the limo ride with him, she probably just wanted to scare him is all."

Maria's attention sparked. "What do you mean by that?"

Avery stared into her coffee. "There were a lot of women upset with Hale for obvious reasons. Maybe some of them just got fed up and they wanted to put a little scare into him. Only…"

"Only what, Avery?"

"Only one of them got carried away. Or…one of them wanted me to go down in a big, big way."

"Who? Who would want you to go down, Avery? And who would want to scare Hale?"

"You've got all kinds of evidence, Detective, you're going to have to tell me."

"I need you to tell me, Avery. All we have is Lana and you say no way."

She shook her head. "I can't because I don't know. I only heard rumors. Rumors that some women wanted to get together to stop Hale. They were supposed to only go so far. I said I'd help, but—I had him followed, had the photos to blackmail him—but that was the last I heard of it."

Maria came out of her seat as the door opened and Avery's attorney Bruce Milo stormed in in his golf clothes.

"That's it, interview is over."

"She's under arrest and she's been made aware of her rights," Maria said.

"Yes, I'm aware of the charges and of your so-called evidence against my client." His face was red from the sun, and a stark tan line had formed around his eyes where he'd worn his sunglasses.

"First degree murder for Hale Medley and Lana Gold," he said as if repeating. He looked at her and his eyebrows shot up, and then out came a laugh. "Good luck with that, Detective. Avery, hang tight, I'll see you at the arraignment."

Avery nodded and appeared weak. Maria had never thought she'd see the day when Avery Ashland looked weary and weak. Perhaps she was human after all.

"The girls," she finally said. "I'm worried about the girls. Please tell them I'm all right. And that I'll be home soon."

"Of course."

He looked to Maria. "I assume you will treat her well?"

"You have my word."

"Somehow that doesn't comfort me," he said, walking back out.

Maria looked at Avery with pure desperation. "Avery, please tell me all you know. I can help you. Let me help you. Give me names, a name, any name."

Bruce peaked back in. "You've helped enough, Detective. Avery, say no more."

Maria left Avery, and Finley entered to recuff her and lead her out. Maria watched silently as he led her away to be processed and placed in custody. She'd always had a good feeling watching perp after perp take their walk, but this one felt different. It didn't feel... right. Somehow, though she wasn't sure how, she knew there was more to the story. Would they ever know the whole truth? Or would Avery Ashland remain silent and spend the rest of her life in prison?

CHAPTER TWENTY-EIGHT

How do you plead, Ms. Ashland?" the judge, who sounded loud and baritone, asked.

Avery stared straight ahead, thinking of nothing but her nieces. Around her, life spun on, but she wanted nothing of it. She only wanted to hold her nieces.

A firm nudge from Bruce forced her back into reality. "Say you're not guilty, for God's sake," he whispered.

She threw back her shoulders and looked up at the judge, who looked very small in his oversized robe and oversized bench. His eyes were bearing down on her, and she considered staring back, but she had little strength left to fight.

"Not guilty," she managed, trying to remain upright. She hadn't eaten and she was beginning to feel it. Bruce embraced her and eased her back into her seat. There was grumbling and mumbling from the courtroom behind her. The press had not been allowed in, but she'd recognized several people she knew, including Nadine, who'd looked ashen and heartbroken. Across the aisle from her, she'd seen Bryce and friends of both Avery and Lana. More than a few glared at her as if she were guilty and right where she belonged. And the others looked at her anxiously, whispering to each other like crazed onlookers. She understood their anxiety. Any one of them could be standing where she was.

Bruce nudged her again, demanding her attention.

The prosecution spoke. "Your honor, we'd like the defendant to be held in custody until trial. Defendant has the means and the motive to leave the country."

Bruce interrupted. "Your honor, my client has no criminal record, she's an upstanding citizen, no threat to anyone, and let's not even get into her charity work. We recommend she be released on own recognizance."

The judge sat back in his seat and contemplated.

"Bail will be set at one million dollars." He pounded his gavel and dismissed them.

Avery swallowed hard. "I can go home?"

"As soon as we make bail."

"Well, make it, damn it."

"I will, Avery."

"No, you don't understand. The girls. They're probably scared and God knows what they've heard."

He closed his briefcase as people moved around them. "Avery, you'd better start concentrating on yourself here. You're in some serious shit."

"You said you would handle it."

"And I'm trying. But you're not helping. Whatever you told the detective, it's got her up in arms, and they're on my ass to speak to you again. To offer you a deal. You know what that means? They still think you're guilty. And a deal would mean time. As in prison time. And I'm not even going to get into what will happen if this goes all the way to trial and the jury thinks you're guilty. You're looking at life."

She didn't speak. She didn't know what to say. She didn't need to ask why or how things had gotten this way. She knew it was mostly her and her behavior. She hadn't cooperated and she'd only angered guys like Finley who were gunning to put her away. But all her life she'd managed to handle things, to maneuver extremely well and outwit her opponent. Even if she'd been in the wrong. So how was she losing now when she'd done nothing?

She closed her eyes. "Just get me home and let me think. I can't spend another night using a piece of bread as a pillow in that cell with crazy women."

He nodded and she was led out in cuffs in her black-and-white striped uniform. A pattern she hoped she'd never have to see again.

❖

"What do you mean I can't see them?" Avery yelled into the phone. She slammed it down when her sister again went off about her being charged with murder and then began hinting at her guilt. She picked up the phone, pressed the end button again and again, and then threw it across the room. All she wanted to do was to hold her nieces and comfort them. But her sister wouldn't allow it.

She crumbled onto the couch and placed her head in her hands. Tears forms and slipped down her cheeks. The heat of them surprised her. She'd rarely cried in her life, and she wasn't used to the feeling of rawness and tightness in her throat or the warmth and saltiness of the tears. All of it infuriated her at how weak it all made her feel.

"Avery?" Nadine entered the room and touched her shoulder. "Are you all right? What was that noise?"

"I threw the phone," she said with a sigh. She wiped her eyes. "I'm not allowed to see the girls."

Nadine saw her face and handed her some tissue. "Oh, I'm sorry."

Avery pushed away the tissue. "Just when I think this whole thing can't get any worse, it does. I may go to prison, Nadine. Prison."

Nadine eased down next to her. "I have faith that that won't happen." She patted her knee. "Because you didn't kill anyone."

"How do you believe me when no one else does?"

Nadine gave a soft smile. "I've known you since you were four, Avery Ashland. I've seen you through many things, and you know many of them I didn't agree with. But I know your heart. It's hard and stubborn and guarded, but it isn't a bad heart. You aren't a monster or a murderer. You're just a pain in the ass."

Avery laughed and wiped more tears. "I wasn't expecting to hear that one."

"It's the truth. I've stayed on because I love you like you were my own, and I want what's best for you. But you don't make it easy."

Avery wrapped an arm around her and held her close. "Oh, Nadine. All those years of nonsense and playing around. I should've listened to you. I should've listened."

"It's never too late to change, Avery."

"No, I guess it isn't. But I feel like it's too little too late. I can't have the woman I want, I can't see the girls, and I'm probably going to jail." She threw up her hands. "What else do I have to lose?" She rose and crossed to the bar where she downed a shot of whiskey.

Nadine turned. "You've already made plans for a party, haven't you?"

"I called a few friends."

"I don't think it's wise, Avery. You should lay low, behave."

"Someone is playing with me, Nadine. They want me to go down. This may be the only way for me to find out who it is. And if not, at least I have one last hoorah before it all comes tumbling down."

Nadine stood and crossed to her. She took her hand. "Promise me you'll be careful."

"I will."

Nadine kissed her hand. "I wish I could believe you."

"I do too."

Chapter Twenty-nine

Maria checked her phone and tried calling again, but Samantha didn't answer. Frustrated, she tossed the phone next to her and rubbed her face. It was nearing ten and she was tired and looking forward to some serious rest. Even though she'd been on desk duty, she'd been super busy with evidence and with organizing direction on two new cases.

Even so, her mind always went back to Avery Ashland and the unanswered questions. She'd hoped Samantha could answer some. But she hadn't been able to reach her. Was she avoiding her? Had she moved on already? Her brother had said she was known to be a player. But Maria hadn't sensed a fuck and run vibe from her. And why had she been at Avery's? Could it really be mere coincidence that they'd met?

She didn't buy it.

Avery had seduced her purposely.

To get to her. She was sure of it. What it did though, was anger her and cause resentment. Is that what Avery wanted? To play games?

Wasn't she tired of those games?

Maria shook her head and rubbed Horace who purred like the old man he was. She stroked his long curly mustache and snuggled down with him. Maybe she'd give in and crash on the couch for a while. Maybe she wouldn't even bother with the bed.

But her phone rang and she jerked back to attention. The number was new yet familiar. She answered.

"Detective Diaz."

"Detective?" The caller was female, and she sounded fragile yet determined.

"Yes?"

"You must come to Euphoria tonight. Your presence is needed."

Maria stood. "My presence is needed? Why? Who is this?"

Hesitation.

"Please. You must come. You're the only one who can keep her safe."

"Who is this?" She searched her mind frantically.

"If you don't come, I'm afraid something bad will happen to her."

And suddenly she knew. Her heart dropped. "Nadine?"

The phone went dead.

Chills spread out across Maria's body, and she felt the hair prickle on the back of her neck. What was going on at Euphoria? She dialed Finley and left him a voice mail. She told him about the call and said she was going to check it out. She was off the case, yes. Technically, they all were. It was in the D.A.'s hands now. But Nadine sounded frightened and like she had nowhere else to turn. She looked to Horace who stood very still watching her.

"I've got to go," she said more to herself than to him. "I have to see what's going on." She grabbed her keys and left him and his big yellow-eyed stare.

And the whole way to the resort, she tried to convince herself she was doing the right thing.

"Oh, my God. She isn't. Please tell me she isn't." Maria pulled up to the valet and handed her keys off to a young gentleman. Around her, guests hurried inside, dressed to the nines. And all wore masks, setting off her already amplified anxiety. "What's going on tonight?" she asked another attendant.

"Ms. Ashland's private farewell party."

"Farewell party?"

He eyed her as she walked up the stairs. "Yes, do you have an invitation?"

"I have a feeling I'm wanted here."

"Ma'am?"

She waved him off. "Nothing. She knows me." She pointed inside at the desk clerk she and Finley had become all too familiar with. Kelly waved her inside but held her up.

"I'm sorry, Detective, but you aren't on the list this evening." She sounded apologetic and looked a little nervous herself.

"Really?" Maria glanced around at the women in ball gowns and men in tuxedos. "You guys going to be able to run a tight ship with all these disguises?"

The young woman's face fell, but she said nothing.

"Listen, Nadine called me. Asked me to come. She's concerned."

The young woman hesitated and then blew out a long breath. She stamped Maria's hand and handed over a mask. "You need this."

Maria took it and covered her face. "Thanks."

The young woman nodded and Maria touched her hand. "Please. Don't tell Ms. Ashland I'm here."

"But—"

"Where is she? I'll find her and tell her myself."

"Fourth floor. But it's strictly off limits to most guests. She'll know it's you the second you step off the elevator."

Maria stiffened at the memory of her last visit to that floor. "That's okay." She thanked her and walked on. She wove between dancing guests and kept her mask up to her face. She heard people make comments about her attire and many believed her to be staff. One woman asked her for more champagne. It was just as well though; she didn't want them aware of her presence. And if she could help it, she'd hide herself from Avery for as long as she could until she knew exactly what it was that was going on. A farewell party sounded dubious and suspicious, as if Avery was going to run away or something worse. She was determined to get to the bottom of it.

She stepped into the elevator and pressed four. She rode up alone. Her phone rang from her hip, but she silenced it. If it was Finley he'd have to wait. She couldn't afford to be talking to him while staking out the goings-on on the fourth floor. She texted him, confirmed her location, and said she'd call soon. The elevator stopped as she slipped the phone into her pocket.

She moved slowly, surprised at the absence of security. She cocked her head as she heard laughter. Then, as she continued to move, she heard the moans of pleasure. She moved slowly down the blue lit hall and came to a stop at the first room. She checked the door and found it locked. She moved on, and the moans were growing closer. But door after door was closed and locked.

She came to the landing and edged the corner. When she snuck a look, her breath shook by the sight of Avery, who was tied to a thick cushioned chair with two women covered head to toe in leather and face masks, devouring her between her parted legs. Avery was moaning softly and Maria pulled back, tried to make sense of the scene, and then looked again. Avery was nude and sweat coated with her arms thrown to her side and her legs splayed over the armrests. Rope was wrapped around her chest, and torso, and though she was moaning as if she were enjoying the pleasure, her eyes were heavy and unfocused.

Maria had an urge to interrupt to make sure Avery was okay, but Avery caught sight of her first and shook her head. The women didn't see and continued. The short one laughed and moved to stand by Avery's head. She stroked her face and her hair.

"There, there, darling. Just relax and let go. Feel the pleasure. I know you love it. Always have." She knelt and kissed her.

The other woman stopped and pushed away. She remained on her knees. "Quit, babying her, for God's sake."

Avery moaned and tried to move.

"I can't help it. She's still so divine, even after all these years."

"Well, I've had enough. I think she's drugged enough now. She can't fight back." She stood and approached the shorter woman. She tugged her in for a firm embrace. "Besides, I'm getting jealous."

The shorter woman laughed playfully. "No need, my princess. I'm all yours." They kissed long and deep. And when they pulled away, the shorter woman spoke again. "I'm afraid I can't stay for much longer. You know I can't stand to watch the rough stuff."

"Yes, I know. But this one's not going to be rough. She's simply going to fall asleep with a sweet little suicide note on her lap, claiming responsibility for both Lana and Hale."

"Oh, it's all too perfect isn't it? We get rid of Hale and that little whore Lana, all while blaming Avery. It's like we won the lottery three times."

The tall woman laughed and reached out to pinch and twist Avery's nipple. Avery moved slightly but only made a small noise.

"She's almost gone," the taller one said. "You'd better go and change and rejoin the party."

The shorter one nodded, and Avery surprised them by making a loud noise as she looked toward Maria.

The masked women turned and saw her.

"Shit, what's she doing here?"

Avery groaned as if it was hard to speak. "Run, Maria."

The taller woman rushed her, and Maria turned. She ran down the hall, but her legs felt like they were filled with cement. She grunted and ran harder, but she could feel the woman gaining on her. It was just like in her nightmare. She couldn't get away. And when she felt the woman grab her ponytail, she cried out. But she was yanked backward and then something jabbed her side causing immediate shock and pain. She felt it again and again, and then… darkness.

Maria opened her eyes and blinked against the black. Her lashes felt crushed, and she knew she was blindfolded. She tried to speak but choked against what felt like a ball gag. Panicked, she inhaled quickly, desperate for what little breath she could get through her nose. She moved her hands and found her wrists and ankles bound. She cried out as best she could and shook her whole body.

"Cop bitch is freaking out," a voice said. She recognized it as the taller masked woman who had chased her.

"Some tough one she is," another voice, the one she assumed was the shorter woman, said.

Maria pulled harder against her restraints and groaned.

"She's going to choke on her own saliva."

"Let her."

"No, we need her. This is perfect."

Suddenly, Maria was freed from her blindfold. She blinked and focused, but the women were still disguised.

The taller one approached. "I'm taking out your gag, but if you scream…" A large serrated blade was held to her throat. The woman loosened the gag, and it fell to the ground. Maria could feel her own saliva sliming her chin. She swallowed a few times to gain control and then searched the room. Avery was still in the chair, but she wasn't bound. She appeared to be unconscious.

"What did you do to her?" Maria asked, voice raspy.

"Who, Avery?" The shorter woman laughed. "She's just taking a little nap thanks to those handy little muscle relaxers we used on Hale and Lana."

"You're killing her?" Maria struggled, desperate to break free. She had to get out, get Avery, call for help. Then she remembered Finley. Oh God, would he come? Surely, he would. If she could just hang on. But Avery didn't appear to have much time. "Do you really think killing Avery will solve all your little problems?"

The women laughed.

The one with the knife drew closer. "We're not only going to kill Avery; we're going to kill you, too."

She stepped up and touched her neck with the blade. "We're just going to make it look like Avery killed you."

Maria glared at her, tried to place the voice. She saw the green eyes, the black slicked back hair.

"Melanie Prague."

Melanie removed the mask and smiled. "Well, what do you know, the cop's not so dumb after all." She wiped the sweat from her brow. "Sorry, Detective, I know you're sick and all, and you deserve an honorable death…but I'm afraid it's going to be messy, just like Hale."

Maria struggled and laughed. "It's too late, Melanie. We know Avery was set up. I just came here to tell her. And my partner, he's downstairs. He'll be up any minute."

"She's bluffing," the shorter one said.

But Melanie seemed anxious. Maria continued to struggle, and she was about to call out when she saw Avery move. On wobbly looking legs, Avery stood from the chair and tackled the shorter woman to the floor. Melanie whipped around and rushed them, but Avery wrapped an arm around the shorter woman's throat and pulled her into a stand. Avery backed away toward Maria, holding the shorter woman as hostage.

"Don't do it, Melanie, or I'll snap her neck."

Melanie laughed. "You think I care? Do it. It's just another death to blame on you."

"Bullshit, I know you care. You're in love with her just as I once was. And I know when you're in love, you take it very seriously."

"You don't know shit, Avery."

Avery fought to remain standing. Her eyes appeared like they were struggling to stay open. She turned slightly and reached up with one hand, but she couldn't undo Maria's bind. She refocused on the woman in her arms.

"You here that, Bryce? She doesn't care if I kill you."

"I heard her." Bryce tore off her mask. "But I don't believe her. I know she loves me."

Melanie shook her head. "I don't love anyone. Not anymore. You, like the others, just helped me to rid my life of Hale and ultimately, Avery. She's played her last game."

"No way." Bryce shook her head. "We did this together. We're in love. Darling, please. Come back to your senses."

"Together? I had to do all the dirty work."

Bryce began to panic. "Melanie, please. Don't do this."

But Melanie charged them and Bryce tore away from Avery to meet her head-on. They fell to the floor and rolled. Avery turned and unfastened Maria's binds, managing to free her hands. She went to unfasten her ankles, but Melanie, who had stabbed Bryce, stood with knife in hand. She rushed Avery.

"Avery, look out!" Maria shouted.

Avery stood and turned just as Melanie stuck out her knife.

"No!" Maria screamed and reached out to tear Avery away. Avery fell to the floor with her, and Maria saw the blood on her torso and tugged her farther away from Melanie. But Melanie grinned and stalked toward them.

"Time to say good-bye to Avery, Detective. We've all had to at one point or another. Because Avery will have no one. Right, Avery?"

Avery slumped against Maria as the blood poured from her wound. Maria covered it as best she could. Avery looked up at her.

"I'm sorry, Maria. I'm—I only wanted to be with you."

Maria squeezed her tight, and Melanie's face contorted with evil and she held up her knife with both hands.

"Fucking bitch." She took a step toward them, and a shot rang out. She jolted. Another shot and she jolted again, this time collapsing. She fell crookedly with the knife in her hand and blood oozing from her mouth.

Finley hurried to her and kicked the knife away. He looked to Maria who was still holding tight to Avery.

"When this shit is over," he said, breathless, "remind me to kick your ass."

Maria nodded and looked down at Avery. "She's hurt badly," she said.

Finley rested his hands on his knees as more cops rushed the room.

Avery looked up at her with tears in her eyes. "Tell me, Maria. Tell me, what's wrong with you?"

Maria fought back against the tightness in her throat and the pain in her side. She cradled Avery's head in one hand and pressed on her wound with the other.

"Please, trust me enough to tell me. I—I won't hurt you. Could never. Hurt you."

Maria knelt closer. "I have MS, Avery. Multiple Sclerosis."

Avery closed her eyes. "I'm so sorry. Sorry for—everything." She opened her eyes and touched Maria's face. "I just want to love you. But I understand why—you won't let me." She drifted away and Maria held her tighter, panicked. She looked to Finley.

"Fins, she's innocent. She really is."

He stared at them for a long moment as if letting it sink in and then shook his head and knelt down next to them to help put pressure on the wound.

"Ain't that a bitch," he whispered, waving the emergency services over to them. "Ain't that a bitch."

CHAPTER THIRTY

"Auntie Avery!" her nieces shouted as they ran into the penthouse and into her open arms.

"Hey!" She embraced them tightly and winced slightly from the pain. "Oh, be careful, I'm still a little sore from where I got hurt."

The girls looked up at her. "You're okay thought, right?"

"Yes, I'm just fine." She tousled the Rory's hair. "Nothing to worry about."

"You won't have to go away again? Even to the hospital?" Kylie asked.

"No, baby. I'm home for good."

They squeezed her again, and she wiped a stray tear from her eye. It was funny how much she'd cried the last couple of weeks. Tears seemed to come easier now, and while she knew it was good for her, according to Nadine and a therapist, she still had a hard time accepting them. She inhaled sharply and straightened.

"Why don't you go check out your room? There's a surprise."

"Really?" They bounced up and down and then took off across the living room to the hallway. She heard them shriek with excitement when they reached their shared bedroom.

"Think they like it?" she asked Nadine.

"I think they love it," she said. She took Avery gently by the arm and led her to the couch where she helped her ease down. Then she brought a tray with tea and mugs and set it on the coffee table.

"I don't ever want them to know what happened," Avery confessed. She'd been thinking about it a lot, and the thought of her nieces someday reading about the murders and her involvement with the parties and the investigation made her cringe. It was the main reason why she'd decided to make some changes in her life.

"Try not to think about that right now."

"It's difficult." Nadine handed her a mug, and Avery steeped her tea and took a sip. It was ginger lemon, and it helped to settle her stomach which had been upset since her attack. Melanie Prague had almost succeeded in killing her, stabbing her in her torso, and nearly missing her liver. The nightmares were still prominent, and she was reminded each and every time she moved.

"All you can do is lead the best life you can, love them to pieces, and talk to them when the time comes."

Avery touched Nadine's arm before she moved away. "Thank you, Nadine. For everything. I love you."

Nadine searched her eyes, and Avery could tell she was surprised at the serious words.

"I know you do, Avery." She smiled. "I love you."

She fluffed a pillow and placed it behind her back. Then she covered her with a new fleece throw blanket. The girls would probably never notice that the old one was gone. And that was just as well.

Avery glanced around at her home and noted the fresh clean smell of it, and the nice yet cozy organization. It had taken Nadine a week to rearrange all that was taken for evidence and returned. She'd also scrubbed the house from top to bottom as if the attack had happened in the penthouse rather than the fourth floor.

The girls ran back into the room with their dolls in their hands. "The dollhouse is so awesome, Auntie Avery."

"Yeah! We love it. And we're gonna play with it all night long!"

"Maybe even sleep in it."

"Yeah!"

Avery laughed, so glad she'd chosen a good gift for them. She wanted them distracted from all the work going on at the resort.

So she'd hired a contractor to come in and build a large dollhouse, making sure to include it into the architecture of their room.

"Sounds like fun. When I'm all healed and better, I'll join you."

They squealed with delight. "Okay, but you need your own dolls."

"I'll have to get some then."

But Rory approached, stroked her doll's hair, and then handed it over. "Here, Auntie Avery. You can have Guinevere."

Avery took the doll and touched her niece's cheek. "Love, you don't have to give me your doll."

"She'll help you feel better."

Avery smiled. "Okay. I promise to take very good care of her. But for now, why don't you care for her for me? And play with her until I can. That way she can have some fun."

Rory smiled. "Okay." She took the doll and they ran off to play.

Avery stared after them, wistful.

"To be so young and innocent."

Nadine sat and joined her for some tea. "Uh-huh."

"Was I ever so innocent?"

"No."

Avery laughed. "You could've fibbed for my benefit."

"No point. You know you were full of piss and vinegar."

They sipped their tea in silence. "I wish the phone would ring," Avery said. "I guess you find out who your real friends are in a case like this."

"Yes."

No one had called since she'd been home from the hospital, and only her business acquaintances had sent flowers while she recovered. The people she'd thought were her friends had been silent. It seemed she and Euphoria were something to avoid. However, she was surprised when they'd reopened just how many reservations had been made by the wealthy from all over the world.

"I think you're better off," Nadine said softly, "without those people."

Avery stared out the large windows. "I think you're right." She stirred her tea. "I'm not going to be the same person I was, Nadine. I can't. It almost killed me."

"I know."

"I want good people in my life."

"You will have them. But first...you have to be a good person."

Avery nodded. "I am. I mean...Lying there in the hospital, going over all that had happened. The lies, the games, the ultimate betrayal of people I thought I knew and cared about...I think for the first time, I really understood and knew who I wanted to be."

Nadine sipped her tea and listened.

"I think I've always tried to be someone I'm not. Someone my father wanted. Tough, cold. Take no prisoners. And then with women, I was unobtainable. The ultimate catch who couldn't be caught. But it was so empty. My God, I was just running in circles."

She closed her eyes. "Until Maria."

"Detective Diaz."

"Yes. It all began to change with her."

"Have you spoken to her?"

"No. And I wonder if she'll ever speak to me again."

"Why wouldn't she?"

"Because of the mess I made. The mess I was a part of. I could've just told her from the get-go that I knew someone was planning on scaring Hale. That women were fed up. I could've given her names, even if I didn't know for sure about anyone other than Lana."

"But you were protecting Lana."

"I tried. A lot of good that did me."

"Avery. I honestly think if you would've named names...they would've killed you."

She considered the remark. "I don't know. Maybe eventually they would have. I just can't believe they hated me that badly. To go through all that to frame me."

"They wanted Hale gone. You were just an added bonus."

"Maybe."

Avery shook her head as feelings of guilt, shame, and anger came. "God, three women I trusted."

"Don't go there, Avery. They were crazy, and don't forget how easily they turned on each other."

Avery set her mug down on the table. "Will I ever get over this?"

"No. But you will get through it."

"How?"

"By taking it one day at a time. And by being a good person."

Avery sighed. "I don't even know where to start."

"You can start with Detective Diaz. There's a lot there that needs to be said."

Avery again stared out the window. "She's got a lot on her plate. Work, the MS. God, and I just made things so much more complicated for her."

"Tell her that. Tell her how you feel about it. She needs to hear it, Avery."

"How much could an apology help?"

"You'd be surprised. And not only that, but you need to tell her how you feel about her. Don't expect anything, just tell her. For both your sakes."

Avery stared out the window. She watched the sun sparkle and glint off the buildings of Las Brisas. So much had changed in such a short amount of time. She looked back to her dear, dear friend and mother figure. She smiled.

"I think, as always, Nadine, that you're right."

CHAPTER THIRTY-ONE

Iow have you been?" Finley asked over his favorite greasy Chinese. "You've been quiet. Thought I was going nuts. Paige is up in arms, says I'm acting crazy without you."

"New partner that bad?" Maria asked, taking a bite of kung pao chicken. It was flavorful, but it wasn't all white meat like she preferred.

Finley shrugged. "She's all right, I guess. Stubborn. Just like you."

Maria laughed. "You don't deserve any less."

"I guess not." He forked a thick wad of noodles into his mouth and slurped up the few strands that went awry.

"I've been okay," Maria said, shrugging herself. She smiled politely as the waitress refilled her iced tea. "I'm changing my diet, eating more greens and fruits and veggies. And I work out with a physical therapist. So far, so good. Just the damn stiffness in my leg is bothering me."

Finley chewed while nodding. "You think you'll be able to come back full fledge?"

She pushed her food around. "I honestly don't know. It's only been about a month. I have five months left on my medical leave." She sipped her tea. "But the doctor says things are looking good so far. My strength is good and my stamina is better." Her mind went to that last night at Euphoria and how she couldn't get away when she'd needed to. It almost cost her her life. Luckily, Melanie had only used a stun gun on her. "To be honest…I still worry. You deserve a healthy partner. One who can save your ass when needed."

He grinned. "There's no one like you, Maria. There never will be."

"Thank God for that," she said with a laugh.

"No, seriously. I hope you do return, even if it's just at head-quarters. We need you."

She nodded. "I'm pretty sure I need you all too." She took another bite and Finley eyed her curiously for her egg roll. She passed it over. "It's been strange…being away. Horace is in heaven. I think he's going to propose."

Finley took a big bite out of her egg roll and sipped his iced tea. "I know you love that damn cat."

She smiled.

He swallowed and this time he pushed around his food. "Say, listen. Have you heard anything from you-know-who?"

She looked away. "No."

"Surprised?"

"A little."

"Yeah, me too. I've been meaning to tell you…she contacted me. Called the wife, actually. Went on and on about me saving her life. She even thanked me. And I think…she might've cried a little."

Maria felt her face flush as the sting of jealousy overcame her. She hadn't heard a word from Avery since that night when she'd seen her to the ambulance.

"Well, I didn't go visit her, you know, in the hospital."

"You were in a bad place," Finley said. "Plus, your own health was shit. You couldn't get out of bed for days."

"She doesn't know that."

He seemed lost in thought as he looked beyond her. "So tell her."

"Whoa." She sat back. "You're telling me to call her?"

He shrugged.

"Finley, you hate this woman."

"I didn't hate her…I just thought she was a selfish bitch. That and a killer."

"Yes, there was that wasn't there?"

"Damn right. You can't blame me for that. She looked guilty as hell. And somehow she almost pranced around with it as if she were proud."

"You're still jealous over her sexual confidence."

He coughed. "What?"

"She overwhelmed you with her powers of seduction and you couldn't handle it. I don't think most men can. Take Hale for instance."

"I am not Hale, and I don't like the comparison, thank you very much."

"I'm just saying."

"Me? What about you? You—"

"All right, all right. It's not something I'm proud of."

"You're saying it was bad?"

"No. I'm saying I was irresponsible. I've had to confess that to my superiors once already. I'd rather not hash through it again."

He took another big bite of noodles. "Suit yourself. I'm just glad the press has moved on."

"You and me both."

"The sarge was right though. This was one big motherfucker of a case. It made us, you know."

"Made you, maybe." She played with her food again. "I'm afraid I don't yet know what it's done to me."

He covered her hand with his own. "It made you a legend. You'll see. Your instincts about her were right in the end. Despite the mounting evidence. And that's something you can't learn or buy."

She offered a smile but didn't totally feel it.

"Wanna come over and see S.J. walk? It's a riot. We can't get enough of it." He smiled like the proud papa he was.

She wiped her mouth with her napkin. "I can't. I'm meeting Samantha in an hour."

"Samantha? Really?"

"Yes."

He tsked. "She's a player. Ignored you for weeks."

"I know. And now that I'm semi-famous and in the papers, she wants to see me again."

"So, what gives?"

"I don't know. I just want to tell her to her face I'm not interested."

He shook his head and motioned for the waiter for the check.

"Always a smartass. That's my Maria."

"That's right and don't you forget it."

"I don't think, my dear, that's even humanly possible."

Maria reached for her cane and stood from the couch. It had been an hour since she'd politely told Samantha that they shouldn't see each other again. Samantha had tried to explain why she'd seen Avery and she swore that not much had happened, but Maria didn't totally believe her innocent motives. It didn't really matter anyway because they weren't exclusive, but she knew she couldn't see her again. The sex had been great, yes, but she wanted the whole package. And she wouldn't settle for anything less.

She stared into the setting sun shining a brilliant gold into her front drapes. She walked as best she could with her stiff leg over to the window and closed the curtains and then walked to the door to bolt it.

She engaged the lock and saw that there were two messages on her old answering machine. She rarely answered her home phone and rarely paid attention to the machine. She pressed play and sighed as her mother's voice pleaded with her to come stay with them while she was on the mend. And if she'd at least have someone in her life, they wouldn't worry so much and on and on. Maria deleted the message and waited for the next one.

There was a long pause after the beep. Finally, she heard a woman's voice. One she recognized at once.

"Hey, uh, it's me. I'm not brave enough to leave this message on your cell phone so I called this number hoping to get a voice mail…"

The message went on, but there was a soft knock on her door. She stopped the message, unlocked the door, and pulled it open. She inhaled sharply at Avery Ashland, who had just been speaking on her machine, and now stood on her front stoop.

"Avery," she breathed.

Avery pulled off her shades and smiled softly. It wasn't over-confident or seductive in intent. It was just a wonderful, kind smile.

Maria almost swooned.

"Hi," Avery said.

Maria shook her head, truly shocked to see her and her obvious change in demeanor. "Hi."

"I left you a message, and when I didn't hear back…"

"I was just now listening to it."

"Oh." She slid an elegant hand into her gray dress slacks and slid her shades back onto her head. Her blond hair was tightly pulled into a ponytail, and she looked paler than usual in a black shimmering short-sleeved blouse.

"Please, come in," Maria stammered, stepping aside. Avery inched by her, and Horace jumped from the back of the couch to purr and weave between her legs.

Maria closed and locked the door and knelt carefully to scoop him up. "Please, excuse him. He thinks he's the welcoming committee."

Avery laughed and scratched his head. "He's cute."

Maria placed him back onto the couch and walked with her cane to offer Avery a seat.

"Please, make yourself comfortable."

But Avery didn't move. She looked anxious, a little hesitant even. "I don't think I can sit right now."

Maria stared at her, searching for clues.

"Did you listen to the whole message?"

"No, you knocked on the door."

Avery touched her temple. "Okay. Okay." She finally looked at her. "I'm sorry I haven't been in touch."

Maria caught the sincerity in her voice. She'd never seen her or heard her like this.

"I'm sorry too. I should've checked on you in the hospital."

Avery stepped toward her. "No, don't." She stopped and closed her eyes. "I should've come by long before this. Long before. But really, Maria, I'm a coward. That's why I played games, slept around. I was hiding. Protecting myself from having true feelings. And now—Maria. I—I'm. I've only ever said this to one other woman, and let me tell you, what I feel for you is so much stronger. So much so that I can hardly take it. I feel like my heart's going to burst right out of my chest. Maria…I'm in love with you. I came to tell you I'm in love with you. The phone message, it says the same, but I was too chicken shit to come here and tell you in person."

Maria clenched her cane and stared incredulously. Her other hand found its way to cover her heart. She fought for breath.

"I—don't know what to say."

Avery took another step closer. "You don't have to say anything. Just—let me hold you. All I want to do is hold you. I think I just might die right here on the spot if I don't."

Maria blinked as if what she were hearing and seeing weren't real. "You want to hold me?"

Avery nodded. "More than anything." She took another step and brushed Maria's hair from her face. "May I?"

Maria whispered, "Yes."

Avery took her gently in her arms and pressed her long, lean body to hers. Maria closed her eyes and inhaled her unique scent. Hints of amber and citrus and other heart-fluttering things she couldn't name. Her heart pounded and she leaned into her and felt Avery's own heartbeat with her free hand. It was racing faster than hers.

"You're trembling," Maria said.

"I can't help it."

Her breath in Maria's ear sent shockwaves of desire right through her. Her skin came alive and she heated. "Me neither."

Avery continued to brush her hair away from her cheek and ear. "I've wanted nothing but this for weeks on end. To be still with you, feel you, inhale you. God, you smell good." She lightly kissed Maria's neck, and Maria made a small noise of approval. "And I can't forget how it felt to touch you. How wet you were. So hot and slick. I see your face as you came. I see it in my dreams."

"Avery," Maria said, unsure how to respond. She'd thought of it too. In fact, she'd thought of little else while lying in her bed late into the night. "I can't be your lover. I can't do that. I'm not built that way."

"What way?"

"Sex with no attachment. No matter how hot it might be. I can't help but—feel for you."

Avery stared into her eyes. "I don't want just sex, Maria. I want you. All of you."

Maria inhaled a shaky breath. "Oh God, Avery, I don't know. I'm still reeling from the case, from what happened—"

"And who you think I am?"

Maria fell silent.

"I'm not that person. I'm—"

"I know who you are. The way you care about your nieces and Nadine. Somehow I know."

Avery smiled. "Yes, that's who I am. Who I want to be. I'm not going to hide anymore."

Maria smiled in return. "That sounds nice."

"I'm glad you think so."

"Can I kiss you, Maria?"

Maria nodded softly. "Yes, please."

Avery leaned down and captured her lips with her own. The heat between them galvanized and turned into fire as they kissed and captured and tugged and explored. Maria stood as tall as she could and clung to Avery, letting her cane fall to the floor.

"Avery," she said between kisses.

"Yes."

"I can no longer stand."

Avery lifted her and carried her down the hall. "Where's the bedroom?"

"You're getting warmer. At the end on your left."

Avery carried her into the master bedroom and placed her on the bed. She knelt to kiss her again, but Maria stopped her.

"Wait," Maria said. "I want to see you. Undress you."

Avery straightened and looked into her eyes.

"Yes, like that. Look at me while you undress."

Avery slid her hands to the hem of her blouse and lifted it slowly over her head. Maria took in her white lace bra and the lean muscles of her torso. A tiny freckle sat just above her navel, and Maria had the urge to kiss it.

"Your slacks," Maria said, her voice low and raspy with desire.

Avery followed her lead and unbuttoned her slacks. She lowered them to her feet and stepped out of them carefully. She stood before her in matching bra and panties, breathing as if she were running a marathon.

"You're exquisite," Maria managed. "As if you were sculpted." She reached out and ran her fingertips up and down her sides. Avery shivered and her eyes flashed.

"I don't think I can keep going this slow," Avery said.

Maria ran her eyes down her body. "Why? Are you as wet as I am?"

Avery answered by leaning in and pressing her hungry mouth to Maria's. She plunged in with her hot tongue and eased her back onto the bed. Maria held her fast and wrapped her legs around her, needing to feel the pressure of her against her aching flesh.

"Oh yes, Avery. Yes. Take me. Take me now."

Maria arched herself, offering her neck for feeding. Avery latched on and bit and nibbled her way down. When she reached the fabric of her shirt, Avery simply tore it away. When her mouth covered her bra, Avery quickly shoved it up and over her head.

"Suck them," Maria said, offering her aching nipples. "Suck them hard." Avery took a nipple in her mouth and sucked so hard Maria nearly came in her pants. She arched off the bed and tangled her hands in Avery's hair as she moved from one hard nipple to the other, groaning like an animal as she did so. Maria scratched her back and managed to unhook her bra. When it was free, she tugged her upward and took Avery's nipple in her mouth and sucked in most of her taut breast.

Avery rocked into her, eyes clenched. Maria's mouth smacked as she released and captured the other breast. Both of them found each other's hot centers and rubbed, milking one another for the ultimate contact of flesh on flesh.

"I'm going to come," Avery said, still rocking.

Maria stopped her movement and released her breast. "No, not yet. Take off your panties."

Avery stood hurriedly and stripped off her panties. Then she did the same to Maria, yanking off her pants and panties together. "Am I being too rough?"

"No. God no. Honestly, I don't even care. I want you that badly."

Avery crawled back on top of her and met her mouth for a long, deep kiss. Bare, muscled thighs found bare, aching flesh, and they moved against one another, teasing, promising.

"I'm going to taste you now," Avery said. "I can't wait."

"Neither can I," Maria said. "Turn and bring yourself to me."

Avery paused, looked into her eyes, and then turned and backed herself to Maria's face. When she felt her warm hands lead her hips to her, she lowered herself to Maria's glistening flesh and fed.

Maria called out and squeezed her tight. She eased her back to her mouth and captured her swollen red tip in her mouth and sucked. Avery cried out and refastened to her, and they fed off one another, taking and giving and taking and giving. They swirled and sucked and bobbed and teased, both of them until they were moaning and crying into one another ready to crest and explode.

"I'm coming," Avery said, shoving her hips back faster and harder.

"Mm, come, baby. Come with me." Maria sucked her wet flesh and thrust her own hips into Avery's mouth, ready to come herself.

They peeked and exploded together, both of them taking in as much flesh as they could. They gave until they could no longer move or breathe. Both moaning and contracting, muscles out of control.

"Oh, God," Maria finally breathed. "Fucking hell."

Avery detached and crawled from her, turning to rest with Maria in her arms. "I want more," Avery said. "I can't get enough of you."

Maria laughed. She felt so free and warm, like she was tingling from head to toe, the stiffness in her leg long forgotten. "I'm not sure how much I can take. My body is still twitching."

Avery ran the tip of her finger along Maria's lips. "When it comes to you, I think I'm insatiable."

Maria turned into her. "Really? I think I can get on board with that."

"You think so?"

"Mm-hm. I, uh, haven't really had very much in the way of orgasms in a long while. I don't like doing it myself."

"You're kidding?"

Maria shook her head. "Nope."

"God, I could die just imagining you trying." She shifted a little and parted Maria's legs. "Did you use your fingers?" She toyed with the curl of dark hair framing her flesh, ever so lightly touching it. Maria shivered and clung to her.

"Uh-huh. And the showerhead."

"The showerhead? Oh, that will be fun." She kissed her, softly, slowly, and lowered her fingers to either side of her moist clit, causing it to swell once again. She stroked as she kissed her, long and slow and painfully delicate.

"You're still so wet. I want to taste it. Taste it all. Think you can handle that?" She moved her fingers lower still and found her slickness, bringing it up to rub her clit. Over and across and around and around, until Maria was helplessly bucking in a rhythm with her.

"Avery," she said. "You make me crazy. Oh God. Yes, God."

"Yes, love, say my name. You have no idea what it does to me to hear you say my name."

"Avery, Avery!" Just as she was about to come, Avery positioned herself between her legs, inserted two fingers, and fucked her while she fed off her engorged clit. Maria screamed into the twilight, hips raised, fingers knotted in Avery's hair. She came and she came and she came. And just when she thought it might end, Avery stopped, slid her pinky into Maria's ass and fucked her some more, long and deep and slow.

Maria let out a low growl of approval and clenched the bedclothes. "Oh fuck," she managed. "Jesus, yes, Avery."

"You like that?" She fucked her harder, faster. "You're so beautifully tight. I can't get enough. God, Maria, when you come, say my name, say it like—say it like you love me."

Maria looked into her eyes and burst into oblivion. All reality completely left her, and from a distance, she heard herself crying out for Avery, crying out and begging her for more, more, more. She tore at the bed covers, thrashed from side to side, and bucked like a madwoman. Avery was fucking her to heaven and above, so deep inside, pushing and pulling, so good, so insanely fucking good it was like a dream. The best dream she'd ever had with the blond goddess between her legs, giving her every imaginable pleasure with one hand. It was magical; Avery was magical. And when she stilled, her heart still thudded and her breath came in wild spurts. Her hands hurt to open and stretch.

"Maria, Maria?" Avery was gently calling to her. Gently removing herself from her.

Maria met her gaze. "Mm?"

"Are you okay?"

She closed Maria's legs and pulled a stray sheet up over her body. She rested next to her on her elbow.

"I think I just died and came back to earth." Maria turned into her and nestled against her. "You blew me away."

Avery brushed her hair with her fingers. "I want to do so much more."

Maria laughed. "I want you to too. But we have all the time in the world now."

Avery kissed her. "And I don't want to waste a minute of it."

"We won't." Maria kissed her back. "I promise."

CHAPTER THIRTY-TWO

When Maria entered Avery's penthouse, she found her standing at the large windows, her beautiful body in silhouette just as it had been the first time she'd met her. Only now instead of holding a cigarette, she was holding a glass of water and looking out at the world as if she were lost in its beauty.

"I want a photo of you, just like that," Maria said.

Avery startled, turned, and then smiled. "Nadine let you in?"

"Mm-hm."

"Damn, I was hoping to hear you. I wanted a quick make out session in the hallway." She grinned and walked toward her in loose cream slacks and a cream and black patterned vest that hugged her upper body like a second skin. Maria wanted to devour her on the spot.

"You look yummy," Maria said as Avery kissed her, oh so softly, and with a tantalizing hit of her cologne. "Smell yummy too."

Avery groaned and leaned in to nibble her neck. "So, do you, Ms. Diaz." She slapped her ass. "You all set?"

Maria nodded. "Horace is at my mother's, house is all locked up, and my luggage is all downstairs."

"Wonderful." Avery kissed her again. "I'm so glad you're coming."

"Mm, me too." Maria kissed her back. Just then, a door banged, and Avery's nieces came tearing into the living room.

"Maria's here!" They threw themselves against her, and Maria nearly toppled.

"Hi, guys." She hugged them in return, thrilled that they liked her so much. And when she looked at the warm smile on Avery's face, her heart warmed. "Are you excited to go?"

They screeched and bounced up and down. "Yeah!"

"Yeah!"

Avery tousled their hair. "Go get your pillows and blankets for the plane." The girls took off to their bedroom.

"Wow, I don't think I've ever been so excited to go to Disney World than I am right at this moment," Maria said. "Their excitement is infectious."

Avery tugged her in for an amorous embrace. "You, my dear, are what's got me so excited. You're infectious." She inhaled her neck and nibbled her jaw, causing Maria's skin to come alive.

"Please tell me we have our own room," Maria said, kissing Avery's jaw in return. She was already so wet she could hardly stand.

"Oh, we have a whole suite with adjoining rooms with Nadine and the girls. Once they turn in, we'll have all the privacy we want."

"Mm, yes, that sounds very promising."

Avery pulled back and stared into her. "Thanks for understanding that I needed to do this with the girls."

Maria touched her face. "I completely understand."

"I promise to sweep you off your feet as soon as you're available again. Paris, the Caribbean, you name it."

"Avery, I'm fine. And you already sweep me off my feet."

"Really?"

"Yes. Literally."

Avery swept her up into her arms. "Like this?"

Maria playfully pounded on her shoulder. "Yes! Now put me down." She did so and Maria squeezed her hand. "Thank you for understanding my limitations."

Avery smiled. "I've got everything all set at the resort. If you need a scooter, you've got it. If you need anything, it will be there. I'll make damn sure."

"I'm all right for now, but those wild nights with you—phew."

Avery laughed. "Well, we can go slow and gentle. Painfully slow if you want."

Maria shivered. "Dear God, what you do me." They kissed.

The girls ran back into the room, arms full of blankets and pillows. Nadine followed with her purse slung over her shoulder. She already had on a straw hat and sunscreen, Maria could smell it.

"Okay, off to the plane!" Avery shooed everyone out the door and then looked back for Maria.

"Ready?"

"Avery Ashland," Maria said, taking her hand, "I've never been more ready."

THE END

About the Author

Ronica Black lives in the desert southwest with her menagerie of animals and her menagerie of art. When she's not writing, she's still creating, whether that be drawing, painting, or woodworking. She loves long walks into the sunset, rescuing animals, anything pertaining to art, and spending time with those she loves. When she can, she enjoys returning to her roots in North Carolina, where she can sit on the front porch with her family, catch up on all the gossip, and enjoy a nice cold Cheerwine.

Ronica is a two-time Golden Literary Society winner and a three-time finalist for the Lambda Literary Awards.

Books Available from Bold Strokes Books

Breakthrough by Kris Bryant. Falling for a sexy ranger is one thing, but is the possibility of love worth giving up the career Kennedy Wells has always dreamed of? (978-1-63555-179-2)

Certain Requirements by Elinor Zimmerman. Phoenix has always kept her love of kinky submission strictly behind the bedroom door and inside the bounds of romantic relationships, until she meets Kris Andersen. (978-1-63555-195-2)

Dark Euphoria by Ronica Black. When a high-profile case drops in Detective Maria Diaz's lap, she forges ahead only to discover this case, and her main suspect,aren't like any other. (978-1-63555-141-9)

Fore Play by Julie Cannon. Executive Leigh Marshall falls hard for Peyton Broader, her golf pro...and an ex-con. Will she risk sabotaging her career for love? (978-1-63555-102-0)

Love Came Calling by CA Popovich. Can a romantic looking for a long-term, committed relationship and a jaded cynic too busy for love conquer life's struggles and find their way to what matters most? (978-1-63555-205-8)

Outside the Law by Carsen Taite. Former sweethearts Tanner Cohen and Sydney Braswell must work together on a federal task force to see justice served, but will they choose to embrace their second chance at love? (978-1-63555-039-9)

The Princess Deception by Nell Stark. When journalist Missy Duke realizes Prince Sebastian is really his twin sister Viola in disguise, she plays along, but when sparks flare between them, will the double deception doom their fairy-tale romance? (978-1-62639-979-2)

The Smell of Rain by Cameron MacElvee. Reyha Arslan, a wise and elegant woman with a tragic past, shows Chrys that there's still beauty to embrace and reason to hope despite the world's cruelty. (978-1-63555-166-2)

The Talebearer by Sheri Lewis Wohl. Liz's visions show her the faces of the lost and the killers who took their lives. As one by one, the murdered are found, a stranger works to stop Liz before the serial killer is brought to justice. (978-1-63555-126-6)

White Wings Weeping by Lesley Davis. The world is full of discord and hatred, but how much of it is just human nature when an evil with sinister intent is invading people's hearts? (978-1-63555-191-4)

A Call Away by KC Richardson. Can a businesswoman from a big city find the answers she's looking for, and possibly love, on a small-town farm? (978-1-63555-025-2)

Berlin Hungers by Justine Saracen. Can the love between an RAF woman and the wife of a Luftwaffe pilot, former enemies, survive in besieged Berlin during the aftermath of World War II? (978-1-63555-116-7)

Blend by Georgia Beers. Lindsay and Piper are like night and day. Working together won't be easy, but not falling in love might prove the hardest job of all. (978-1-63555-189-1)

Hunger for You by Jenny Frame. Principe of an ancient vampire clan Byron Debrek must save her one true love from falling into the hands of her enemies and into the middle of a vampire war. (978-1-63555-168-6)

Mercy by Michelle Larkin. FBI Special Agent Mercy Parker and psychic ex-profiler Piper Vasey learn to love again as they race to stop a man with supernatural gifts who's bent on annihilating humankind. (978-1-63555-202-7)

Pride and Porters by Charlotte Greene. Will pride and prejudice prevent these modern-day lovers from living happily ever after? (978-1-63555-158-7)

Rocks and Stars by Sam Ledel. Kyle's struggle to own who she is and what she really wants may end up landing her on the bench and without the woman of her dreams. (978-1-63555-156-3)

The Boss of Her: Office Romance Novellas by Julie Cannon, Aurora Rey, and M. Ullrich. Going to work never felt so good. Three office romance novellas from talented writers Julie Cannon, Aurora Rey, and M. Ullrich. (978-1-63555-145-7)

The Deep End by Ellie Hart. When family ties become entangled in murder and deception, it's time to find a way out... (978-1-63555-288-1)

A Country Girl's Heart by Dena Blake. When Kat Jackson gets a second chance at love, following her heart will prove the hardest decision of all. (978-1-63555-134-1)

Dangerous Waters by Radclyffe. Life, death, and war on the home front. Two women join forces against a powerful opponent, nature itself. (978-1-63555-233-1)

Fury's Death by Brey Willows. When all we hold sacred fails, who will be there to save us? (978-1-63555-063-4)

It's Not a Date by Heather Blackmore. Kade's desire to keep things with Jen on a professional level is in Jen's best interest. Yet what's in Kade's best interest...is Jen. (978-1-63555-149-5)

Killer Winter by Kay Bigelow. Just when she thought things could get no worse, homicide Lieutenant Leah Samuels learns the woman she loves has betrayed her in devastating ways. (978-1-63555-177-8)

Score by MJ Williamz. Will an addiction to pain pills destroy Ronda's chance with the woman she loves or will she come out on top and score a happily ever after? (978-1-62639-807-8)

Spring's Wake by Aurora Rey. When wanderer Willa Lange falls for Provincetown B&B owner Nora Calhoun, will past hurts and a fifteen-year age gap keep them from finding love? (978-1-63555-035-1)

The Northwoods by Jane Hoppen. When Evelyn Bauer, disguised as her dead husband, George, travels to a Northwoods logging camp to work, she and the camp cook Sarah Bell forge a friendship fraught with both tenderness and turmoil. (978-1-63555-143-3)

Truth or Dare by C. Spencer. For a group of six lesbian friends, life changes course after one long snow-filled weekend. (978-1-63555-148-8)

A Heart to Call Home by Jeannie Levig. When Jessie Weldon returns to her hometown after thirty years, can she and her childhood crush Dakota Scott heal the tragic past that links them? (978-1-63555-059-7)

Children of the Healer by Barbara Ann Wright. Life becomes desperate for ex-soldier Cordelia Ross when the indigenous aliens of her planet are drawn into a civil war and old enemies linger in the shadows. Book Three of the Godfall Series. (978-1-63555-031-3)

Hearts Like Hers by Melissa Brayden. Coffee shop owner Autumn Primm is ready to cut loose and live a little, but is the baggage that comes with out-of-towner Kate Carpenter too heavy for anything long term? (978-1-63555-014-6)

Love at Cooper's Creek by Missouri Vaun. Shaw Daily flees corporate life to find solace in the rural Blue Ridge Mountains, but escapism eludes her when her attentions are captured by small town beauty Kate Elkins. (978-1-62639-960-0)

Somewhere Over Lorain Road by Bud Gundy. Over forty years after murder allegations shattered the Esker family, can Don Esker find the true killer and clear his dying father's name? (978-1-63555-124-2)

Twice in a Lifetime by PJ Trebelhorn. Detective Callie Burke can't deny the growing attraction to her late friend's widow, Taylor Fletcher, who also happens to own the bar where Callie's sister works. (978-1-63555-033-7)

Undiscovered Affinity by Jane Hardee. Will a no strings attached affair be enough to break Olivia's control and convince Cardic that love does exist? (978-1-63555-061-0)

Between Sand and Stardust by Tina Michele. Are the lifelong bonds of love strong enough to conquer time, distance, and heartache when Haven Thorne and Willa Bennette are given another chance at forever? (978-1-62639-940-2)

Charming the Vicar by Jenny Frame. When magician and atheist Finn Kane seeks refuge in an English village after a spiritual crisis, can local vicar Bridget Claremont restore her faith in life and love? (978-1-63555-029-0)

Data Capture by Jesse J. Thoma. Lola Walker is undercover on the hunt for cybercriminals while trying not to notice the woman who might be perfectly wrong for her for all the right reasons. (978-1-62639-985-3)

Epicurean Delights by Renee Roman. Ariana Marks had no idea a leisure swim would lead to being rescued, in more ways than one, by the charismatic Hudson Frost. (978-1-63555-100-6)

Heart of the Devil by Ali Vali. We know most of Cain and Emma Casey's story, but *Heart of the Devil* will take you back to where it began one fateful night with a tray loaded with beer. (978-1-63555-045-0)

Known Threat by Kara A. McLeod. When Special Agent Ryan O'Connor reluctantly questions who protects the Secret Service, she learns courage truly is found in unlikely places. Agent O'Connor Series #3. (978-1-63555-132-7)

Seer and the Shield by D. Jackson Leigh. Time is running out for the Dragon Horse Army while two unlikely heroines struggle to put aside their attraction and find a way to stop a deadly cult. Dragon Horse War, Book 3. (978-1-63555-170-9)

Sinister Justice by Steve Pickens. When a vigilante targets citizens of Jake Finnigan's hometown, Jake and his partner Sam fall under suspicion themselves as they investigate the murders. (978-1-63555-094-8)

The Universe Between Us by Jane C. Esther. Ana Mitchell must make the hardest choice of her life: the promise of new love Jolie Dann on Earth, or a humanity-saving mission to colonize Mars. (978-1-63555-106-8)

Touch by Kris Bryant. Can one touch heal a heart? (978-1-63555-084-9)